Todd Andrews

"I woke up that morning, then, slugged my rye, looked around my room, got quietly out of bed, and dressed for the office.... I'm sure I splashed cold water on my face, rinsed my mouth out, wiped my reading glasses with toilet paper, rubbed my chin to persuade myself that I didn't need shaving, patted my hair down in lieu of combing it.... It was at some moment during the performance of this ritual—the instant when the cold water hit my face seems a probable one— that all things in heaven and earth came clear to me, and I realized that this day I would make my last; I would destroy myself on this day ..."

ALICE JAMES: A Biography by Jean Strouse
AN UNKNOWN WOMAN by Alice Koller
AT PLAY IN THE FIELDS OF THE LORD
   by Peter Matthiessen
THE BEGGAR MAID by Alice Munro
THE BELL JAR by Sylvia Plath
CANCER WARD by Alexander Solzhenitsyn
THE CONFESSIONS OF NAT TURNER by William Styron
DARKNESS VISIBLE by William Golding
DELTA OF VENUS Erotica by Anaïs Nin
THE DIVINERS by Margaret Laurence
THE END OF THE ROAD by John Barth
FAR TORTUGA by Peter Matthiessen
THE FIRST CIRCLE by Alexander I. Solzhenitsyn
THE FLOATING OPERA by John Barth
GILES GOAT-BOY by John Barth
THE GOLDEN NOTEBOOK by Doris Lessing
GOODBYE, COLUMBUS by Philip Roth
THE HILL OF EVIL COUNSEL by Amos Oz
THE HOUSE ON PRAGUE STREET by Hana Demetz
HOUSEKEEPING by Marilynne Robinson
HUNGER OF MEMORY by Richard Rodriguez
THE LONG MARCH by William Styron
LOST IN THE FUNHOUSE by John Barth
THE MEMOIRS OF A SURVIVOR by Doris Lessing
THE MIDDLE GROUND by Margaret Drabble
MY LIFE AS A MAN by Philip Roth
MY MICHAEL by Amos Oz
THE NEEDLE'S EYE by Margaret Drabble
NIGHT OF THE AUROCHS by Dalton Trumbo
ONE DAY IN THE LIFE OF IVAN DENISOVICH
   by Alexander Solzhenitsyn
PORTNOY'S COMPLAINT by Philip Roth
THE REALMS OF GOLD by Margaret Drabble
SET THIS HOUSE ON FIRE by William Styron
THE SNOW LEOPARD by Peter Matthiessen
SOMETIMES A GREAT NOTION by Ken Kesey
THE STONE ANGEL by Margaret Laurence
THE SUMMER BEFORE THE DARK by Doris Lessing
AN UNKNOWN WOMAN by Alice Koller
V. by Thomas Pynchon
VISION QUEST by Terry Davis
A WEAVE OF WOMEN by E. M. Broner
WHEN SHE WAS GOOD by Philip Roth
WHERE THE JACKALS HOWL by Amos Oz
A WOMAN OF THE FUTURE by David Ireland
WRINKLES by Charles Simmons

THE FLOATING OPERA
John Barth

BANTAM BOOKS
TORONTO · NEW YORK · LONDON · SYDNEY

This low-priced Bantam Book
has been completely reset in a type face
designed for easy reading, and was printed
from new plates. It contains the complete
text of the original hard-cover edition.
NOT ONE WORD HAS BEEN OMITTED.

THE FLOATING OPERA

A Bantam Book / published by arrangement with
Doubleday & Company, Inc.

PRINTING HISTORY

THE FLOATING OPERA was originally published by
Appleton, Century Crofts, Inc., in 1956.
The Doubleday edition was revised by the author.
Doubleday edition published May 1967

Bantam edition / July 1972

2nd printing . . . . . May 1973	5th printing . . . . . . May 1976
3rd printing . . . . March 1974	6th printing . . . . March 1977
4th printing . . . . . June 1975	7th printing . . . . August 1978
	8th printing . . . . April 1980

Bantam Windstone edition / April 1981
10th printing . . . October 1983

Windstone and accompanying logo of a stylized W
are trademarks of Bantam Books, Inc.

ISBN 0-553-24098-6

Published simultaneously in the United States and Canada

Bantam Books are published by Bantam Books, Inc. Its trademark, consisting of the words "Bantam Books" and the por-
trayal of a rooster, is Registered in U.S. Patent and Trademark
Office and in other countries. Marca Registrada. Bantam
Books, Inc., 666 Fifth Avenue, New York, New York 10103.

PRINTED IN THE UNITED STATES OF AMERICA

H   19 18 17 16 15 14 13 12 11 10

prefatory note to the revised edition

The Floating Opera was written in the first three months of 1955; its companion-piece, *The End of the Road*, in the last three months of the same year. The *Opera* was my first novel; I was twenty-four, had been writing fiction industriously for five years, and had had—deservedly—no success whatever with the publishers. One finally agreed to launch the *Opera*, but on condition that the builder make certain major changes in its construction, notably about the stern. I did, the novel was published, critics criticized the ending in particular, and I learned a boatwright little lesson. In this edition the original and correct ending to the story has been restored, as have a number of other, minor passages. *The Floating Opera* remains the very first novel of a very young man, but I'm pleased that it will sink or float now in its original design.

John Barth

contents

i tuning my piano

To someone like myself, whose literary activities have been confined since 1920 mainly to legal briefs and *Inquiry*-writing, the hardest thing about the task at hand—*viz.*, the explanation of a day in 1937 when I changed my mind—is getting into it. I've never tried my hand at this sort of thing before, but I know enough about myself to realize that once the ice is broken the pages will flow all too easily, for I'm not naturally a reticent fellow, and the problem then will be to stick to the story and finally to shut myself up. I've no doubts on that score: I can predict myself correctly almost every time, because opinion here in Cambridge to the contrary, my behavior is actually quite consistent. If other people (my friend Harrison Mack, for instance, or his wife Jane) think I'm eccentric and unpredictable, it is because my actions and opinions are inconsistent with *their* principles, if they have any; I assure you that they're quite consistent with *mine*. And although my principles might change now and then—this book, remember, concerns one such change—nevertheless I always have them a-plenty, more than I can handily use, and they usually hang all in a piece, so that my life is never less logical simply for its being unorthodox. Also, I get things done, as a rule.

For example, I've got this book started now, and though we're probably a good way from the story yet, at least we're headed toward it, and I for one have learned to content myself with that. Perhaps when I've finished describing that particular day I mentioned before—I believe it was about June 21, 1937—perhaps when I reach the bedtime of that day, if ever, I'll come back and destroy these pages of piano-tuning. Or perhaps not: I intend directly to introduce myself, caution you against certain possible interpretations of my name, explain the significance of this book's title, and do several other gracious things for you, like a host fussing over a guest, to make you as comfortable as possible and to dunk you gently into the meandering stream of my story—useful activities better preserved than scrapped.

To carry the "meandering stream" conceit a bit further, if I may: it has always seemed to me, in the novels that I've read now and then, that those authors are asking a great deal of their readers who start their stories furiously, in the middle of things, rather than backing or sidling slowly into them. Such a plunge into someone else's life and world, like a plunge into the Choptank River in mid-March, has, it seems to me, little of pleasure in it. No, come along with me, reader, and don't fear for your weak heart; I've one myself, and know the value of inserting first a toe, then a foot, next a leg, very slowly your hips and stomach, and finally your whole self into my story, and taking a good long time to do it. This is, after all, a pleasure-dip I'm inviting you to, not a baptism.

Where were we? I was going to comment on the significance of the *viz.* I used earlier, was I? Or explain my "piano-tuning" metaphor? Or my weak heart? Good heavens, how does one write a novel! I mean, how can anybody stick to the story, if he's at all sensitive to the significances of things? As for me, I see already that storytelling isn't my cup of tea: every new sentence I set down is full of figures and implications that I'd love nothing better than to chase to their dens with you, but such chasing would involve new figures and new chases, so that I'm sure we'd never get the story started, much less ended, if I let my inclinations run unleashed. Not that I'd mind, ordinarily—one book is as good as another to me—but I really do want to explain that day (either the 21st or the 22nd) in June of 1937 when I changed my mind for the last time. We'll have to stick to the channel, then, you and I, though it's a shoal-draught boat we're sailing, and let the creeks and coves go by, pretty as they might be. (This metaphor isn't gratuitous—but let it go.)

So. Todd Andrews is my name. You can spell it with one or two *d*'s; I get letters addressed either way. I almost warned you against the single-*d* spelling, for fear you'd say, "*Tod* is German for death: perhaps the name is symbolic." I myself use two *d*'s, partly in order to avoid that symbolism. But you see, I ended by not warning you at all, and that's because it just occurred to me that the double-*d Todd* is symbolic, too, and accurately so. *Tod* is death, and this book hasn't much to do with death; *Todd* is almost *Tod*—that is, almost death—and this book, if it gets written, has very much to do with almost-death.

One last remark. Were you ever chagrined by stories that seemed to promise some revelation, and then cheated their way out of it? I've run more times than I'd have chosen to into stories concerning some marvelous invention—a gravity-defier, or a telescope powerful enough to see men on Saturn, or a secret weapon capable of dislocating the solar system—but the mechanics of the gravity device are never explained; the question of Saturn's inhabitation is never answered; we're not told how to build our own solar-system dislocators. Well, not so this book. If I tell you that I've figured some things out, I'll tell you what those things are and explain them as clearly as I can.

Todd Andrews, then. Now, watch how I can move when I really care to: I'm fifty-four years old and six feet tall, but weigh only 145. I look like what I think Gregory Peck, the movie actor, will look like when he's fifty-four, except that I keep my hair cut short enough not to have to comb it, and I don't shave every day. (The comparison to Mr. Peck isn't intended as self-praise, only as description. Were I God, creating the face of either Todd Andrews or Gregory Peck, I'd change it just a trifle here and there.) I'm well off, by most standards: I'm a partner in the law firm of Andrews, Bishop & Andrews—the second Andrews is me—and the practice nets me as much as I want it to, up to perhaps ten thousand dollars a year, maybe nine, although I've never pushed it far enough to find out. I live and work in Cambridge, the seat of Dorchester County, on the Eastern Shore of Maryland. It's my home town and my father's—Andrews is an old Dorchester name—and I've never lived anywhere else except for the years I spent in the Army during the First World War and the years I spent in Johns Hopkins University and the University of Maryland Law School afterwards. I'm a bachelor. I live in a single room in the Dorset Hotel, just across High Street from the courthouse, and my office is in "Lawyers' Row" on Court Lane, one block away. Although my law practice pays my hotel bill, I consider it no more my career than a hundred other things: sailing, drinking, walking the streets, writing my *Inquiry*, staring at walls, hunting ducks and 'coons, reading, playing politics. I'm interested in any number of things, enthusiastic about nothing. I wear rather expensive clothing. I smoke Robert Burns cigars. My drink is Sherbrook rye and ginger ale. I read often and unsystematically—that is, I have my own system, but it's unorthodox. I am in no hurry. In short, I live my life—or have lived it, at least, since 1937—in much the same manner as I'm writing this first chapter of *The Floating Opera*.

I almost forgot to mention my illnesses.

The fact is, I'm not a well man. What reminded me of it just now was that while I was daydreaming about the name *Floating Opera*, sitting here at my table in the Dorset Hotel, surrounded by the files of my *Inquiry*, I commenced drumming my fingers on the table, in rhythm with a galloping neon sign outside. You should see my fingers. They're the only deformity in a body otherwise serviceable and, it has in my life been whispered to me, not unlovely. But these fingers. Great clubbed things: huge, sallow, heavy nails. I used to have (probably still have) a kind of subacute bacteriological endocarditis, with a special complication.

Had it since I was a youngster. It clubbed my fingers, and now and then I get weak, not too often. But the complication is a tendency to myocardial infarction. What that means is that any day I may fall quickly dead, without warning—perhaps before I complete this sentence, perhaps twenty years from now. I've known this since 1919: thirty-five years. My other trouble is a chronic infection of the prostate gland. It gave me trouble when I was younger—several kinds of trouble, as I'll doubtless explain somewhere later—but for many years now I've simply taken a hormone capsule (one milligram of diethylstilbestrol, an estrogen) every day, and except for a sleepless night now and then, the infection doesn't bother me any more. My teeth are sound, except for one filling in my lower left rear molar and a crown on my upper right canine (I broke it on a ferryboat railing in 1917, wrestling with a friend while crossing the Chesapeake). I'm never constipated, and my vision and digestion are perfect. Finally, I was bayoneted just a little bit by a German sergeant in the Argonne during the First World War. There's a small place on my left calf from it, where a muscle atrophied, but the little scar doesn't hurt. I killed the German sergeant.

No doubt when I get the hang of storytelling, after a chapter or two, I'll go faster and digress less often.

Now then, the title, and then we'll see whether we can't start the story. When I decided, sixteen years ago, to write about how I changed my mind one night in June of 1937, I had no title in mind. Indeed, it wasn't until an hour or so ago, when I began writing, that I realized the story would be at least novel-length and resolved therefore to give it a novel title. In 1938, when I determined to set the story down, it was intended only as an aspect of the preliminary study for one chapter of my *Inquiry*, the notes and data for which fill most of my room. I'm thorough. The first job, once I'd sworn to set that June day down on paper, was to recollect as totally as possible all my thoughts and actions on that day, to make sure nothing was left out. That little job took me nine years—I didn't push myself—and the notes filled seven peach baskets over there by the window. Then I had to do a bit of reading: a few novels, to get the feel of the business of narrating things, and some books on medicine, boat-building, philosophy, minstrelsy, marine biology, juris-prudence, pharmacology, Maryland history, the chemistry of gases, and one or two other things, to get "background" and to make sure I understood approx-imately what had happened. This took three years—rather unpleasant ones, because I had to abandon my usual system of choosing books in order to do that comparatively specialized reading. The last two years I spent editing my recollections of that day from seven peach baskets down to one, writing commentary and interpretative material on them until I had seven peach basketsful again, and finally editing the com-mentary back down from seven peach baskets to two, from which I intended to draw comments rather at random every half hour or so during the writing.

Ah, me. Everything, I'm afraid, is significant, and nothing is finally important. I'm pretty sure now that my sixteen years of preparation won't be as useful, or at least not in the same way, as I'd thought: I under-stand the events of that day fairly well, but as for commentary—I think that what I shall do is try not to comment at all, but simply stick to the facts. That way I know I'll still digress a great deal—the temptation is always great, and becomes irresistible when I know the end to be irrelevant—but at least I have some hope of reaching the end, and when I lapse from grace, I shall at any rate be able to congratulate myself on my intentions.

Why *The Floating Opera?* I could explain until Judgment Day, and still not explain completely. I think that to understand any one thing entirely, no matter how minute, requires the understanding of every other thing in the world. That's why I throw up my hands sometimes at the simplest things; it's also why I don't mind spending a lifetime getting ready to begin my *Inquiry*. Well, *The Floating Opera*. That's part of the name of a showboat that used to travel around the

Virginia and Maryland tidewater areas: *Adam's Original & Unparalleled Floating Opera*; Jacob R. Adam, owner and captain; admissions 20, 35, and 50 cents. The *Floating Opera* was tied up at Long Wharf on the day I changed my mind, in 1937, and some of this book happens aboard it. That's reason enough to use it as a title. But there's a better reason. It always seemed a fine idea to me to build a showboat with just one big flat open deck on it, and to keep a play going continuously. The boat wouldn't be moored, but would drift up and down the river on the tide, and the audience would sit along both banks. They could catch whatever part of the plot happened to unfold as the boat floated past, and then they'd have to wait until the tide ran back again to catch another snatch of it, if they still happened to be sitting there. To fill in the gaps they'd have to use their imaginations, or ask more attentive neighbors, or hear the word passed along from upriver or downriver. Most times they wouldn't understand what was going on at all, or they'd think they knew, when actually they didn't. Lots of times they'd be able to see the actors, but not hear them. I needn't explain that that's how much of life works: our friends float past; we become involved with them; they float on, and we must rely on hearsay or lose track of them completely; they float back again, and we either renew our friendship—catch up to date—or find that they and we don't comprehend each other any more. And that's how this book will work, I'm sure. It's a floating opera, friend, fraught with curiosities, melodrama, spectacle, instruction, and entertainment, but it floats willy-nilly on the tide of my vagrant prose: you'll catch sight of it, lose it, spy it again; and it may require the best efforts of your attention and imagination—together with some patience, if you're an average fellow—to keep track of the plot as it sails in and out of view.

ii the dorchester explorers' club

I suppose I must have waked at six o'clock, that morning in 1937 (I'm going to call it June 21). I had spent a poor night—this was the last year of my prostate trouble. I'd got up more than once to smoke a bit, or walk about my room, or jot some notes for my *Inquiry*, or stare out the window at the Post Office, across High Street from the hotel. Then I'd managed to fall asleep just before sunrise, but the light, or whatever, popped me awake on the tick of six, as it does every morning.

I was just thirty-seven then, and as was my practice, I greeted the new day with a slug of Sherbrook from the quart on my window sill. I've a quart sitting there now, but it's not the same one; not by a long shot. The habit of saluting the dawn with a bend of the elbow was a hangover from college-fraternity days: I had got really to enjoy it, but I gave it up some years ago. Broke the habit deliberately, as a matter of fact, just for the exercise of habit-breaking.

I opened my eyes and bottle, then, and took a good pull, shook all over from head to toe, and looked at my room. It was a sunny morning, and though my window faces west, enough light reflected in to make the room bright. A pity: the Dorset Hotel was built in the early eighteen hundreds, and my room, like many an elder lady, looks its best in a subdued light. Then, as now, the one window was dappled with little rings of dust from dried raindrops; the light-green plaster walls were filigreed with ancient cracks like a relief map of the Dorchester marshes; an empty beef-stew can, my ashtray, was overflowing butts (I smoked cigarettes then) onto my writing desk—a bizarre item provided by the management; the notes for my *Inquiry*, then in its seventh year of preparation, filled a mere three peach baskets and one corrugated box with MORTON'S MARVELOUS TOMATOES printed on the end. One wall was partially covered, as it is yet, by a Coast & Geodetic Survey m..p of Dorchester County—not so annotated as it is now. On another hung an amateur oil painting of what appeared to be a blind man's conception of fourteen whistling swan landing simultaneously in the Atlantic during a half-gale. I don't recall now how I came by it, but I know I let it hang through inertia. In fact, it's still over there on the wall, but once while drunk my friend Harrison Mack, the pickle magnate, drew a kind of nude on top of it in crayon. All over the floor (then, not now) were spread the blueprints of a boat that I was building at the time in a garage down by the range lights on the creek; I'd brought the prints up to do some work on them the day before.

It seems to me that any arrangement of things at all is an order. If you agree, it follows that my room was as orderly as any room can be, even though the order was an unusual one.

Don't get the impression that my life, then or now, is "bohemian" or "left bank." If I understand those terms correctly, it isn't. In the first place, by 1937 I wasn't enthusiastic about any kind of art, although I was and am mildly curious about it. Neither was my room dirty or uncomfortable—just crowded. It was probably the day before the maids came to clean: they spoil my orderliness by putting things "straight"—that is, out of sight. Finally, I live too well to be called a bohemian. Sherbrook rye costs $4.49 a quart, and I use a lot of quarts.

So. It's really a quite adequate room, and I'm still here. I woke up that morning, then, slugged my rye, looked around my room, got quietly out of bed, and dressed for the office. I even remember my clothes, though that date—the 21st or 22nd—escapes me, after sixteen years of remembering: I wore a gray-and-white seersucker suit, a tan linen sports shirt, some necktie or other, tan stockings, and my straw boater. I'm sure I splashed cold water on my face, rinsed my mouth out, wiped my reading glasses with toilet paper, rubbed my chin to persuade myself that I didn't need shaving, and patted my hair down in lieu of combing it—sure, because I've done these things, in that order, nearly every morning since perhaps 1930, when I moved into the hotel. It was at some moment during the performance of this ritual—the instant when the cold water met my face seems a probable one—that all things in heaven and earth came clear to me, and I realized that this day I would make my last; I would destroy myself on this day.

I stood erect and grinned at my dripping face in the mirror.

"Of course!"

Exhilaration! A choked snicker escaped me.

"For crying out loud!"

Momentous day! Inspiration, to have closed my eyes on the old problem; to have opened them on the new and last and only solution!

Suicide!

I tiptoed from the room to join my colleagues in the hall, the charter members of the Dorchester Explorers' Club, for coffee.

Like the hotels of many small towns, the Dorset is bigger than it need be. Most of its fifty-four rooms are empty in the wintertime, and even with the addition of the several all-summer visitors who move in when the weather warms, there are enough rooms left empty on an average night to accommodate any traveling circus or muskrat-trappers' convention that might come through town unexpectedly. The owners are able to stay in business, one might guess, only because the building was paid for several generations ago, and willed to the present operators unencumbered; because overhead and maintenance costs are very low; and because a number of elderly ladies and gentlemen unfortunate enough to have outlived their welcome in this world are forced by circumstances to make the hotel their last stopover on the road to the next. These supernumeraries, especially the men among them, comprise the Dorchester Explorers' Club—meetings every morning from 6:15 until 6:45. The D.E.C., founded and named by myself, is still extant, though of the charter members only I remain alive.

That morning, as I remember, just two others were present: Capt. Osborn Jones, an eighty-three-year-old retired oyster dredger crippled by arthritis, and Mister Haecker, seventy-nine, former principal of the high school, then pensioned and, though in good health, devoid of family—the end of his line. Because Capt. Osborn had difficulty with stairs, we met in his room, on the same floor as mine.

"Morning, Cap'n Osborn," I said, and the old man grunted, as was his habit. He was dressed in a shiny gray cap, a nondescript black wool sweater, and blue denims washed nearly to whiteness.

"Morning, Mister Haecker," I said. Mister Haecker wore his usual spotless and creaseless black serge, a silk necktie, and a clean if somewhat threadbare striped shirt.

"Good morning, Todd," he answered. I remember he was lighting his first cigar of the morning with one hand and stirring coffee with the other. I had purchased a one-burner hot plate for the Club some months before, and by mutual consent it remained in Capt. Osborn's room. "Good and hot," he said, handing me a cup of coffee.

I thanked him. Capt. Osborn commenced swearing steadily, in a monotone, and striking his right leg with his cane. Mister Haecker and I watched him while we sipped our coffee.

"Can't wake her up, huh?" I offered. Every morning, as soon as Capt. Osborn dressed and sat down, his leg went to sleep, and he pounded it until the blood circulated. Some mornings it took longer than others to get the job done.

"Drink your coffee, Captain," Mister Haecker said

in his very mild voice. "It will do more good than all your temper."

Capt. Osborn grew dizzy from the exertion; I saw him grip his chair arms to steady himself. He sighed, between clenched teeth, and took the coffee that Mister Haecker held out to him, grunting his thanks. Then, without a word, he deliberately poured the steaming stuff all over the delinquent leg.

"Hey there!" Mister Haecker exclaimed with a frown, for such displays annoyed him. I, too, was startled, afraid the coffee would scald the old fellow, but he grinned and struck once more at the leg with his cane.

"Smack her good," I urged admiringly.

Capt. Osborn gave up the struggle and settled back in his chair, coffee still steaming and dripping from his trouser leg onto the floor.

"Awright," he said, breathing heavily, "awright. I'm goin' to die. But I want to do it all at oncet, not a piece at a time." He regarded the leg with disgust. "God damn leg." He kicked his right foot with his left. "Pins and needles, feels like. One time I could buck and wing with that leg. Even steered my boat with 'er, standin' on the other and holdin' a donkey rope in each hand! No more, sir."

"Wouldn't be so bad if he'd die in installments," I said to Mister Haecker, who was fixing the Captain another cup of coffee. "Maybe the undertaker'll bury him a piece at a time, and we can pay him a little each month."

This about Capt. Osborn's senility was a running joke in the Explorers' Club, and as a rule Mister Haecker, for all his primness, joined in the bantering, but this morning he seemed preoccupied.

"You *are* going to die, Captain," he said solemnly, giving Capt. Osborn the fresh coffee, "just as Todd says. But not for a spell, we trust. In the meantime you're an old man, same as I. Just old age, is all. Why buck it? There's not a thing in this world you can do about it."

"Ain't nothing I can do about it," Capt. Osborn admitted, "but I ain't got to like it."

"Why not?" Mister Haecker pressed. "That's just what I want to know."

"Why'n hell should I?" Capt. Osborn snorted. "Can't work and can't play. Jest spit tobacco and die. You take it; I don't want it." He drew a handkerchief from his sweater pocket and blew his nose violently. The cushions of his chair, the drawers of his table, the pockets of his sweater and trousers—all were stuffed with damp or drying handkerchiefs: the Captain, like many watermen, suffered from acute sinusitis, aggravated by the damp air of Dorchester County, and would have nothing to do with doctors. His only therapy was the half-tumblerful of Sherbrook that I gave him every morning before I left the hotel. It kept him mildly drunk until near noon, by which time his sinuses were less congested.

"Well," Mister Haecker said, "wise men have never run down old age. Let me read you a quote I copied down from a book yesterday, just to read you."

"Oh, my. Oh, my."

"He's going to convert you, Cap'n Osborn," I warned.

"Hee, hee!" the old man chuckled. He always thought it tremendously funny when I suggested that he was a backslider.

"No," Mister Haecker said, spreading open a folded strip of paper and holding it to the light. "This is something I copied down from Cicero, and I want you to hear what Cicero says about being old. Here's what Cicero says, now: ' ... *if some god should grant me to renew my childhood from my present age, and once more to be crying in my cradle, I should firmly refuse.* ...' There, now. I guess Cicero ought to know. Eh?"

"I expect so," Capt. Osborn said, not daring to contradict flatly the written word.

"Well, now," Mister Haecker smiled. "Then I say let's make the most of it. How does it go? *The last of life, for which the first was made.* Don't you think so?" He looked to me, for support. "Don't *you* think so?"

"Don't ask me, Mister Haecker; I'm still in the first."

"Listen," Capt. Osborn said, in that tone employed by old men to suggest that, having indulged long enough the nonsense of others' opinions, they are about to get down to the truth. "Ye see this here arm?" He held out his bony right arm. "Well, sir, they could tie me to a cottonwood tree this minute, and hitch a team to this here arm, and they could pull 'er out slow by the roots, God damn 'em, and I'd let 'em, if they'd make me forty again, with a season's pay in my pocket and all summer to live. Now, then!"

He sat back exhausted in his chair, but his face was triumphant.

"Do you think that's right?" Mister Haecker pleaded to me. "Is that the way you'd feel?"

"Nope," I said. Mister Haecker brightened considerably, but Capt. Osborn glared.

"Ye mean ye'd spend yer time readin' nonsense to yerself?" he asked incredulously.

"Nope," I said. Now Mister Haecker seemed disappointed too.

"Well, what's your opinion about it?" he asked glumly. "Or don't you have one?"

"Him!" Capt. Osborn snuffled with laughter and phlegm. "That one's got opinions on ever'thing!"

"Oh, I've got one," I admitted. "Matter of fact, I woke up with it this morning."

"Woke up with it, did ye!" Capt. Osborn cackled. "I bet it's a hot one, now!"

Mister Haecker waited patiently, though without much relish, to hear my opinion, but he was spared it, because Capt. Osborn's laughter turned into coughing and choking, as it sometimes did, and the two of us had to clap him on the back until, still sputtering, he caught his breath. As soon as he could breathe normally again, I left the club meeting to fetch him his glass of rye from my room, for it seemed to me he needed his medicine badly.

Light step! I wanted to dance across the hall! My opinion? My opinion? S U I C I D E ! Oh, light step, reader! Let me tell you: my whole life, at least a great part of it, has been directed toward the solution of a problem, or mastery of a fact. It is a matter of attitudes, of stances—of masks, if you wish, though the term has a pejorativeness that I won't accept. During my life I've assumed four or five such stances, based on certain conclusions, for I tend, I'm afraid, to attribute to abstract ideas a life-or-death significance. Each stance, it seemed to me at the time, represented the answer to my dilemma, the mastery of my fact; but always something would happen to demonstrate its inadequacy, or else the stance would simply lose its persuasiveness, imperceptibly, until suddenly it didn't work—quantitative change, as Marx has it, suddenly becoming qualitative change—and then I had the job to face again of changing masks: a slow and, for me, painful process, if often an involuntary one. Be content, if you please, with understanding that during several years prior to 1937 I had employed a stance that, I thought, represented a real and permanent solution to my problem; that during the first half of 1937 that stance had been losing its effectiveness; that during the night of June 20, the night before the day of my story, I became totally and forcibly aware of its inadequacy—I was, in fact, back where I'd started in 1919; and that, finally and miraculously, after no more than an hour's predawn sleep, I awoke, splashed cold water on my face, and realized that I had the real, the final, the unassailable answer; the last possible word; the stance to end all stances. If it hadn't been necessary to tiptoe and whisper, I'd have danced a *trepak* and sung a *come-all-ye!* Didn't I tell you I'd pull no punches? That my answers were yours? *Suicide!* Poor Mister Haecker, he must wait to learn my opinion (wait, wretched soul, I fear, for Judgment Day), but not you, reader. *Suicide* was my answer; my answer was *suicide*. You'll not appreciate it before I've laid open the problem; and lay it open I shall, a piece at a time, after my fashion—which, remember, is not unsystematic, but simply coherent in terms of my own, perhaps unorthodox, system.

Then, for heaven's sake, what is my system? Patience, friend; it's not my aim to mystify or exasperate you. Remember that I'm a novice at storytelling—even if I weren't, I'd do things my own way. I suggest you substitute this question for yours: Why didn't I carry Capt. Osborn's rye with me when I first left my room, so that I shouldn't need to return for it? There's a more specific question, and a more reasonable, and a less prying, and its answer involves the answer to the other. I didn't take the rye with me in the first place because it wasn't my habit to do so, and one of the results of my eye-opening answer was that this day—this June 21 (I'm almost certain)—should, because of its very momentousness, be lived as exactly like every other day of my recent life as I could possibly live it. Therefore, although I knew very well that Capt. Osborn would need his medicine, I left it in my room and returned for it after coffee, as was my practice.

Is this an answer? More to the first question than to the second; you still don't know how the practice originated, any more than I do, but you know that my system for living this extraordinary day was to live it as ordinarily as possible, though every action would necessarily be charged with a new significance. And similarly, my method in telling this story will be to set down the events of that day as barely as possible, for I know that in the telling I'll lose the path often enough for you to learn or guess the whole history of the question, as the audience to my untethered showboat pieces together the plot of their melodrama—and I swear by all the ripe tomatoes in Dorchester that when the excitement commences, the boat will be floating just in front of you and you shan't miss a thing.

So, then. I crossed the hall to my room, opened the door softly, and tiptoed inside to fetch the glass of rye. My intention was to rinse the drinking glass out, fill it half full, and leave as quickly as possible, but as soon as I turned the faucet at the washbasin, and it sounded its usual A♭ above high C, Jane Mack opened her marvelous green eyes and sat up in my bed: her hair, brown and sleek as a sable's, fell around her shoulders, and the bed sheet slid to her hips; she raised her right arm to push the hair back; the movement flattened her stomach and lifted one of her breasts in a way that flexed my thighs to watch. I was still holding the quart of Sherbrook in my right hand and the glass in my left. Jane asked me, in a sleepy voice, whether it was eight o'clock yet; I told her it was not. She scratched her head, yawned, flopped back on the pillow, sighed, and, I think, went to sleep again instantly. The sheet was still at her hips, and she lay with her back to me. I believe that a small warm breeze was moving through the room, and I remember clearly that a little ray of sunlight reflected from something outside and streaked brilliant across the sun-browned skin of her, where her waist grew smallest above the round angle of her hip, thrust up by the hard mattress of my bed. I drank Capt. Osborn's medicine myself, as was *not* my practice, poured him another dose, and tiptoed out.

iii coitus

If you're still with me, I shan't even bother explaining why I couldn't tell you that Jane Mack was my mistress until after I'd announced that this day was a momentous one; either you're familiar with the business of climaxes and anticlimaxes, in which case no explanation is necessary, or else you know even less about storytelling than I do, in which case an explanation would be useless. She was, indeed, my mistress, and a fine one. To make the triangle equilateral, Harrison Mack was my excellent friend, and I his. Each of the three of us loved the other two as thoroughly as each was able, and in the case of Jane and Harrison, that was thoroughly indeed. As for me—well, I'll explain in a later chapter. And Harrison was quite aware of the fact that between 1932 and 1937 his wife spent many, many hours in my room and in my bed. If he didn't know that I had made love to her exactly six hundred seventy-three times, it's because Jane neglected to keep score as accurately as I did.

I'll explain it now: it's a good yarn, and Capt. Osborn can wait a chapter for his rye.

I first met Harrison Mack in 1925, at a party given by a classmate of mine from the University of Maryland Law School. It was a drunken affair held somewhere in Guilford, a wealthy section of Baltimore. At the time, I shall explain, I was in the early throes of a spell of misanthropic hermitism, which lasted from 1925 until 1930. I had, for various reasons, renounced the world of human endeavors and delights, and although I continued my legal studies (principally through inertia), I was having no more to do with my fellow man and his values than I had to. Rather a saint, I was, during those five or six years—a Buddhist saint, of the Esoteric variety. It was one of my provisional answers to the peculiar question of my life, and long after I'd outgrown it I still remembered that stance with pleasure.

For one thing, it made me appear mysterious, standing aloof in a bay window, smoking a cigarette with an air of quiet wisdom while all around me the party screamed and giggled. Some quite pleasant people, Harrison Mack among them, reasoned that I must have answers that they lacked, and sought me out; women thought me charmingly shy, and sometimes stopped at nothing to "penetrate the disdainful shell of my fear," as one of their number put it. Often as not, it was they who got penetrated.

On the night of this particular party I found myself being made friends with by a great handsome fellow who came over to my window, introduced himself as Harrison Mack, and stared out beside me for nearly an hour without speaking: some time afterwards I observed that Harrison involuntarily adopts, to a great extent, the mood and manner of whomever he happens to be with—a tendency I admire in him, for it implies that he has no characteristic mood or manner of his own. We talked after a while, brusquely, of several things: the working class, prohibition, law, the Sacco-Vanzetti affair, and Maryland. Harrison, it turned out, was well off; his father, Harrison Mack Senior, was president of a pickle company. Since the cucumbers that were ultimately transmogrified into Mack's Pickles were grown on the Eastern Shore, whence they were carried as whole pickles to the Baltimore plant for fancy processing, the Macks had summer homes sprinkled about the peninsula, and Harrison was no stranger to the haunts of my youth. We talked aloofly of pickles and wealth.

Harrison—a fine, muscular, sun-bronzed, gentle-eyed, patrician-nosed, steak-fed, Gilman-Schooled, soft-

spoken, well-tailored aristocrat—to his family's understandable alarm was a communist at the time. Not a
parlor communist, either: an out-and-out leaflet-writing
revolutionary who had sold his speedboat, his Stutz
automobile, and God knows what else, to live on when
his father disinherited him; who spent ten hours a day
writing and distributing party-line penny dreadfuls
among factory workers, including the employees of the
Mack Pickle factories; who took his lumps with the rest
when strikebreakers or other kinds of bullies—
including certain salaried employees of the Mack
Pickle factories—objected to his activities; who was at
the moment engaged to marry the woolliest-looking
specimen of intellectual Bolshevism I've ever laid un-
believing eyes upon, because she was ideologically
pure; and whose only remaining streak of good sense,
as far as I could see that night, was his refusal to
become actually a dues-paying member of the Party,
for fear it might prove a liability to the execution of his
schemes.

As it happened, Harrison did precisely, if accidental-
ly, the only thing that could possibly have induced me
to like him that night: he made it obvious from the
beginning that he liked me a great deal. He was an
engaging fellow, still is, and I saw nothing amiss in a
saint's having one friend. The sheer oppositeness of his
enthusiasm from anything I myself could conceivably
have been enthusiastic about at that time—though I
had been interested enough in social reform not too
long before—drew me to him, and, as I learned later,
he was attracted by my "transcendent rejection" (his
term) of the thing that meant life to him. In short, we
were soon friends, and walked blindly to my rooms at
dawn for more drink, singing the *Internationale* in
French through the mansioned and junipered roads of
Guilford.

I knew him well for the next year, or until my
graduation from law school. I was a saint throughout
the whole period—indeed, that mask endured for four
more years—and although we argued sometimes for
days, neither of us was rational enough to be convinced

of the other's position. I say this because I know for
certain that all the major mind changes in my life have
been the result not of deliberate, creative thinking on
my part, but rather of pure accidents—events outside
myself impinging forcibly upon my attention—which I
afterwards rationalized into new masks. And I suspect
that Harrison simply assumes, in time, the intellectual
as well as the manneristic color of his surroundings.

For example, when we said goodbye in 1926—I to
set up practice in Cambridge, he to assist a Party press
in Detroit—I thought I detected an ideologically im-
pure attitude in him toward his leaflet-writing colleagues. He had, in fact, come to loathe them, and, it
seemed to me, had begun to prefer refuting the *Men-
sheviki* with me in my room to supporting the *Bol-
sheviki* with them in some dirty factory. He was not at
all enthusiastic about his new assignment, and I think
he would have washed his hands of the whole business, but that such a defection would have given his
arguments for universal brotherhood a hollow ring. Our
separation upset Harrison more than me, whose nirvana
could hardly be ruffled by such a mundane circum-
stance as losing a friend.

I saw him next in 1932, under quite different
circumstances. I had been admitted as a partner in the
firm of Andrews & Bishop, and throughout 1927 and
1928 I enriched myself and the firm at the rate of
perhaps forty dollars a month—the folks of Cambridge
very wisely trust no new doctors or lawyers, even fifth-
generation natives of the county. I was living with my
father, a widower, in his house in East Cambridge. In
1929 Dad lost all his savings and property on the stock
market, and the next year he hanged himself with his
belt from a floor joist in the basement. After that I
made more money from the firm, despite the depres-
sion, since Dad's clients more or less inherited me as
their lawyer, and when the family house and lot, a
summer cottage at Fenwick Island, Delaware, and one
or two timber properties down the county had been
sold toward meeting Dad's debts, I moved into Room
307 of the Dorset Hotel, where I've lived ever since.

And I became a cosmic cynic, although I didn't bother to mention the fact to Harrison when I saw him again, any more than I'd told him before, in so many words, that I was a saint.

He walked into my office in Lawyers' Row, next to the courthouse, one afternoon, very solemnly, and put a bottle of gin on my desk. He had grown stouter and a bit tired-looking, but was still bronzed and handsome.

"I'm back," he said, indicating the gin, and for the rest of the afternoon we drank tepid gin and walked the several streets of Cambridge, renewing our friendship.

"What happened to your revolution in Detroit?" I asked him once. "I notice they're still making cars out there."

"Ah," he shrugged, "I got fed up with the fuzzy bastards."

"And the brotherhood of man?" I asked him later.

"To hell with the brotherhood of man!" he replied. "I wouldn't want those guys for field hands, much less brothers."

"What about Miss Moscow?" I asked later yet, referring to his fiancée of 1926.

"Free lover," he snorted. "I believed all men were brothers; she thought all men were husbands. I gave the whole mess up."

And so he had, for it became apparent, as he talked, that he was in fact a saint these days, of the sort I'd been earlier. He was having little to do with the world's problems any more.

"Social justice?" I asked him.

"Impossible to achieve, irrelevant if achieved," he answered, and went on to explain that men aren't worth saving from their capitalist exploiters.

"They'd be just as bad if they were on top," he declared. "Worse, in fact: we present capitalists are gentlemanly beasts, and my comrades were beastly beasts."

It was the "inner harmony" of the "whole man," he told me, that mattered. The real revolution must be in the soul and spirit of the individual, and collective materialistic enthusiasms only distracted one from the disorder of his own soul.

"Marxism," he said, "is the opiate of the people."

He insisted I come to his house for dinner.

"To Baltimore?" I exclaimed. "Tonight?"

He blushed. "I'm living here now, Toddy." He explained that upon his recanting the Marxist heresy, his father had reinstated him in the Mack family's good graces and excellent credit ratings, and put him in charge of all the cucumber patches and raw processing plants on the Shore.

"We bought a house in East Cambridge," he said, "on the water. Just moved in. Come help us warm it."

"Us?"

"I'm married," he said, blushing again. "Loveliest thing you ever saw. Janie. Ruxton and Gibson Island, you know, but sensible. You'll love each other."

Well. I went to Harrison's house that evening, when we were good and drunk, and I recall saying "For pity's sake!" when I found that he'd bought Dad's old house—the one in which I was born and raised, and which I'd abandoned in disgust.

"Didn't know it was your family's place till I'd bought it and searched the title," Harrison claimed, beaming. He was happy about the whole thing: he'd heard since about Dad's debts and the fact that I'd lost the house along with the other property, and it gave him pleasure to have rescued it, so to speak, from unclean hands, and to be able to invite me to make it my home as often as I wished. I thanked him, and without much appetite followed him inside.

Jane, perhaps twenty-six at the time, met us at the door with an indulgent smile, and we were introduced. She was indeed "Ruxton and Gibson Island," a combination of beauty and athleticism. She wore a starched sundress and looked as if she'd just stepped from a shower after a swim. Her dark brown hair, almost black, was dried by the sun, as was her skin. That night she kept reminding me of sailboats, and has ever since. I think of her as perched on the windward washboard of a racing sailboat, a Hampton or a Star, perhaps tending the jib sheet, but certainly squinting against the sun in a brilliant blue world—a sun that heats the excellent timber beneath her thighs, and dries the spray on her face and arms, and warms the Chesapeake wind that fans her cheeks, fluffs her hair, and swells the gleaming sails. And in fact her skin, particularly across the plateau of her stomach, did indeed, I later learned, smell of sunshine, and her hair of salt spray; and the smell of her in my head never failed for five years to give me that giddy exhilaration which as a boy I always felt when I approached Ocean City on a family excursion, and the first heady spume of Atlantic in the air made my senses reel. To be sure, she insisted it was simply the result of not washing her hair as often as she should: she was in fact an ardent sailor.

For dinner we were served chicken breasts and some vegetable or other. Harrison was too drunk to bother with small talk; he ate and gave polite orders to the maid. And I was too full of gin and Jane to do much besides stare at the chickens' breasts and hers. Luckily, Harrison had told her that I was shy—his impression of my former sainthood—and so she interpreted as a timid inability to look her in the face what was actually a hushed and admiring if somewhat drunken ogling directly beneath. I've no idea what was said that evening, but I remember clearly that, as frequently used to happen when my sexual passions were aroused and unsatisfied, my ailing prostate gave me pain that night, and I was unable to sleep.

Of course I wanted to make love to her—I can't think of any attractive girl I ever saw in my youth whom I didn't wish to take to bed, and young Mrs. Mack was, if somewhat grave like her husband, a good deal more lovely and sensible than most of the women I'd encountered in my thirty-two years. Nor had I scruples about adultery—I was a cynic, remember. Still, I know that left to myself I'd never have carried my attentions beyond ogling her and telling her, half seriously, in Harrison's presence, that I was in love with her: I simply didn't choose to prejudice my friendship with Harrison, whom I really enjoyed, or to do anything

which, if successful, might disturb what appeared to be
a pleasant marriage. There could, I decided during the
first weeks of what turned out to be a close friendship
between the three of us, be no doubt that in their sober
fashion Jane and Harrison were in love with each other.

But the matter was taken out of my hands one
August weekend. Harrison had acquired one of his
father's summer cottages, on Todd Point, downriver
from Cambridge, and the three of us often spent week-
ends there, sailing, swimming, fishing, drinking, and
talking. On the morning of the second Saturday in
August he and Jane roused me out of bed in the hotel,
loaded me into their roadster with themselves and two
cases of beer, and set out for the cottage. It struck me
during the ride that they were unusually, even deliberately, exuberant: Harrison roared risqué songs at the
top of his voice; Jane, sitting in the middle, had her
arms around both of us; husband and wife both called
me "Toddy boy." I sighed to myself, resolved not to
wonder, and emptied three bottles of beer before we
finished the fifteen-mile trip to the cottage.

All morning we swam and drank, and the exaggerated liveliness and good-fellowship continued without
letup. It was decided that after lunch we would load
the rest of the beer into the Macks' sailboat—a beamy,
clinker-built knockabout—and sail to Sharp's Island, in
the Bay at the mouth of the Choptank, in order to sail
back again. Harrison gave Jane a long goodbye kiss and
set off to find ice, which he declared we needed in
quantity; Jane set her bathing-suited self to washing
the lunch dishes, and I went to sleep on the Macks'
bed in the cottage's one bedroom. The absence of
Harrison—the first time he'd left us alone together, as it
happened, because of my supposed shyness—was con-
spicuous, and on my way to sleep I was acutely conscious of Jane's presence on the opposite side of the
plywood partition. I fell asleep imagining her cool
brown thighs—they must be cool!—brushing each other, perhaps, as she walked about the kitchen; the gold
down on her upper arms; the salt-and-sunshine smell of
her. The sun was glaring through a small window at

the foot of the bed; the cottage smelled of heat and resinous pine. I was tired from swimming, sleepy from beer. My dream was lecherous, violent—and unfinished. Embarrassingly. For I felt a cool, real hand caress my stomach. It might have been ice, so violently did my insides contract; I fairly exploded awake and into a sitting position. I believe it was "Good Lord!" I croaked. I croaked something, anyhow, and with both hands grabbed Jane, who sat nude—unbelievable!—on the edge of the bed; buried my face in her, so startled was I; pulled her down with me, that skin against mine; and *mirabile dictu!* I did indeed explode, so wholly that I lay without sense or strength.

Damned dream, to wake me helpless! I was choked with desire, and with fury at my impotence. Jane was nervous; after the first approach, to make which had required all her courage, she collapsed on her back beside me and scarcely dared open her eyes.

The room was dazzlingly bright! I was so shocked by the unexpectedness of it that I very nearly wept. Incredible, smooth, tight, perfect skin! I pressed my face into her, couldn't leave her untouched for an instant. I quiver even now, twenty-two years later, to write of it, and why my poor heart failed to burst I'm unable even to wonder.

Well, it was no use. I fell beside her, maddened at my incapacity and mortified at the mess I'd made. That, it turned out, was the right thing to do: my self-castigation renewed Jane's courage.

"Don't curse yourself, Toddy." She kissed me—sweetness!—and stroked my face.

"No use," I muttered into her.

"We'll see," she said lightly, entirely self-possessed now that I seemed shy again: I resolved to behave timidly for the rest of my life. "Don't worry about it. I can fix it."

"No you can't," I moaned.

"Yes I can," she whispered, kissing my ear and sitting up beside me.

Merciful heavens, reader! Marry Ruxton and Gibson Island, I charge you! Such an imaginative, athletic, informed, exuberant mistress no man ever had, I swear: she burst frequently into spontaneous, nervous laughter. . . .

Enough. I don't really believe in chivalry any more than in anything else—but I shan't go further. Enough to know that we were soon able to commit jubilant adultery. Afterwards we smoked and talked.

"How about Harrison?" I asked.

"All right."

"All right?"

"Yes."

"How?"

"He doesn't mind."

"*Doesn't* or *won't?*"

"Doesn't."

"He knows?" I asked incredulously.

"Approves."

"Don't you love each other?"

"Of course," she said. "Don't be silly."

"What the hell!"

"We talked it over," she explained, embarrassed again. "Harrison thinks the world of you, and I do, too. We don't see why a woman can't make love to somebody she likes a lot, just for the pleasure of it, without a lot of complications. Do you?"

"Of course not," I said quickly.

"That's how we felt," she said. I was becoming curious and a bit amused. "Harrison and I love each other completely," Jane went on, speaking very solemnly and scratching a fly bite on one leg. "So much that neither of us could possibly ever be jealous. If you thought for a minute that I didn't love him because of what I've done, I'd die."

"Nonsense," I assured her, just as solemnly. "I understand everything."

"Thank heaven." She sighed and rested her head on me. "We talked it over for a long time. I was scared to death. I still don't know if I should've done it, but Harrison is wonderful. He's so *objective*."

"I've loved you since the first time I saw you," I

said, and though I intended it to sound convincing, the solemnity of it made me blush.

"I wish you wouldn't say that," Jane said. "I don't think there's got to be any love in it. I like you a lot, as a friend, but that's all, Toddy."

"Not for me."

"I mean it," she said. "I enjoyed making love to you, and I hope you liked it, too. That's plenty enough, I think, without falsifying it with any romance."

"I agree, if that's how you want it," I said sedately. "You were the finest thing in the world."

She cheered up a lot, then. She went to the icebox for beer—I noticed there was at least fifty pounds of ice inside—and when I came up behind her, held her against me, and nuzzled the back of her neck, she laughed and pressed my hands more tightly against her with her own.

"I don't know how I'll be able to face Harrison," I said, in order to please her.

"Oh, you mustn't be embarrassed, Toddy. He's wonderful about this. He was as eager as I was. He really thinks you're fine."

"He's amazing," I said. She seemed afraid that I wouldn't appreciate his marvelousness. "He's a regular saint."

"He admires you a lot." Her back was toward me while she opened the beer.

"But he's better in every way than I am," I declared to the calendar on the wall. "How can I ever pay him back?"

Now I confess that this last was a loaded question; barrister that I am, I was curious to learn the extent to which Harrison had suggested to his wife that she go to bed with his friend.

"He doesn't expect any payment," she assured me. "I mean, I don't either. You mustn't feel obliged at *all*, Toddy. The thing is to not make much of it; it was just for the pleasure of it; that's all."

"I can't believe that any man could go on liking another man, though, after that," I said doubtfully.

"I swear he will, Toddy!" Jane cried, very urgently

for one determined to make light of the whole matter. "How can I convince you? Honest, it was as much his idea as mine!"

I shook my head to indicate either the difficulty anyone might have in comprehending such an unorthodox situation, or the awe that an ordinary, unthinking, weak-willed mortal such as myself necessarily felt before such saintly generosity as Harrison Mack's.

"Cheer up," Jane smiled, and kissed me on the nose as she handed me my beer. I was certain my attitude had been the best possible one. She was in control, sheltering and encouraging me. Somewhat self-consciously, but apparently for my benefit, she slipped off the robe she'd covered herself with and began donning lithely the bathing suit she'd stripped off to come to me earlier. The show, I supposed, was part of the gift from Saint Harrison. It was a dazzlingly good show, and I drank it in with my beer.

After I'd calmed a little from the shock of being seduced, I sat in an old glider on the little screened porch of the cottage to watch the Choptank through the pines. Jane came through, smiled at me as though to say again, "Please don't worry, now; I swear Harrison approves," and walked down the lawn and out on the pier to the sailboat. I watched her then with pleasure as she pumped the bilge, sponged the hull and deck, and bent the mainsail and jib to the spars. Everything she did was graceful, efficient, and lust-provoking. I shook my head in astonishment at the whole business.

I heard the car drive up, and a moment later Harrison entered through the rear of the cottage. He made a noisy business of putting the unnecessary ice away, and after a while came out on the porch with me, handed me yet another beer, and sat on the glider. He was, of course, embarrassed, and despite himself made an exaggerated show of everything: lighting his cigarette and mine, taking deep draughts of the beer, stretching out his legs, sighing, yawning. No question but that he knew very well I had made love to his wife. We rather avoided looking either at each other or at Jane, whose rangy body was much before us. I smiled at the notion of Harrison's pulling a revolver from his shirt and laying me out with three slugs of lead. I began recalling all the violent consequences of adultery I'd ever heard of as a lawyer and a reader of tabloid newspapers. Was this hospitable prostitution something novel, or did one simply never hear of it?

"Well," Harrison croaked, in a voice that I believe was meant to be hearty, "we can either keep quiet about it, like gentlemen, or talk frankly about it, like I'd like to, to make sure we understand each other."

"Sure," I said, and began peeling the label off my beer bottle.

"She makes love well, doesn't she?" Harrison grinned.

"Oh, yes indeed!" I said.

There was a silence that Harrison didn't let last more than an instant.

"I want you to know it's all right with me, Toddy," he said, his voice still unnatural. "I approved of it as much as Janie did. She likes you a lot, you know, and I do too. I think it was a swell idea she had."

I was certain now that it had been Harrison's idea.

"Janie and I love each other completely," he went on, wishing I'd help him. "We're not stupid enough to be affected by things like jealousy or conventions. [*Pause*] You can have sexual attractions apart from love. We both enjoy love-making. [*Pause*] If I was attracted to any girl, Janie wouldn't be silly enough to object to me going to bed with her, because she knows there wouldn't be any love in it."

"Of course not," I said.

"It's like playing tennis," Harrison laughed. "Just for the fun and exercise. Some guys would get jealous if their wife played tennis with another man, or danced with him. Actually, I guess kissing is a more serious offense than love-making, because it's no fun in itself, but just a symbol of something else."

I shook my head in apparent awe.

"*Don't feel obligated*," Harrison laughed. "For Christ's sake don't thank me for anything. Just enjoy it.

The thing is, don't make too much of it. It gets all out of proportion."

Well, I wasn't making anything out of it.

"Are any of us any different than we were?" he went on.

"I am," I said solemnly. It was clear to me that whether he realized it or not, Harrison very much wanted thanking and being obliged to; I decided to make him feel very good.

"Oh, sure," he grinned. "But you know what I mean."

"But you don't know what *I* mean," I said. "It was my first time."

"What?"

"That's right." I stared at my peeled beer bottle. "I was a virgin."

"No!" he breathed, realizing that this enormous fact was not to be laughed at. "How old? Thirty?"

"Thirty-two," I said. "I had prostate trouble for a long time."

Harrison glanced out to where Jane was walking back up the pier toward the cottage.

"Well say," he said, "I hope we didn't do anything you didn't like." He was extremely impressed and flattered.

"No," I said. "It was fine, Harrison. Of course I've nothing to compare it with."

"Well listen," he said quickly, for Jane was coming near. "For Christ's sake don't feel obligated to me. I thought it was a swell idea. I did it—we did it— because we like you. And don't get the idea—I've heard of guys like this—don't get the idea I'm the kind of guy that has to push his wife off on his friends."

"Of course not."

"Well, here comes Janie," he said, relieved. "Cheer up, now. And for Christ's sake *don't feel obligated*."

"All right," I said.

The breeze that afternoon was stiff, and a quietude settled on the three of us. For my part, I did a lot of staring at nothing, as though preoccupied with my thoughts. Harrison and Jane assumed that I was meditating on the great thing that had happened to me, and they were flattered and uneasy, and spoke in cheerful voices about nothing. Harrison, I could see, was bursting to tell Jane I'd been a virgin. Both behaved protectively and with exaggerated consideration for my feelings: it was, let me assure you, a real and thoroughgoing generosity in the Macks that I smiled at inwardly—nothing false about it except the manifestations, and that falsification was due to the strained situation, which I was aggravating by my silence. I could pretty much see where the thing was leading.

May I explain?

Really, you see, Harrison and Jane were quite ordinary people, only a little more intelligent and a lot better-looking and richer than most. They had few friends, by their own choice, preferring to be on intimate terms with just one or two people. There was nothing affected in Jane's warmth—she was naturally disposed to affection—and Harrison's intelligence, while somewhat disoriented and not really keen, was capable of convincing both of them that most social conventions are arbitrary. Yet I knew Harrison well enough to know that his emotions were often at variance with his intelligence—he realized the irrational nature of race prejudice, for example, but couldn't bring himself to like Negroes—and I supposed Jane had similar conflicts. Doubtless they'd thought about this move for a long time, each titillated with the adventure; perhaps they'd discussed it in bed together, in the dark, where their embarrassment—or eagerness—wouldn't show. Neither would want to appear overenthusiastic, I imagine, for fear of making the other suspicious—that Jane was dissatisfied or Harrison perverted, neither of which suspicions was true. I'm sure they'd worked out every detail, savoring the deed before it was committed, imagining my surprise and pleasure, and my gratitude. I really liked Harrison, and for that reason I was sorry he'd initiated the affair, because I anticipated certain unpleasant consequences from it. But it was done: Jane was officially my mistress for a while—I was sure she'd be back for more—and I resolved to enjoy the thing while it lasted, for she was all that a man, shy or otherwise, could want in a bed partner.

These were the things I thought as we rounded Todd Point and sailed on a close reach directly for Sharp's Island. Jane was at the tiller—an excellent helmsman, of course—I tended the jib sheet, and Harrison lay supine in the bilge beside the centerboard trunk, his feet forward, the mainsheet in one hand and a cigar in the other, talking to Jane, on whose bare feet his head rested. We took a swim when we reached the island, got stung by sea nettles, talked a bit about politics, and smoked cigarettes. After a while I pled fatigue and lay down to sleep on a blanket on the sand. Jane and Harrison declared they were going to walk around the island.

The time came when I felt her hand, but I had heard her returning up the beach, and so lost no manliness through surprise. I pulled her down beside me at once and kissed her.

"Where's Harrison?" I asked her.

"Other side of the island," she said, and I had the bathing suit half off her before she could add, "he's getting firewood."

"Let's go in the trees," she said, a little nervously. "They could see us from Cook's Point if they had field glasses."

"Never mind," I said. "Let's oblige me."

"Don't say that," she said.

Harrison came back as it was getting dark, dragging after him a roped bundle of firewood, and found us sitting dressed and talking on the blanket. He was not so cheerful as before, and set about silently and busily to build the fire, his stooped back half-accusing me of letting him do all the work. I let him do all the work. He remained morose throughout the rest of the evening and during the run back to the cottage. Jane made some attempt at cheerfulness, but lapsed into silence when she got no response. I watched them benignly, wondering what had happened to everyone's objectivity.

By next day the mood was gone, replaced by

Harrison's usual cheerfulness; but its existence, though short-lived, was, I thought, indicative of chinks in the saintly armor. Of course, I tend to see significances in everything.

"*It was just for the pleasure of it; that's all,*" Jane had told me.

"*You can have sexual attractions apart from love,*" Harrison had told me.

Yet: "The truth is, I do love you in a way, Toddy," Jane said a week later in my hotel room. "Not the same way as I love Harrison, but it's more than just friendship; and it makes love-making more fun, doesn't it?"

"Of course," I said.

And: "A woman can love two or several men in the same way at the same time," Harrison declared after that, one night at dinner at his house, "or in different ways at the same time, or in the same way at different times, or in different ways at different times. The 'one-and-only-and-always' idea is just a conventional notion."

"Of course," I said.

Nor was I being especially hypocritical, although I'd just as readily agreed earlier to the proposition that love is separable from copulation, and copulation from love. The truth is that while I knew very well what copulation is and feels like, I'd never understood personally what love is and feels like. Are the differences between, say, one's love for his wife, his mistress, his parents, his cats, his nation, his hobby, his species, his books, and his natural environment differences in kind, or merely in degree? If in kind, are the kinds definable to the point of intelligibility? If in degree, is the necessarily general definition which can cover them all so general as to be meaningless? Is this thing a fact of nature, like thirst, or purely a human and civilized invention? If he is in love who simply decides to say, "I am in love," then love I'd never known, for often as I'd said, "I am in love," I'd said it always to women who expected to hear it, never to myself. As for copulation, whether between humans or other sorts of animals, it makes me smile.

Despite which fact, I could assent without qualm
to either of the Macks' sets of propositions, for they
speak only of "a person," not of everybody; who was I
to say that "a person" can or cannot divorce love from
copulation, when I didn't comprehend love? That "a
person" can or cannot love several others at once, when
I didn't comprehend love? Assenting even simultaneously to contradictory propositions has never especially
troubled me, and these of the Macks weren't simul-
taneous. I was not and am not interested in the truth or
falsehood of the statements.

What I *was* interested in, when I thought of it now
and then in the weeks that followed, was the fact that
the Macks had so changed their minds, because it
corresponded to my speculations about the course of
the affair. I scarcely regarded myself as involved in it
at all: my curiosity lay entirely in the character of
Harrison and, to a lesser degree, of Jane. When I'd got
home that August weekend after losing my chastity, I
did a bit of conjecturing, supplementing my conjec-
tures with notes. Here is one of the outlines I wrote of
Harrison's psychic process:

ANTE COITUM FELIX

    I Desire for adventure.
   II Titillation at idea of extra-marital sex.
  III Reluctance to suggest idea to wife.
  IV Love for friend—suggests idea of ex.-mar. sex
        for wife with friend.
   V Titillation at idea.
  VI Objective discussion with wife of jealousy,
        adultery, *etc.*
 VII Planning of actual affair betw. friend and
        wife.

THE ACT

VIII Desperate objectivity: *"Don't feel obli-
        gated!"*
  IX Real wrestling with jealousy, despite intellec-

tual tolerance. Unusual demands on wife's affections.

X Moodiness at wife's enjoyment of affair, and refusal to hear of her canceling it.

XI Insistence that wife continue affair with friend, and mounting jealousy when she does.

XII Desultoriness except when wife asks what's up; then cheerfulness and objectivity, necessarily, or wife will end affair and chance for martyrdom.

Stages I through X, if not XII, were matters of history, easily enough inferred by the time I wrote the list. But I went on as follows:

POST COITUM TRISTE

XIII Wife, to reassure herself, decides she loves friend "in a way."

XIV Husband doubts friend appreciates enormity of his good fortune.

XV Both h. & w. become more demanding of friend; he is their property. Jealous of him, if not of each other.

XVI Want declarations of love from friend.

XVII *Friend refuses*—friendship cools.

XVIII Active dislike of friend for his ingratitude.

XIX Suspension of affair.

XX Period of mutual silence: h. & w. love each other more than before, in self-defense.

This was as far as I could see with any certainty, but from there I outlined a number of possible directions that the business might take:

I Permanent disaffection (probable)

II Resumption of affair on original basis (quite possible)

III Resumption of affair on part of wife, against husband's will (very doubtful)

IV Resumption of qualified affection, but no
more sex (quite possible)

I made other outlines, as well, in the days that
followed, but this one, at least as far as Stage XX,
proved the most accurate. First of all, as I have already
suggested, when the horns on Harrison's brow were but
a few days old, Jane and I contrived to lengthen them a
bit, whether at his instigation or not I can only guess.
I had returned to my room for a nap after lunch, as
was my practice even then. She was waiting for me,
and not long afterwards she said, "The truth is, I do
love you in a way, Toddy. Not the same way as I love
Harrison, but it's more than just friendship; and it
makes love-making more fun, doesn't it?"

"Of course," I said.

I was sitting on the edge of my bed. She was
standing directly in front of me. I believed she wanted
me to tell her that I loved her.

"I love you," I said. I was right: she did want to
hear it.

During the next year or so the affair went on
strongly. Janie actually began spending every Tuesday
and Friday night in my room—fantastic, so to schedule
it!—and Harrison dropped into the office at least twice
a day. They insisted that I take dinner with them
every night, and Harrison even suggested that I move
in with them.

"You can have your old bedroom back," he said.
"I've always felt it was the Andrews' house, and that
we were the guests."

The mention of my old bedroom, where I'd slept
from age zero to age seventeen, reminded me of a
certain adventure, and I laughed.

"I can't help it," Harrison smiled, a little abashed.

"No, no, it's not that," I grinned. But I turned his
proposal down, to be sure. Incredible! Yet he was, I'm
sure, more manly in every way than I—it was a matter
of sheer generosity, I swear!

Well, the thing soon commenced getting out of
hand, as I'd feared. Jane was as lovely and skillful as

ever, but she was too loving, too solicitous. Harrison was planning a summer trip to the Bahamas for the three of us. Jane spoke vaguely for a while of my marrying some *intelligent* girl, but soon spoke of it not at all. Harrison mentioned it once too, with the implication that the four of us would live precisely like one happy family. All this out of the excess of their love for me. It was time to take measures.

Once he stopped in my office when I happened to be preparing a suit *a vinculo matrimonii* for Dorothy Miner, a plump Negro girl of eighteen, who picked crabs at one of the seafood houses. She was an entirely uneducated girl, a friend of mine, and she was arranging a divorce from her husband of a month, one Junior Miner, who had abandoned her. Dorothy's skin, teeth, and eyes were excellent, and she snapped her gum. Our relationship was Platonic.

"Hi, Harrison," I greeted him. "This is Dorothy."

Dorothy grinned hello and snapped a salute.

"How d'you do," Harrison said, scarcely noticing her. "Coming for lunch, Toddy?"

Recently he'd been taking me to lunch uptown.

"In a few minutes," I said. "Dorothy here is divorcing her husband, and I'm handling her suit."

"Oh?" He sat in one of the chairs, lit a cigar, and prepared to read a magazine.

I peered into the waiting room. The secretary had already gone to lunch.

"She's poor," I went on, "so I take it out in trade."

Harrison flinched as though I'd slapped him and, blushing deeply, looked at me with a twisted smile.

"Are you kidding?" He looked surreptitiously at Dorothy, who at my statement had clapped her hand over her mouth to hold down laughter and chewing gum.

"No indeed," I grinned. "I'm getting to be real good at this business. Isn't that so, Dorothy?"

"Whatever you say, Mister Andrews," Dorothy giggled; it was a tremendously funny joke.

"What the hell, Toddy!" Harrison laughed sharply.

"As a matter of fact," I said, moving toward her, "I believe her bill is overdue right now."

Dorothy giggled and fussed with her hair. But she rose uncertainly from her chair, brushed her skirt flutteringly, and stood facing me.

"Aw, say, Toddy!" Harrison croaked, getting up from his chair.

"Excuse me," I said. "You go on to lunch; I'll be along in a minute."

"What the hell, Toddy!" Harrison exclaimed, aghast and angry. "I'll see you later!" He left the office as fast as he could, actually perspiring from his humiliation and embarrassment. I went to the window and watched him hurry up the sidewalk.

Dorothy, meanwhile, watched my face for some clue. "What you up to, Mister Andrews?" she demanded, bursting into giggles after the question.

I don't recall my answer, but I'm sure Dorothy laughed at whatever it was, since she thought me mad. I went to join Harrison.

"What the hell, Toddy!" he said during lunch, for perhaps the third time. "I'd have felt cheap!"

He was apologizing for what he feared I'd call his prudery, to be sure, and perhaps even chastising himself for having missed his chance; but more than that he was, I saw, deeply insulted.

"I'm not prejudiced; I just couldn't have anything to do with a Negro girl," is what he said, but *"You've been unfaithful to Jane and to me; you've defiled yourself and us in that black hussy"* is what he meant.

"Do you make a practice of that?" he asked me.

"Sure of 'em pay in eggs," I said blithely. "But a man can use just so many eggs."

"Aw, hell, Toddy."

"What's the matter, man?" I laughed. "Don't you want me to put what I've learned into practice?"

"You may do anything you want to, of course," Harrison said. "I've said that all along."

"Hell, Harrison, you knew I wasn't a virgin, and Jane did, too. What did you think I'd been doing for thirty-two years?"

But of course they didn't know; they'd believe anything I told them. Harrison could only shake his head. His appetite was gone.

"You mustn't take things seriously," I said cheerfully. "No matter how you approach it, everything we do is ridiculous." I laughed again, as I do every time I remember what happened in my bedroom when I was seventeen.

"Friendship's not a ridiculous thing," Harrison said, full of emotion. "I don't see why you've decided to hurt Jane and me."

"Friendship may or may not be ridiculous," I said, "but it sure is impossible."

"No, it's not," Harrison said. He was very near tears, I think, and it looked ridiculous in a robust fellow like him. "I just wish you hadn't hurt us. There wasn't any reason to. I'm not angry. I just wish you hadn't done it."

"Nonsense," I said. "I didn't say anything."

"Do you think love is ridiculous?" Harrison asked.

"Everything is ridiculous."

"Why'd you lie about being a virgin? There wasn't any reason to."

"You deserved that for expecting to hear it, and being pleased when you heard it," I said.

Harrison practically slumped on the table. I really believe I had destroyed his strength.

"You don't like us," he declared hopelessly.

"Buck up, man, this is degrading!" I said. "What difference does anything make? Of course I was acting, but you all wanted an act. How do you think Jane would've felt if I'd told her the truth? I'm on your side."

"The hell you are," Harrison grumbled; he was angry enough at me now to get up and walk out of the restaurant. He even left me with the check.

It was Tuesday, and there was a good chance that Jane was in my room, waiting for me to come up for my nap. I took my time, strolling down to Long Wharf before heading toward the hotel, so that Harrison could rescue her from my clutches. When finally I went in, no one was there, but I thought I detected the smell of her skin in the air. Perhaps it was my imagination. I sighed and, for the first time since that August weekend, really relaxed. It was a pity: the Macks were agreeable people, and they would have a bad day.

iv the captain's confession

Now, what was I doing? I believe I didn't explain how Jane got to be back in my bed again by 1937, did I? Well, I'll finish the story later, as we go along: I've stayed close to the plot for a good long time now. Wait: looking back I see that the whole purpose of the digression was to explain why it was that I was incapable of great love for people, or at least solemn love. And I see I didn't explain it yet, at that. Good Lord! The last half of this book, I'm afraid, will be nothing but all these explanations I've promised and postponed. Let's forget all this for the moment and get Capt. Osborn his glass of rye, which I've been holding all this time, before he dies of thirst and old age.

Very well: I tiptoed from my room, so as not to disturb Jane again from her slumbers, and took the old rascal his drink, which he threw down neat with much sputtering and fuming.

"Ah, that's a good boy, son," he grinned upon finishing. Already his face was regaining its color. "If yer headed out, why I'll jest take yer arm, sir."

Mister Haecker had watched us listlessly all this time. That morning he seemed more nervous and preoccupied than usual, and—I swear this isn't all hindsight—I believe I suspected just then that for some reason or other this June 21 or 22 was going to be as momentous a day for him as for me.

"I'm headed out right now, Cap'n," I said. Capt. Osborn wheezed to his feet and limped over to take my arm, so that I could help him down the steps.

"Going out today, Mister Haecker?" I asked.

"No, son," Mister Haecker sighed. He looked as if he would say more; as if, in fact, the "more" were filling his head to bursting. One terrible look he flashed me, of pure panic; I've not forgotten it. I waited a moment for it to come. "No," Mister Haecker said again, flatly this time, and rose to return to his room.

Capt. Osborn and I left then, and started the slow descent of the stairs. I tried carefully to feel every step, so full was I of the wonder of this day; of my new and final answer, and my stupidity at not having thought of it years ago.

But I am not a thinker, nor have I ever been. My thinking is always after the fact, the effect of my circumstances, never the other way round.

"This is step number nine," I said to myself. "Isn't it a nice step? This is step number ten, as you go down, or eighteen as you come up. Isn't it grand? This is step number eleven, or seventeen . . ." and so on. There was plenty of time to enjoy each step for its particular virtues, because of Capt. Osborn's lameness. I was having a fine time.

On step number seventeen going down, or eleven coming up, Capt. Osborn pinched my arm, the one supporting him, and chuckled softly. "How was it last night, Toddy boy?"

I looked at him in amused surprise. "What?"

The Captain chortled. "Ye don't s'pose a nosy old dog like me don't know what's up, do ye?" He poked me with his elbow, and actually winked.

"You lecherous old bastard!" I grinned. "I bet you've been listening at my door!"

"Naw, boy, I got ears for that kind o' carryin's-on. Shucks! Don't think I give a durn about it, boy. I'd have 'em up to my room by the clutch if I weren't most dead."

I said nothing, wondering only why he'd bothered to tell me about it.

"I been listenin' to you and her for a right smart while now," he said seriously, but with his eyes twinkling. "She's a fine gal, and a frisky-lookin' one. You know how it is when yer old."

"How is it?"

Capt. Osborn snorted and smacked me on the shoulder. "Well, sir, I jest couldn't go on a-listenin' to ye any more, Toddy boy, without ye knew about it. 'Tweren't noways fair. I even left my door open some nights, now that's how wicked I am. Ye can think what ye like; I done told ye now and it's off my chest."

He seemed really relieved—of course he was a little drunk, too.

"How long have you been listening?" I asked him. "Since 1932?"

"Durn near," Capt. Osborn admitted glumly. "I swear I never did no more'n leave my door open, though. I don't care, Toddy; ye can hate me if ye want."

Now he didn't dare to look me in the eye. He was unable to speak for shame. We were near the bottom of the steps.

"So you think she's frisky-looking, do you?" The change in my voice gave him courage, but he still felt bad.

"I've had a bunch o' women, Toddy," he whispered to me solemnly. "My wife, God rest her poor soul, was a fine woman, despite she weren't no beauty; and a waterman—well, ye run into lots o' floozies round the boats, want to help a drudgeman spend his wad. Some of 'em was mighty lively, too, for a small town, sir! And I been to the city, and the fancy houses, I won't lie." He smiled at the memory, then grew solemn again. "But I swear to God as I'm standin' here before ye this minute, may He smite me dead if I'm a-lyin', I never in my life seen a woman could hold a candle to that gal o' yourn, Toddy. She's a beauty, I declare!"

"You old goat," I said after a minute.

"I shan't do it no more, Toddy," he said wretchedly.

"Indeed you shan't." I laughed, and his spirits were soon restored. I had had a magnificent idea, an idea such as one should have every day. Oh, it was going to be a lovely momentous day. "Good morning to you, Cap'n," I said when we reached the lobby. "I may go by your corner later on today. I'm going to pay my bill now."

But Capt. Osborn wasn't ready to let me go yet. He held on to my arm and chewed his coffee-stained mustache for a minute, composing what he had to say. I waited respectfully, for I was in no hurry at all.

"Do you believe that malarky o' Haecker's?" he asked finally, a little suspiciously. " 'Bout how nice it is to git old?"

"No."

"I sleep light," he said after a moment, looking past me to the street door. "Some days I don't sleep a wink from one day to the next, sir, but I don't git tired, or I guess I'm the same tired all the time, sleep or no. Ye git that way when yer old; ye don't need sleep 'cause ye ain't able to do nothin' when yer awake to tire ye out no more'n ye already are. An old man hears what he ain't s'posed to hear, and don't hear half what he ought to. I've heard you and that young lady till I wanted to holler, if my head wasn't clogged up with the catarrh and my lights a-burnin' with the bronchitis and my joints stiff with the rheumatism, and I'd cuss myself for listenin', and couldn't stop to save me. I'd cuss myself for not gittin' up to close the door, but when yer old as me, gittin' up is a chore, and ye got to sort o' collect yerself, and then ye jest wait all day to git back in bed, but can't sleep 'cause ye know that sooner or later that there bed ye was so hot to crawl into is goin' to be the last time ye'll crawl into it. That ain't no fit lullaby to git sung to sleep with, Toddy! And when I'd git up and go to the door, why I could jest hear ye all the plainer, and I'd tell myself that right there was somethin' I'll never do again on this earth!"

He paused for breath; I was astonished at his volubility.

"Well, sir, Haecker might be right; he's a sight smarter'n me, but I swear I can't see one durn thing to this *old* business. The sinus keeps a-fillin' yer nose till yer fit to drown, and yer eyes water, and yer legs go to sleep if ye set still, and yer bones pain ye if ye move. I'd rather be forty and feel good and be dumb as a post, and be fit to do work, than to feel all day like I weren't rightly alive, and hurt all the time and have to blow my nose till it's sore, and crack a cane on my legs to keep the blood a-goin', even if I knew all there was to know."

"Mister Haecker's just a kid," I smiled, delighted to hear Capt. Osborn talk.

"He ain't but seventy and fit as a fiddle," the old man snorted. "I'd of said the same thing at seventy if I'd of commenced to think about it, which I didn't commence to think about it till I was eighty. And I can tell you today it's an awful thing to think about, this *dyin'*, and I would rather be chokin' from the sinus, and not fit to git out o' bed no more, and use a bedpan and eat dry toast, than to be dead, sir! Any man tells ye yer goin' to git to like the idea jest 'cause yer old, he's lyin' to ye, and I want to tell ye right now, when the time comes I am goin' to cuss and holler."

Well, he went on in that vein, and I remember it all, but that's enough of Capt. Osborn for now—perhaps you don't enjoy old men as I do. When he had said his piece—and completely forgotten, I'm certain, what he'd been apologizing for—he went out into the street to take his place on the loafers' bench uptown with his cronies in the sunshine. I loved him, if I loved anyone, I think; death for him would be the hyphenated break in a rambling, illiterate monologue, a good way for it to be if you're most people. He was fooling himself and not fooling himself about it, so that ultimately he wasn't fooling himself at all, and hence it wasn't necessary to feel any pity for him. I felt much sorrier, in my uninvolved way, for Mister Haecker, with his paeans to old age and gracious death: he was really fooling himself, and one could anticipate that he would someday have a difficult time of it. In the meanwhile, he must spend all his energies shoring up his delusion, and do it, moreover, alone, for his intensity and prudishness found him no friends; Osborn, on the contrary, sniffed and wheezed and creaked and spat, and cursed and complained, and never knew a gloomy day in his life.

I remembered my little plan and went to the registration desk. Jerry Hogey, the manager, was on duty. He was a friend of mine, and it was due to his understanding of the world that Jane had been able to come to my room despite hotel policy at any time for the last five years. I bid him good morning as usual, and borrowing a sheet of hotel stationery from him, scribbled a note to Jane.

"This is for the young lady, Jerry," I said, folding it and giving it to him.

"Sure."

Then, as I had done every morning since 1930 (and still do), I wrote out a check for one dollar and fifty cents payable to the Dorset Hotel, for the day's lodging.

v a *raison de coeur*

That's right, I pay my hotel bill every day, and reregister every day, too, despite the fact that the hotel offers weekly and monthly and even seasonal rates for long-term guests. It's no eccentricity, friend, nor any sign of stinginess on my part: I have an excellent reason for doing so, but it is a *raison de coeur*, if I may say so—a reason of the heart and not of the head.

Doubly so; literally so. Listen: eleven times the muscle of my heart contracted while I was writing the four words of the preceding sentence. Perhaps six hundred times since I began to write this little chapter. Seven hundred thirty-two million, one hundred thirty-six thousand, three hundred twenty times since I moved into the hotel. And no less than one billion, sixty-seven million, six hundred thirty-six thousand, one hundred sixty times has my heart beat since a day in 1919, at Fort George G. Meade, when an Army doctor, Captain John Frisbee, informed me, during the course of my predischarge physical examination, that each soft beat my sick heart beat might be my sick heart's last. This fact—that having begun this sentence, I may not live to write its end; that having poured my drink, I may not live to taste it, or that it may pass a live man's tongue to burn a dead man's belly; that having slumbered, I may never wake, or having waked, may never living sleep—this for thirty-five years has been the condition of my existence, the great fact of my life: had been so for eighteen years already, or five hundred forty-nine million, sixty thousand, four hundred eighty

heartbeats, by June 21 or 22 of 1937. This is the enormous question, in its thousand trifling forms (Having
heard tick, will I hear tock? Having served, will I
volley? Having sugared, will I cream? Itching, will I
scratch? Hemming, will I haw?), toward answering
which all my thoughts and deeds, all my dreams and
energies have been oriented. This is the problem
which, having answered it thrice before without solv-
ing it, I had waked this one momentous morning with
the key to, gratuitously, gratis, like that! This question,
the fact of my life, is, reader, the fact of my book as
well: the question which, now answered but yet to be
explained, answers, reader, everything, explains all.

Well, perhaps not all, or at least perhaps not clearly. It doesn't directly explain, for example, why I chose
and choose to pay my bill daily, every morning, instead
of weekly or seasonally. Don't think, I beg you, that I
fear not living to get my money's worth if I pay too far
ahead: lose money I might, but fear losing it, never.
There's nothing in me of Miss Holiday Hopkinson, my
ninety-year-old neighbor and senior member of the
D.E.C., who buys her one-a-day vitamin pills in the
smallest bottles—for her, the real economy size—and
sleeps fully dressed, her arms folded funereally upon
her chest, so as to cause, by her dying, the least possible trouble for anybody. No, I pay my buck-fifty
every morning to remind myself—should I ever forget!—
that I'm renting another day from eternity, remitting
the interest on borrowed time, leasing my bed on the
chance I may live to sleep on it once more, for at least
the beginning of another night. It helps me maintain a
correct perspective, reminds me that long-range plans,
even short-range plans, have, for me at least, no value.

To be sure, one doesn't want to live as though
each day may be his last, when there is some chance
that it may be only his next. One needs, even in my
position, something to counter-balance the immediacy
of a one-day-at-a-time existence, a life on the installment plan. Hence my *Inquiry*, properly to prepare even
for the beginning of which, as I see it, would require
more lifetimes than it takes a lazy Buddhist to attain

Nirvana. My *Inquiry* is timeless, in effect; that is, I proceed at it as though I had eternity to inquire in. And, because processes persisted in long enough tend to become ends in themselves, it is enough for me to an hour's work, or two hours' work, on my *Inquiry* every night after supper, to make me feel just a little bit outside of time and heartbeats.

So, I begin each day with a gesture of cynicism, and close it with a gesture of faith; or, if you prefer, begin it by reminding myself that, for me at least, goals and objectives are without value, and close it by demonstrating that the fact is irrelevant. A gesture of temporality, a gesture of eternity. It is in the tension between these two gestures that I have lived my adult life.

vi maryland beaten biscuits

Now you know my secret, or an important part of it.
No one else—except Dr. Frisbee, I suppose—ever
knew it, not even my excellent friend Harrison. Why
should I have told him? I never told him I was a saint,
and yet he became one himself soon enough afterwards. I never told him in so many words that I was a
cynic, and yet he's one today, as far as I know. If I had
told him of my heart condition he'd only have tried to
acquire one too, and I've no particular wish to make
anyone unhappy. No, I long ago learned that one's
illnesses are both pleasanter and more useful if one
keeps their exact nature to himself: one's friends, uncertain as to the cause of one's queer behavior and
strange sufferings, impute to one a mysteriousness often
convenient. Even Jane never suspected my ailing
heart, and though she well knew—from how many
painful nights!—that something was wrong with me, I
never told her about my infected prostate, either. As a
result, she often attributed to herself failures in our
intercourse that were incontestably mine, and Jane—
proud Jane—is never lovelier or more desirable than
when contrite.

　　Enough: I paid my hotel bill, then, and stepped
onto High Street just as the clock on the People's Trust
building struck seven. Already the air was warm; it
promised to be a blistering day, like the day before,
when temperature and humidity both were in the
nineties. Very few people were about yet, and only an
occasional automobile wandered down the quiet ex-

panse of the street. I crossed diagonally against the traffic—to the corner of Christ Episcopal Church, whose lovely stones were softly greened, and strolled from there down the left side of High Street toward Long Wharf, eating my breakfast as I walked.

I recommend three Maryland beaten biscuits, with water, for your breakfast. They are hard as a haulseiner's conscience and dry as a dredger's tongue, and they sit for hours in your morning stomach like ballast on a tender ship's keel. They cost little, are easily and crumblessly carried in your pockets, and if forgotten and gone stale, are neither harder nor less palatable than when fresh. What's more, eaten first thing in the morning and followed by a cigar, they put a crabberman's thirst on you, such that all the water in a deep neap tide can't quench—and none, I think, denies the charms of water on the bowels of morning? Beaten biscuits, friend: beaten with the back of an ax on a sawn stump behind the cookhouse; you really need a slave system, I suppose, to produce the best beaten biscuits, but there is a colored lady down by the creek, next door to the dredge builder's. . . . If, like a condemned man, I had been offered my choice from man's cuisine for this my final earthly breakfast, I'd have chosen no more than what I had.

Few things are stable in this world. Your morning stomach, reader, ballasted with three Maryland beaten biscuits, will be stable.

High Street, where I walked, is like no other street in Cambridge, or on the peninsula. A wide, flat boulevard of a street, gently arched with edge-laid yellow brick, it runs its gracious best from Christ Church and the courthouse down to Long Wharf, the municipal park, two stately blocks away. One is tempted to describe it as lined with mansions, until one examines it in winter, when the leaves are down and the trees gaunt as gibbets. Mansions there are—two, three of them—but the majority of the homes are large and inelegant. What makes High Street lovely are the trees and the street itself. The trees are enormous: oaks and cottonwood poplars that rustle loftily above you like pennants atop mighty masts; that when leaved transform the shabbiest houses into mansions; that corrugate the concrete of the wide sidewalks with the idle flexing of their roots. An avenue of edge-laid yellow bricks is the only pavement worthy of such trees, and like them, it dignifies the things around it. Automobiles whisper over this brick like quiet yachts; men walking on the outsized sidewalk under the outsized poplars are dwarfed into dignity. The boulevard terminates in a circular roadway on Long Wharf—terminates, actually, in the grander boulevard of the Choptank. Daniel Jones, upon whose plantation the city of Cambridge now rests, put his house near where this street runs. Colonel John Kirk, Lord Baltimore's Dorchester land agent, built in 1706 the town's first house near where this street runs. There are slave quarters; there are porch columns made of ships' masts; there are ancient names bred to idle pursuits; there are barns of houses housing servantless, kinless, friendless dodderers; there are brazen parades and bold seagulls, eminence and imbecility; there are Sunday pigeons and excursion steamers and mock oranges—all dignified by the great trees and soft glazed brick of the street. The rest of Cambridge is rather unattractive.

As was my custom, I strolled down to the circle and over beside the yacht basin. The river was glassy and empty of boats, too calm to move the clappers of the bell buoy out in the channel, a mile away. A single early motor truck inched across the long, low bridge. The flag above the yacht club predicted fair weather. With a great sense of well-being I tossed the last hard half of my breakfast biscuits at a doubler crab mating lazily just beneath the surface. As was *their* custom, the gentleman did the swimming while the soft lady beneath, locked to him with all her legs, allowed him his pleasure, which might last for fourteen hours. Crabbers refer to the male and female thus coupled as one crab, a "doubler," just as Plato imagined the human prototype to be male and female joined into one being. My biscuit landed to starboard of the lovers, and the gentleman slid, unruffled, six inches to port, then submerged, girl friend and all, in search of the missile that had near scuttled his affair. I laughed and made a mental note to make a physical note, for my *Inquiry*, of the similarity between the crabbers and Plato, and to remind Jane that there were creatures who took longer than I.

I lit my first cigar and completed the circle, coming around to the side nearest the creek. Work was commencing in the lumber mill and shipyard across the creek mouth from where I stood: a weathered bugeye, worn by forty or fifty years of oyster-dredging, was hauled up on the railway, and a crew of men scraped barnacles and marine growth from her bottom. I surveyed the scene critically and with pleasure, but no more intently than usual, despite the fact that I might never see it again, for I was determined to preserve the typicality of this great day. I had knocked the first ash from my cigar and was preparing to walk part way up High Street to the garage where my boat lay a-building, when my satisfied eye caught something new in the picture: a brightly lettered poster tacked to a piling at the farthest corner of the wharf, where the creek joined the river, and at the foot of the piling a small package or bale tied with a string. I walked over to investigate.

ADAM'S ORIGINAL & UNPARALLELED FLOATING OPERA, announced the poster; *Jacob R. Adam, Owner & Captain.* 6 BIG ACTS! it went on to declare: DRAMA, MINSTRELS, VAUDEVILLE! *Moral & Refined!* TONIGHT TONIGHT TONIGHT TONIGHT! *Admissions:* 20¢, 35¢, 50¢! TONIGHT TONIGHT! FREE *Concert Begins at 7:30 PM! Show Begins 8:00 PM!*

The bundle at the foot of the piling contained printed handbills advertising the show in more detail; it was obviously dumped there temporarily by the showboat's advance man. I took a handbill from the bundle, stuck it into my coat pocket to read at my leisure, and continued my morning walk.

I smoked my way back onto High Street, the handbill folded in my pocket and my mind preoccupied with scampering ideas as flitting as idle mice. In thirty seconds I'd forgotten all about the poster, the handbill, and ADAM'S ORIGINAL & UNPARALLELED FLOATING OPERA.

vii my unfinished boats

When I think of Cambridge and of Dorchester County, the things I think of, understandably, are crabbing, oystering, fishing, muskrat-trapping, duckhunting, sailing, and swimming. It is virtually impossible, no matter what his station, for a boy to grow to puberty in the County without experiencing most of these activities and becoming proficient in one or two of them.

Virtually, but not entirely. I, for example, though I was not a sheltered child, managed to attain the age of twenty-seven years without ever having gone crabbing, oystering, fishing, muskrat-trapping, duckhunting, sailing, or even swimming, despite the fact that all my boyhood companions enjoyed these pursuits. I just never got interested in them. Moreover, I've never tasted an oyster; I can't enjoy crabmeat; I'd never choose fish for dinner; I detest wild game of any sort, rodent or fowl; and although Col. Henry Morton, who owns the biggest tomato cannery on God's earth, is a peculiar friend of mine, the tomatoes that line his coffers upset my digestion. But lest you conclude too easily that this represents some position of mine, let me add that I *have* done some sailing since I set up my law practice here in 1927—though I still can't handle a sailboat myself—and I'd become, as a matter of fact, something of an expert swimmer by the time of this story. And this *does*, in a small way, reflect a philosophical position of mine, or at least a general practice, to wit: being less than consistent in practically everything, so that any general statement about me will probably be inadequate. To be sure, many people make such statements anyway—I get the impression at times that doing so constitutes a chief activity of the town's idle intelligences—but I have the not-inconsiderable satisfaction of knowing that they're wrong and of hearing them contradict one another (and thereby, I conclude, cancel one another out).

All this, deviously, by way of introduction to my boatbuilding, for my next step, after completing my morning stroll around Long Wharf, was to turn off High Street into an alley running down to the creek. There, in a two-car garage loaned me by a friend and client of mine, every morning I did an hour's work on the boat I'd been building for some years.

My boats—what shall I say of them? In my life I've built two. The first I started when I was perhaps twelve years old. I had devoured every yachting magazine I could lay my hands on, had "sent away" for blueprints and specifications, had tossed and dreamed of hulls and spars and sails until I was dizzy with yearning. To build a boat—that seemed to me a deed almost holy in its utter desirability. Then to provision it, and some early morning to slip quietly from my mooring, to run down the river, sparkling in the sun, out into the broad reaches of the Bay, and down to the endless oceans. Never have I regarded my boyhood as anything but pleasant, and the intensity of this longing to escape must be accounted for by the attractiveness of the thing itself, not by any unattractiveness of my surroundings. In short, I was running *to*, not running *from*, or so I believe.

But I could never be content with anything even remotely within my power to achieve. My father, delighted at the idea of my building a boat, suggested various types of skiffs, scows, prams, dinghies, and tenders, and even a simple catboat: he would help me, of course, with the steaming of the frames and strakes. But what! Go to Singapore in a dinghy? Cap the black growlers of the northern ocean in a row-skiff? For me it was more a problem of choosing between a fifty-foot auxiliary sloop and a fifty-foot auxiliary schooner. The sloop rig, I remember arguing to myself, lent itself more readily to one-man cruising, and I'd not need to rely for help on the indistinct young girls I somehow saw lying about the deck; on the other hand, if in a typhoon, say, I should be dismasted, that would be all, brother, were I to put my eggs in one basket as the sloop rig does. A divided rig—schooner, yawl, or ketch, in the order of my preference—would leave me some hope of limping bravely to port under the remaining mast. To be sure, these delicate arguments had to be kept to myself. I allowed my father to buy me enough lumber for a skiff, and I remember quite clearly regretting then that he and Mrs. Aaron, the current housekeeper, weren't dead, so that I could commence work on my schooner without their scoffing to embarrass me.

Finally I more or less began work on the skiff, declaring it to be a lifeboat for my schooner. Alas! I was clumsy with tools, if deft and ingenious with daydreams. My measurements were wrong, my lines out of plumb and out of symmetry, my saw cuts rough and crooked, my nails askew. All summer I worked on the thing, correcting one error with another, changing the length and shape of a miscut strake to fit a mismeasured frame, laying a split batten over a gaping seam, ignoring fatal errors into nonexistence, covering incompetence with incompetence, and pretending that the mere labor and bulk of the thing would somehow rectify all the fundamental mistakes implied in the very first step (rather, misstep) of construction. I made it known that I desired neither help nor advice, and my father, chalking the cost of the lumber up to my education, left me alone.

When autumn came I lost interest in boatbuilding. Why labor so on a dinghy, when what I wanted was a schooner? And a schooner, of course, I could never build where there were people to watch and scoff. Left to myself, absolutely to myself, I was certain I could build one and surprise everybody with the finished product. But it must be only the finished product that they judge me by, not the steps of construction: there would be a grandeur in the forest, so to speak, transcending and redeeming any puny deficiencies in the individual trees. All through the winter the half-framed hull weathered untouched in the back yard, like a decomposing carcass whose ribs are partly exposed; by spring I was interested in nothing but horses. The skiff remained in the yard, a silent reproach to my fickleness, for perhaps six years. Then one year, while I was in the Army, a hurricane blew the boat off its sawhorses, and the rotting planks sprang from the frames. My father used it for firewood, I believe.

I tell you this story because it's representative of a great many features of my boyhood. My daydreams, my conceptions of how things should be, were invariably grandiose, and I labored at them prodigiously and always secretly. But my talent for doing correctly the small things that constitute the glorious whole was defective—I never mastered first principles—and so the finished product, while perhaps impressive to the untutored, was always mediocre to the knowledged. To how many of my young achievements does this not apply! I dazzled old ladies at piano recitals, but never really mastered the scales; won the tennis championships of my high school—a school indifferent to tennis— but never really mastered the strokes; graduated first in my class, but never really learned to think. And so on: it's a painful list.

Now a deficiency like this, which doubtless stems from overeagerness to shine in the eyes of one's neighbors, can be hard to throw off, and I'm confident I should have it yet, but that the Army cured me of it.

Not the Army as such—heavens no. The Army as such was a terrible experience in every way. I enlisted impulsively in 1917 and realized before the bus left Cambridge what a really distasteful experience I was going to have. And I had it, too: every unpleasant thing that could happen to a soldier in that insane army happened to me, except being gassed and being killed. Certainly I wasn't patriotic. I had no feelings at all about the issues involved, if there were any (I've never been curious enough really to find out).

Well, this isn't a book about my war experiences,

though I could write a good long book about them, and
it wouldn't resemble any war book you've ever read,
either. Except for a single incident—and I mean to tell
you about it at once—my Army career was largely
without influence on the rest of my life. This one
incident, during the battle in the Argonne Forest, I
find significant in two ways, at least: it in some manner
cured the tendency described above, and it provided
me with the second of two unforgettable demonstrations of my own animality.

The Argonne fighting was well under way before
my outfit was sent in to replace a rifle company that
had been destroyed. It was my first and only battle. I
was, of course, inadequate fighting material—what intelligent boy isn't?—but I was no more afraid as the
lorries drove us to the front than were any of my
fellows, and I've never been cowardly, to my knowledge, in matters of physical violence. It was late afternoon when we arrived, and the Germans were laying
down an incredible barrage on our positions. We were
hustled out of the lorries onto the ground, and it was
much as I imagine jumping from an airplane would be:
relative calm, and then bang! horrible confusion. We
were all paralyzed. None of us remembered anything,
not anything that we'd been told. Frightful! Horrifying!
The air, I swear, was simply split with artillery. The
ground—you couldn't stand on it, no matter how loudly
your officers shouted. We all simply fell down: fortunately for us, I guess. I suppose most of you, if you are
men of this century, have experienced the like, or
worse.

I've no idea what we did. Indeed, I've often wondered, if there were many soldiers like me, how the
Allies won the war. God knows how much the government had spent on my training, hurried as it was, and
then I—all of us—simply collapsed. No cowardice, no
fear (not yet); we were simply robbed of muscle by
the noise.

Just before dark, I remember, I found myself belly-
down on a sort of ridge. All around were splintered
tree stumps, three feet high. I had no idea what I was

doing there. The sun was almost down, and there was a great deal of smoke in the air. A number of uniformed figures seemed to be attending to some business of theirs in a hollow below me. The barrage, I think, had ceased, or else I was totally deaf.

"Why," I said to myself, rather drunkenly, "those men are German soldiers. That is the enemy."

I could scarcely believe it. For heaven's sake! German soldiers! It occurred to me that I was supposed to kill them. I didn't even look around to see if the rest of the United States Army was with me; I simply fired my rifle any number of times at the men working in the hollow. None of them dropped dead, or even seemed to notice their danger. It seems to me they should have counterattacked, or taken cover, or something. No, sir. I remember very carefully reloading and firing, reloading and firing, reloading and firing. It was a hell of an easy war, but how in the world did you go about killing the enemy soldiers? And where was everyone else?

The next thing that happened (for scenes changed in this battle as in dreams) happened in the dark. Suddenly it had been nighttime for a while. This time it was I who was in a hollow, on all fours in a shell hole half full of muddy water. I still had my rifle, but it was empty, and if I owned any more ammunition I didn't remember how to put it in the rifle. I was just there, on hands and knees, my head hanging down, staring at the water. Everything was quiet again; only a few flares made a hissing noise as they drifted down through the air. And now there came real fear, quickly but not suddenly, a purely physical sensation. It swept over me in shuddering waves from my thighs and buttocks to my shoulders and jaws and back again, one shock after another, exactly as though rolls of flesh were undulating. There was no cowardice involved; in fact, my mind wasn't engaged at all—either I was thinking of something else or, more probably, I was just stupefied. Cowardice involves choice, but fear is independent of choice. When the waves reached my hips and thighs I opened my sphincters; when they crossed my stomach and chest I retched and gasped; when they struck my face my jaw hung slack, my saliva ran, my eyes watered. Then back they'd go again, and then return. I've no way of knowing how long this lasted: perhaps only a minute. But it was the purest and strongest emotion I've ever experienced. I could actually, for a part of the time it lasted, regard myself objectively: a shocked, drooling animal in a mudhole. It is one thing to agree intellectually to the proposition that man is a species of animal; quite another to realize, thoroughly and for good, your personal animality, to the extent that you are actually never able to oppose the terms *man* and *animal*, even in casual speech; never able to regard your fellow creatures except as more or less intelligent, more or less healthy, more or less dangerous, more or less adequate *fauna;* never able to regard their accomplishments except as the tricks of more or less well-trained beasts. In my case this has been true since that night, and no one—not my father, nor Jane, nor myself—have I been able even for a moment to regard differently.

The other part of the incident followed immediately. Both armies returned from wherever they'd been hiding, and I was aware for the first time that a battle was really in progress. A great deal of machine-gun fire rattled across the hollow from both sides; men in ones and twos and threes stalked or crawled or ran all around, occasionally peering into my shell hole; the flares blazed more frequently, and there was much shooting, shouting, screaming, and cursing. This must have lasted for hours. With a part of my mind I was perfectly willing to join in the fighting, though I was confused; if someone had shouted orders at me, I'm certain I'd have obeyed them. But I was left entirely alone, and alone my body couldn't move. The waves of fear were gone, but they'd left me exhausted, still in the same position.

Finally the artillery opened up again, apparently laying their fire exactly in the hollow, where the hand-to-hand fighting was in progress. Perhaps both sides had resolved to clean up that untidy squabble with high-explosive shells and begin again. Most of the explosions seemed to be within a few hundred feet of my hole, and the fear returned. There was no question in my mind but that I'd be killed; what I feared was the knowledge that my dying could very well be protracted and painful, and that it must be suffered alone. The only thing I was able to wish for was someone to keep me company while I went through with it.

Sentimental? It certainly is, and I've thought so ever since. But that's what the feeling was, and it was tremendously strong, and I'd not be honest if I didn't speak of it. It was such a strong feeling that when from nowhere a man jumped into the mudhole beside me, I fell on him instantly and embraced him as hard as I could. Very sensibly he assumed I was attacking him, and with some cry of alarm he wrenched away. I fell on him again, before he could raise his rifle, but he managed, in our tussling, to run the point of his bayonet into the calf of my left leg, not very deeply. I shouted in his ear that I didn't want to fight with him; that I loved him; and at the same time—since I was larger and apparently stronger than he—I got behind him and pinioned his arms and legs. He struggled for a long time, and in German, so that I knew him to be an enemy soldier. How could I make everything clear to him? Even if I were able to talk to him and explain my intentions, he would certainly think me either a coward or a lunatic, and kill me anyway. He had to understand everything at once.

Of course, I could have killed him, and I'm sure he understood that fact; he was helpless. What I did, finally, was work my rifle over to me with one hand, after rolling my companion onto his stomach in the muddy water, and then put the point of *my* bayonet on the back of his neck, until it just barely broke the skin and drew a drop of blood. My friend went weak—collapsed, in fact—and what he cried in German I took to be either a surrender, a plea for mercy, or both. Not wanting to leave any doubts about the matter, I held him there for several minutes more, perhaps even pressing a trifle harder on the bayonet, until he broke down, lost control of all his bodily functions, as I had done earlier, and wept. He had, I believe, the same fear; certainly he was a shocked animal.

Where was the rest of the U. S. Army? Reader, I've *never* learned where the armies spent their time in this battle!

Now read this paragraph with an open mind; I can't warn you too often not to make the quickest, easiest judgments of me, if you're interested in being accurate. The thing I did was lay aside my rifle, bayonet and all, lie in the mud beside this animal whom I'd reduced to paralysis, and embrace him as fiercely as any man ever embraced his mistress. I covered his dirty stubbled face with kisses: his staring eyes, his shuddering neck. Incredibly, now that I look back on it, he responded in kind! The fear left him, as it had left me, and for an hour, I'm sure, we clung to each other.

If the notion of homosexuality enters your head, you're normal, I think. If you judge either the German sergeant or myself to have been homosexual, you're stupid.

After our embrace, the trembling of both of us subsided, and we released each other. There was a complete and, to my knowledge, unique understanding between us. I, in fact, was something like normal for the first time since stepping out of the lorry. I was aware, now, with all my senses. A great many shells were whistling overhead, but none were bursting very near us, and the hand-to-hand fighting had apparently moved elsewhere.

The German and I sat on opposite sides of the shell hole, perhaps five feet apart, smiling at each other in complete understanding. Occasionally we attempted to communicate by gestures, but for the most part communication was unnecessary. I had dry cigarettes; he had none. He had rations; I had none. Neither had ammunition. Both had bandages and iodine. Both had bayonets. We shared the cigarettes and rations; I bandaged the wound in his neck, and he the wound in my leg. He indicated the seat of his trousers and held his

nose. I indicated the seat of my trousers and did likewise. We both laughed until we cried, and fell into
each other's arms again—though only for an instant this
time: our fear had gone, and normal embarrassment
had taken its place. We regarded each other warmly.
Perhaps we slept.

Never in my life had I enjoyed such intense inti-
macy, such clear communication with a fellow human
being, male or female, as I enjoyed with that German
sergeant. He was a little, grizzled, unlovely fellow, considerably older than I; doubtless a professional soldier.
I saw him more clearly as the day dawned. While he
slept I felt as jealous and protective—I think *exactly* as
jealous and protective—as a lion over her cub. If any
American, even my father, had jumped into the shell
hole at that moment, I'd have killed him unhesitatingly
before he could kill my friend. What validity could the
artifices of family and nation claim beside a bond like
ours? I asked myself. What difference did it make that
we would go our separate ways, never having learned
even the other's name, he to kill other Americans, I
perhaps to kill other Germans? He and I had made a
private armistice. What difference (I asked myself)
did it make even if we were to meet each other again,
face to face, in the numberless chances of war, and
without a smile of recognition, go at each other with
bayonets? For the space of some hours we had been
one man, had understood each other beyond friendship, beyond love, as a wise man understands himself.

Let me end the story. My rhetorical questions, as
you may have anticipated, raised after a while the
germ of a doubt in my mind. To be sure, I understood
perfectly how *I* felt about our relationship. But then, I
had instigated it. My companion had indeed responded, but from beneath the pointed end of my bayonet,
his face down in the mud. Again, he'd not turned on
me, though he'd had many opportunities to do so since
our tacit truce; but, as I remarked, he looked like an
old professional soldier, and I, remember, was only
eighteen. How could I be certain that our incredible
sympathy did not actually exist only in my imagina-

tion, and that he was not all the while smiling to himself, taking me for a lunatic or a homosexual crank, biding his time, resting, smoking, sleeping—until he was good and ready to kill me? Only a hardened professional could sleep so soundly and contentedly in a mudhole during a battle. There was even a trace of a smile on his lips. Was it not something of a sneer?

In the growing light everything seemed less nightmarish. Doubtless the fighting had moved considerably away from our position. Was I in German territory, or was he in Allied territory? He was indeed an unlovely fellow. Common-looking, and tough. No intelligence in his face. Heaven knows he looked incapable of conceiving or appreciating any such *rapport* as I'd envisioned. Hadn't he speared my leg? Of course, I'd jumped him first. . . .

I grew increasingly nervous, and peered out of my hole. Not a living soul was visible, though a number of bodies lay in various positions and degrees of completeness on the ground, in the barbed wire, on the shattered stumps, in other holes. The air was full of smoke and dust and atmospheric haze, and it was a bit chilly. My leg hurt. I sat back in the hole and stared nervously at the German sergeant, waiting for some sign of his awakening. I even took up my rifle (and moved his away), just to be safe. I was getting jumpier all the time, and began to worry that the fear might return.

Finally I decided to sneak quietly out of the hole and make my way to the Americans, if I could find them, leaving the German asleep. A perfect solution! I rose to my feet, holding my rifle and not taking my eyes from the German soldier's face. At once he opened his eyes, and although his head didn't move, a look of terrible alarm flashed across his face. In an instant I lunged at him and struck him in the chest with my bayonet. The blow stunned him, and my weight on the rifle held him pinned, but the blade lodged in his breastbone and refused to enter.

My God! I thought frantically. *Can't I kill him?* He grasped the muzzle of my rifle in both hands, trying to force it away from him, but I had better leverage from my standing position. We strained silently for a second. My eyes were on the bayonet; his, I fear, on my face. At last the point slipped up off the bone, from our combined straining—our last correspondence!—and with a tiny horrible puncturing sound, slid into and through his neck, and he began to die. I dropped the rifle—no force on earth could have made me withdraw it—and fled, trembling, across the shattered hollow. By merest luck, the first soldiers I encountered were American, and the battle was over for me.

That's my war story. I told it—apropos of what? Oh yes, it cured me. In fact, it cured me of several things. I seldom daydream any more, even for an instant. I never expect very much from myself or my fellow animals. I almost never characterize people in a word or phrase, and rarely pass judgment on them at all. I no longer look for the esteem or approbation of my acquaintances. I do things more slowly, more systematically, and more thoroughly. To be sure, I don't call that one incident, traumatic as it proved to be, the single cause of all these alterations in me; in fact, I don't see where some of them follow at all. But when I think of the alterations, I immediately think of the incident (specifically, I confess, of that infinitesimal puncturing noise), and that fact seems significant to me, though I'll allow the possibility of the whole thing's being a case of *post hoc, ergo propter hoc*, as the logicians say. I don't really care.

So, when I was mustered out of service in 1919 and entered Johns Hopkins University, I began to relearn, correctly, a number of things that I'd half-learned before—among them the technique of thinking clearly. I found, for example, that when I handled a tennis racket correctly, I had little aptitude for tennis. On the other hand, my golf game improved considerably. I gave up playing the piano. And, when in 1935 I again took a mild interest in boats, I did everything correctly right from the beginning. Not that I believe, as many people do, that there is some intrinsic ethical value in doing things properly rather than improperly.

I don't subscribe, as an ethical premise, to the proposition that anything worth doing is worth doing well. It's simply that I've been incapable, temperamentally, of doing things otherwise than correctly since 1918, just as prior to then I was very nearly incapable of doing anything just right.

My boat is a thirty-five-foot work boat, "torpedo-backed" and narrow-beamed in the manner of the tong boats used hereabouts. Her frames, keel, and floor timbers are of stout white oak, and her side, deck, and bottom planking of good white cedar. A very seaworthy little craft, carefully, slowly, and correctly built. By this morning in 1937 I'd been working on her for two years, doing perhaps an hour's work each day. Many mornings I remember, I simply sat in the garage and stared at her, thinking out the wisest next move, or at the wall, thinking of nothing.

On this particular morning I laid some floor planking: I'd finished planking the sides and bottom and had turned the hull right side up. As usual, I didn't bother to change my clothes or even roll my sleeves; in hat, coat, and tie I set to work laying $\frac{3}{4}'' \times 3''$ tongue-and-groove cedar planks to the floor beams, fastening them with bronze screws and galvanized wire nails, countersunk and puttied over. I'd cut the planks the day before, so that at the end of my hour most of the deck was laid and I wasn't even sweating. I brushed the knees of my trousers (they weren't dirty, for I kept my wood clean), lit my second cigar of the day, surveyed my work for several minutes, and then left for the office, closing the garage door behind me. If anyone ever took the trouble to finish my boat, I reflected without sorrow, he'd have himself an excellent vessel.

viii   a note, a warning

A note, a warning, if I may?

I got from my father the habit of doing manual work in my good clothes. Dad always made a fetish of it, like the nineteenth-century surgeons who affected evening clothes in the operating rooms and prided themselves on executing difficult surgery without bloodying their starched and studded shirt fronts.

"It teaches a man to be careful," Dad declared, "and to work easily. Hard work isn't always good work."

In the same attire he'd worn that afternoon in court, boutonniere and all, Dad would spade the vegetable garden before supper, spray the catalpa trees for caterpillars (mixing the unslaked-lime spray himself), and perhaps whitewash the foundation piers of the house or hose off the car. He never got dirty or wet, or even ruffled. When one day in 1930 I came home from the office and found Dad in the cellar, one end of his belt spiked to the floor joist and the other fastened around his neck, there was not a smudge of dirt anywhere on him, though the cellar was quite dusty. His clothes were perfectly creased and free of wrinkles, and although his face was black and his eyes were popped, his hair was neatly and correctly combed.

I agree with Dad that doing manual labor in one's office clothes teaches one to work carefully and neatly, and I follow his practice almost consistently. But I suspect that he attributed to the habit some terminal value; it was, I think, related to some vague philosophy of his. With me that is not the case, and I caution you against inferring anything of a philosophical flavor from my practice. There is in my daily routine a great deal that legitimately implies my ideas about things, but you mustn't work from the wrong things or you'll go astray. Perhaps I shouldn't even have mentioned working on my boat in my good clothes.

ix the handbill

I didn't choose the practice of law as my career, except
perhaps passively; it had been assumed from earliest
memory that I was to study for the Maryland Bar and
enter Dad's firm, and I never protested. Certainly I've
never been dedicated to anything, although as with
many another thing I've always maintained a reasonable curiosity about the meanings of legal rules and the
workings of courts.

May I say that I am perhaps the best lawyer on
the Eastern Shore? Perhaps I shouldn't, for you'll take
the statement as self-praise. If I thought the practice of
law absolutely important, then my statement would
indeed be as much a boast as a description; but truth-
fully I consider advocacy, jurisprudence, even justice,
to have no more intrinsic importance than, say, oyster-
shucking. And you'd understand, wouldn't you, that if
a man like myself asserted with a smile that he was the
peninsula's best oyster shucker (I'm not), or cigarette
roller, or pinball-machine tilter, he'd not be guilty of
prideful boasting?

I am the legal equivalent of a general practitioner
in medicine. I handle criminal cases, torts, wills, deeds,
titles, bonds, articles of incorporation—everything that
a lawyer can get his fingers into. I've argued in or-
phans' courts, circuit courts, federal courts, admiralty
courts, and appellate courts—once in the United States
Supreme Court. I seldom lose cases; but then I seldom
plead a case that I'm not fairly happy about to begin
with. I must confess that I pick and choose among my

possible clients, not to find easy cases, but to find interesting ones.

My partners, fortunately for the firm, are not so choosy; they keep fairly busy and earn good incomes. Harry Bishop, of the original Andrews & Bishop, was sixty-three at the time of this story (he died in 1948). He and Dad founded the firm in 1904, when both were fairly young men. Jimmy Andrews—no relation to me— is the other partner. In 1937 he was perhaps twenty-seven or -eight, just beginning his practice, and I'd suggested bringing him into the firm if only for the convenience of being able to use the same letterhead we'd used before Dad hanged himself.

Our office, whither I went at last after my hour of boat-building, is a little frame building. We each have a private office, but we share the same waiting room, lavatory, and secretary.

The last-mentioned, Mrs. Lake, a lady of fifty, was typing when I entered and paid my usual respects.

"No one waiting for me, I suppose?" I asked.

"Mrs. Mack was in," Mrs. Lake said.

"Oh? What for?"

"She left a note," Mrs. Lake said. "I put it on your desk."

I straightened my tie, using the waiting-room mirror.

"No word yet from Charley this morning?"

"Not yet."

Charley was Charley Parks, an attorney whose office was next door to ours. He was an old friend and poker partner of mine, and currently we were on opposite sides in a complicated litigation that had developed out of a trifling automobile accident. The suit was several years old already and hadn't even been tried yet: both parties being wealthy and "litigious," as we barristers say, Charley and I were having a field day fencing with procedural disputes. I'll describe the case eventually.

"How about the pickle barrel?" I asked, stubbing out my cigar in Mrs. Lake's ashtray and picking up my mail from her desk.

"I think there's a letter there from Baltimore," she said.

This had to do with my major case at the moment, another venerable one, involving the contested will of Harrison Mack Senior, the pickle king, who had died in 1935. It too was a labyrinthine affair: suffice it for the moment to say that Harrison had retained me to rescue his jeopardized millions (nearly three million, in fact), and that since January things had been looking up for our adversaries, much to Harrison's concern, if not mine.

I took my letters into my office then and began my last day's work at the law. Two of the letters were advertisements; I threw them out unopened. Another was a check for one thousand seven hundred dollars from William Butler, my client in the automobile litigation mentioned before—an installment on his bill. I put it aside for Mrs. Lake to handle. Another was a personal note from Junior Miner, the ex-husband of the girl in Chapter III, whose divorce I'd handled five years before. It read, in part:

> I will kill you m———g son of a bich if come
> on Pine street m———g son of bich you now
> why. J.M.

I've no idea why Junior deleted that word in his weekly letter to me; perhaps he was prudish. He believed I arranged Dorothy's divorce in order to make her my mistress, and sent me threatening letters of this sort every six or eight days for a number of years. I put this one aside for Mrs. Lake to file with the others, hoping, as I always did on these occasions, that Junior would not be foolish enough to carry out his threat. Our State's Attorney, Jarman James, was an avid Negro-hanger, and it would have distressed me to present him with such an easy case. To be sure, if Junior didn't carry out his threat within the next several hours, he would be safe.

The next letter I recognized at once from my own

handwriting on the envelope—I'd addressed it to my-self. It was postmarked *Baltimore*, and it was, or could be, tremendously important. But I wasn't ready to read it yet; I propped it against my desk lamp.

The other letters had to do with various works in progress. I read them, spending some minutes after each to stare out of my window at the county jail and make mental notes. Then I put them aside and read Jane's message.

> Darling, if you hoped in some way to hurt me again with your note this morning, you failed. I'm not disturbed at all. I will do exactly what you suggest, my dear, if you will see Marvin Rose for a complete physical, to find out why you're such a pansy. Love, Jane.

Really, she had come a long way since I first met her. I must explain that Marvin Rose is a doctor and a golfing friend of mine, and that in naming a visit to him as the condition for her granting my request—remember the note I sent her earlier, by way of Jerry Hogey—Jane believed herself safe: not since 1924 had I visited a doctor except socially, and Jane knew that my refusal to do so was no less strong for its being unreasonable.

Jane's note, too, I put aside for Mrs. Lake to file, first replacing it in its envelope. I think I may safely suggest, reader, that no one—no one—in Cambridge could bring suit against me with reasonable hopes of winning. In cases where I can't persuade judge or jury with rhetoric or legal gambit, I usually have something in my files to do the trick as evidence. Certainly I could foresee no circumstances in which this note might prove useful, especially since my slight involve-ment in the world would be terminated that very day. Despite which fact, I put it aside for Mrs. Lake.

Then I called the doctor.

"I'd like an appointment to see Dr. Rose just before lunch," I told his receptionist.

"I'm sorry, sir, Dr. Rose will be busy until this evening."

"Would you tell him it's Todd Andrews?" I asked. "I want a physical. Maybe he can look at me during his naptime." I knew that Marvin was in the habit of napping in his office, on the examination table, before lunch.

"Hold on." I heard her cover the mouthpiece and speak to Marvin.

"Hello? Todd?" It was Marvin who spoke now.

"Yes. How about a minute of your naptime today, Marv?"

"What the hell, Toddy, you sick?" he asked incredulously.

"Nope."

"Somebody suing me?"

"Nope. I just want an examination."

He was speechless. For years he and I had argued, at golf or over highballs, about medicine and law, or rather health and justice, and although he had no inkling of my cardiac ailments, he knew that I was unhealthy and that I didn't care to consult a physician about it.

"Sure, Toddy, come on up, boy," he laughed. "Say, are you pulling my leg?"

"Nope. I want the whole works. Eleven o'clock?"

"Make it eleven-fifteen," Marvin said. "I want to sharpen my needles and things. I don't get you often."

We talked for a minute or two of other things, and then I went to my files, got out the dossier on the litigation over Harrison Mack Senior's estate, and prepared to begin work in earnest.

But again I interrupted myself. I had bitten the end off my third cigar, and finding my matchbook empty, I slapped my coat pockets to search for another. What I found was the handbill I'd pocketed earlier on Long Wharf and had forgotten to read. I unfolded it and spread it out on my desk.

COMING

BIGGER & BETTER THAN EVER!

ADAM'S

ORIGINAL **A N D** UNPARALLELED

"Ocean-Going"

FLOATING OPERA

Jacob R. Adam, Owner & Captain

AT: Long Wharf, Cambridge, June [21 or 22]

Tickets on Sale All Day at the Ticket Office
ADMISSIONS: 20¢, 35¢, 50¢

* * SEATING CAPACITY 700 * *

LARGEST FLOATING THEATRE ON THE EASTERN SEABOARD

($60,000 Actually Invested to Date)

A
Choice Company
of
Players,
Presenting the Finest in DRAMA,

MUSIC,

MINSTRELS,

VAUDEVILLE

ONE LONG LAUGH!

———

Great Moral Show
The High-Water Mark of Mirth, Melody, & Minstrelsy

A   N
L   E
 L   W

Up-to-date Comedians, Dazzling Dancers,
Cultivated Singers.

MORAL AND REFINED	**GORGEOUS**	Cooled by the breezes of the sea

You Are Cordially Invited to Visit America's
Finest & Safest Floating Theatre During the Day

———

[On the inside of the folded sheet was more information about the virtues of Adam's Floating Opera, and
a program of the evening's entertainment.]

*FREE Concert Begins at 7:30 PM; Show Begins
8:00 PM

PROF. EISEN'S
$7,500 CHALLENGE ATLANTIC &
CHESAPEAKE MARITIME BAND

Composed of the Finest Musicians in the *U.S.A.!*

Listen for the CALLIOPE!

Watch for the BAND PARADE!

EVERY PROMISE MADE
FAITHFULLY KEPT

Come early for the Band Concert and Stay for the
East Coast's Finest Show

✳ *SEE* ✳

THE MARY PICKFORD OF
THE CHESAPEAKE

!! MISS CLARA MULLOY !!

IN
a new, side-splitting one-act comedy

Hilarious!   **THE**   *Heartwarming!*

Moral!

PARACHUTE

GIRL

** ** SEE ** **
The Chaste & Inimitable

ETHIOPIAN TIDEWATER MINSTRELS
U.S.A.'s Greatest Sable Humorists

** ** SEE ** **
J. Strudge, the Magnificent Ethiopian Delineator,
The Black Demosthenes, in
His Original Burlesque Stump Speech

Sweet Sally Starbuck, the Singing Soubrette,
with Melodies of Heart, Hearth,
& Home.

T. Wallace Whittaker, Famous Southern Tenor, Singing
Pastoral Lays of the Corn & Cotton Fields

SPECIAL FEATURE!

Burley Joe Wells, World Renowned Imitator, With His
Impressions of Steam Calliopes, Sawmills, Model-T
Fords, Hound Dogs, and the Famous Race Between
the Sternwheelers *Natchez* & *Robert E. Lee*, Con-
cluding and Climaxing with the Terrible & Terrific
Explosion of the Steamboat *James B. Taylor*, Which
Tragedy Occurred at Natchez-Under-The-Hill, Mis-
sissippi, on February 19, 1892.

Concluding With A

WONDERFUL PANITHIOPLICONICA

DON'T MISS IT!
KEEP YOUR EYE ON THE DATE!

Bring the Kiddies

Approved By Press, Public, & Clergy Alike.

Well. Far be it from me to miss the Wonderful Panithiopliconica.

"Mrs. Lake," I called, "will you telephone Mrs. Mack sometime this morning and ask her if I may take Jeannine to see the showboat when it pulls in?"

"Okay," Mrs. Lake said. "What time?"

"Late this afternoon, I guess. About four? Am I supposed to do anything after four?"

"I'll look. . . . No."

The famous race between the sternwheelers *Natchez* and *Robert E. Lee*. I wouldn't miss it for anything. But I didn't keep my eye on the date, as Capt. Adam's handbill suggested; indeed, I crumpled the bill and threw it away just then, and I've never been able to remember whether all this occurred on the twenty-first or twenty-second of June. To be sure, at some time during the nine years I spent recollecting the events of this day, I could with small effort have gone to the files of the daily *Banner* and dug out the showboat advertisement to fix the date. But I've never bothered to. Is it the Navajo Indians who make it a point always to leave in their woven rugs and other artifacts some slight imperfection, an odd stitch or a bump of clay, in order not to compete with the gods? I think it is. Well, I have no gods, and so I can't justify my shortcomings as do the Navajos. But it has, I must say, seemed unwise to me from the beginning to verify that date. Perhaps I can't explain why.

Indeed, I shan't try.

x the law

That will-o'-the-wisp, the law: where shall I begin to
speak of it? Is the law the legal rules, or their interpretations by judges, or by juries? Is it the precedent or
the present fact? The norm or the practice? I think I'm
not interested in what the law is.

Surely, though, I am curious about things that the
law can be made to do, but this disinterestedly, without involvement. A child encounters a toy tractor,
winds it up, and sets it climbing over a book. The
tractor climbs well. The child puts another book here,
so, and angles the first. The tractor surmounts them,
with difficulty. The child opens the pages of the first
book, leans the second obliquely against it, and places
his shoe behind the two. The tractor tries, strains,
spins, whirrs, and falls like a turtle on its back, treads
racing uselessly. The child moves on to his crayons and
picture puzzles, no expression on his face. I don't know
what you mean, sir, when you speak of justice.

It may be that, like Capt. Osborn, you have come
to believe that I have opinions about everything, absurd ones at that. Very well. But of most things about
which people hold some sort of opinion, I have none at
all, except by implication. What I mean is this: the
law, for example, prescribes certain things that shall
not be done, or certain ways in which things shall be
done, but of most specific human acts it has nothing to
say one way or the other. Yet these extralegal acts, or
most of them, are certainly influenced and conditioned,
implicitly, by the laws pertaining to other things. Peo-

ple, for example, aren't allowed to kill us while we're performing our extralegal acts. In the same way, though I have no opinion one way or the other on whether suicide, for instance, is a sin, I have certain opinions on a few other things that made it possible for me to contemplate suicide in 1937, and actually to resolve to destroy myself.

All right. I have no general opinions about the law, or about justice, and if I sometimes set little obstacles, books and slants, in the path of the courts, it is because I'm curious, merely, to see what will happen. On those occasions when the engine of the law falls impotently sprawling, I make a mental note of it, and without a change of expression, go on to my boat or my *Inquiry*. Winning or losing litigations is of no concern to me, and I think I've never made a secret of that fact to my clients. They come to me, as they come before the law, because *they* think they have a case. The law and I are uncommitted.

One more thing, before I explain the contest over Harrison Mack Senior's will: if you have followed this chapter so far, you might sensibly ask, "Doesn't your attitude—which is, after all, irresponsible—allow for the defeat, even the punishment, of the innocent, and at times the victory of the guilty? And does this not concern you?" It does indeed allow for the persecution of innocence—though perhaps not so frequently as you might imagine. And this persecution *concerns* me, in the sense that it holds my attention, but not especially in the sense that it bothers me. Under certain circumstances, to be explained later, I am not averse to pillorying the innocent, to throwing my stone, with the crowd, at some poor martyr. Irresponsibility, yes: I affirm, I insist upon my basic and ultimate irresponsibility. Yes indeed.

It did not deeply concern me, as I said before, whether Harrison received his inheritance or not, though I stood to profit by some fifty thousand dollars or more if he did. In any world but ours, the case of the Mack estate would be fantastic; even in ours, it received considerable publicity from the Maryland press.

Old man Mack, whom I've come to admire tremendously though I never met him, died in 1935, after years of declining physical and mental health. He left a large estate: stock in the Mack Pickle Co. amounting to 58 per cent of the total shares, and worth perhaps two million dollars in fairly good times; stock in various other business concerns, some more prosperous than others; a large house in Ruxton, another in West Palm Beach, and cottages in Nova Scotia and Maryland (including the one I was seduced in); extensive farmlands, especially cucumber farms, the crop from which was bought by the Mack Pickle Co.; perhaps a hundred thousand dollars in cash; assorted automobiles, cabin cruisers, horses, and dogs, and through the majority stockholdings, the potential presidency of the pickle company, which office carried a salary of twenty-five thousand dollars a year. It was, undeniably, an estate that many people would consider worth going to court about.

Now of the several characteristics of Harrison *père*, three were important to the case: he was in the habit of using his wealth as a club to keep his kin in line; he was, apparently, addicted to the drawing up of wills; and, especially in his last years, he was obsessively jealous of the products of his mind and body, and permitted none to be destroyed.

You perhaps recall my saying that when I first met Harrison Junior, in 1925, he was undergoing an attack of communism, and had been disinherited as a result? It seems that disinheritance, or the threat of it, was the old man's favorite disciplinary measure, not only for his son, but also for his wife. When young Harrison attended Dartmouth rather than Johns Hopkins; when he studied journalism rather than business; when he became a communist rather than a Republican; he was disinherited until such time as he mended his ways. When Mother Mack went to Europe rather than to West Palm Beach; when she chose sparkling burgundy over highballs, Dulaney Valley over Ruxton, Roosevelt and Garner over Hoover and Curtis; she was disinherited until such time as she recanted her heresies.

All these falls from the reinstatements to grace, of course, required emendations of Father Mack's will, and a number of extrafamiliar circumstances also demanded frequent revision of his bequests. His country club admits someone he doesn't like: the club must be disinherited. A pickle-truck driver runs down a state policeman checking on overloaded vehicles: the driver must be defended in court and provided for explicitly in the will. After the old man's death, when his safe was opened, a total of seventeen complete and distinct testamentary instruments was found, chronologically arranged, each beginning with a revocation of the preceding one. He hadn't been able to throw any of his soul-children into the fire.

Now this situation, though certainly unusual, would in itself have presented no particular problem of administration, because the law provides that where there are several wills, the last shall be considered representative of the testator's real intentions, other things being equal. And each of these wills explicitly revoked the preceding one. But alas, with Mr. Mack all other things weren't equal. Not only did his physical well-being deteriorate in his last years, through arthritis to leukemia to the grave; his sanity deteriorated also, gradually, along the continuum from relative normalcy through marked eccentricity to jibbering idiocy. In the first stages he merely inherited and disinherited his relatives and his society; in the second he no longer went to work, he required entertainment as well as care from his nurses, and he allowed nothing of his creation—including hair- and nail-clippings, urine, feces, and wills—to be thrown away; in the last stages he could scarcely move or talk, had no control whatever over his bodily functions, and recognized no one. To be sure, the stages were not dramatically marked, but blended into one another imperceptibly.

Of the seventeen wills (which represented by no means all the wills Mack had written, merely those written since he acquired his mania for preserving things), only the first two were composed during the time when the old man's sanity was pretty much indisputable; that is, prior to 1933. The first left about half the state to Harrison Junior and the other half to Mother Mack, provided it could not be demonstrated to the court that she had drunk any sparkling burgundy since 1920. This one was dated 1924. The other, dated 1932, left about half the estate to Mrs. Mack unconditionally and the rest to Harrison, provided it could not be demonstrated to the court that during a five-year probationary period, 1932-37, Harrison had done, written, or said anything that could reasonably be construed as evidence of communist sympathies. This clause, incidentally, ran through most of the subsequent testaments as well.

Of the other fifteen documents, ten were composed in 1933 and 1934, years when the testator's sanity was open to debate. The last five, all written in the first three months of 1935, could be established without much difficulty, in court, as being the whims of a lunatic: one left everything to Johns Hopkins University on condition that the University's name be changed to Hoover College (the University politely declined); others bequeathed the whole shebang to the Atlantic Ocean or the A.F.L.

Luckily for the majesty of Maryland's law, there were only two primary and four secondary contestants for the estate. Elizabeth Sweetman Mack, the testator's widow, was interested in having Will #6, a product of late 1933, adjudged the last testament: it bequeathed her virtually the entire estate, on the sparkling-burgundy condition described above. Harrison Junior preferred #8, the fruit of early 1934; it bequeathed *him* virtually the whole works, on the clean-skirts condition also described above. Misses Janice Kosko, Shirley Mae Greene, and Berenice Silverman, registered nurses all, who had attended old Mack during the first, second, and third stages, respectively, of his physical invalidity, liked Wills #3, 9, and 12, in that order: therein, apparently, their late employer provided them remuneration for services beyond the line of duty. The final contestant was the pastor of the Macks' neighborhood church: in Will #13 the bulk of the estate was to pass to that church, with the express hope that the richer and more influential organized religion became, the sooner it would be cast off by the people.

It was an edifying spectacle. Mrs. Mack retained Messrs. Dugan, Froebel & Kemp, of Baltimore, to defend her legal rights; her son retained Andrews, Bishop, & Andrews, of Cambridge; the nurses and the minister retained separate attorneys. Everyone was a little afraid to carry the thing to court immediately, and for several months there was a welter of legal nonsense, threats, and counterthreats, among the six firms involved. Five of us joined forces to oust the clergyman from the sweepstakes—it was enough for the three nurses to agree that Mack was definitely insane by the time Will #13 was composed. A month later, by pretty much the same technique, Misses Kosko and Greene induced Miss Silverman to withdraw, on the solemnly contracted condition that should either of them win, she would get 20 per cent of the loot. Then, in a surprise maneuver, Bill Froebel, of Dugan, Froebel & Kemp, produced sworn affidavits from two Negro maids of the Mack household, to the effect that they had seen Miss Greene indulging in "unnatural and beastly" practices with the deceased— the practices were described in toothsome detail—and suggested to that young lady that, should she not decide the contest wasn't worth the trouble, he would release the affidavits to the newspapers. I never learned for certain whether the affidavits were true or false, but in either case they were effective: the additional attraction of several thousand dollars, payable when Mrs. Mack won the case, induced Miss Greene to seek her happiness outside the courts.

The field was cleared, then, in 1936, of half the entries, before the race even began. Only Miss Kosko, Harrison Junior, and Mrs. Mack remained. Each of them, of necessity, must attempt to prove two things: that Father Mack was still legally sane when the will of their choice was written, and that by the time the subsequent wills were written, he no longer could comprehend what he was about. On this basis, Miss Kosko, I should say, had the strongest case, since her will (dated February 1933) was the earliest of the three. But love was her undoing: she retained as her attorney her boy friend, a lad fresh out of law school, none too bright. After our initial out-of-court sparring I was fairly confident that he was no match for either Froebel or myself, and when, late in 1936, he refused on ethical grounds a really magnanimous bribe from Froebel, I was certain.

And sure enough, when the first swords clashed in Baltimore Probate Court, in May of 1936, Froebel was able, with little trouble, to insinuate that the young lawyer was an ass; that the nurse Miss Kosko was a hussy out to defraud poor widows of their honest legacies by seducing old men in their dotage; that Mrs. Mack, out of the kindness of her bereaved heart, had already offered the trollop a gratuity more munificent than she deserved (this news was ruled out as incompetent evidence, of course); and that even to listen tolerantly to such ill-concealed avariciousness was a tribute to the patience and indulgence of long-suffering judges. In addition, Froebel must have offered some cogent arguments, for surrogate courts, even in Baltimore, are notoriously competent, and the judge ruled in his favor. When Froebel then offered Miss Kosko another settlement, considerably smaller than the first, the young barrister accepted it humbly, coming as it did on the heels of his defeat, and didn't even think of appealing the judgment until it was too late.

Then, in June of the same year, Froebel filed suit for Mrs. Mack, charging flatly that Mr. Mack had been of unsound mind when he wrote Will #8, Harrison's will, and never again regained his sanity. If the court so ruled, then Mrs. Mack's will, #6, would become the authentic testamentary instrument, since Miss Kosko was out of the running. If the court ruled against him, then our document, #8, would automatically revoke his.

There was not much difference between Mack's mental state in late 1933 and his mental state in early

1934. I introduced statements from Misses Kosko and Greene that in both years he required them to save the contents of his bedpan in dill-pickle jars, which were then stored in the wine cellar, and I got the impression that the judge—a staid fellow—believed Mack had been insane from the beginning. The newspapers, too, expressed the opinion that there was no particular evidence on either side, and that, besides, it was a disgraceful thing for a mother and her son to squabble so selfishly. All the pressure was for out-of-court settlement on a fifty-fifty basis, but both Harrison and his mother—who had never especially liked each other—refused, on the advice of their attorneys. Froebel thought he could win, and wanted the money; I thought I could win, and wanted to see.

Will #6, remember, gave all the estate to Mrs. Mack, provided she hadn't tasted sparkling burgundy since 1920. Our will left the money and property to Harrison, if he had steered clear of Moscow since 1932, and in addition, bequeathed to Mrs. Mack the several hundred pickle jars just mentioned. Both documents included the extraordinary provision that, should the separate conditions not be fulfilled, the terms were to be reversed.

Froebel's arguments, essentially, were two: (1) That a man has not necessarily lost his business sense if he provides once for a complete reversal of bequests, of the sort seen in Will #6, assuming he is really dead set against sparkling burgundy; but then to reverse himself completely in the space of a few months indicates that something has snapped in his head, since there were no dramatic eternal changes to account for the new will. (2) That the bequest of the pickle jars appeared in no wills before #8, and in all the wills from #8 through #16, and that such a bequest is evidence tending to show that Mack no longer understood the nature of his estate.

"Not necessarily," I suggested. "Suppose he didn't love his wife?"

"Ah," Froebel replied quickly, "but he left the pickle jars to a different person each time, not to Mrs. Mack every time."

"But remember," I said, "he saved the mess because he liked it; the bequest of it, then, is an act of love. Would you call love insane?"

"Indeed not," Froebel answered. "But if he'd loved her, he'd have given her the property as well as the—excrement."

"No indeed," I countered. "Remember that in one will he bequeathed all his money to the church because he disliked the church. Couldn't the bequest to my client be such an act, and the bequest to yours the real gift?"

"It could indeed," Froebel grinned. "Will you say that that's the case?"

"No, I shan't," I said. "I merely suggested the possibility."

"And in doing so," Froebel declared, "you suggest the possibility that Will Number Eight is as insane as Will Number Thirteen, the church will you mentioned. Anyone who bequeaths three millions of dollars as a punishment, I suggest, is out of perspective."

Oh, Bill Froebel was a lawyer. When it came to impromptu legal sophistry, he and I had no equals at the Maryland Bar.

My arguments were (1) that the inclusion of the pickle jars was hardly sufficient evidence of a sudden loss of understanding, when Mack had been collecting them since Will #3 or 4; (2) that therefore the testator was either sane when he composed both instruments to insane when he composed them; (3) that if he was sane both times, Will #8 was official; (4) that if insane both times, some earlier will was official and must be brought forward, or otherwise Mack could be deemed to have died intestate (in which case Harrison would get all the money, Mrs. Mack retaining only dower).

The judge, Frank Lasker of the Baltimore bench, agreed. Froebel appealed the decision through the Court of Appeals to the Maryland Supreme Court, and both appellate courts affirmed the lower court's judgment. It seemed as if Harrison were a wealthy man: all that remained was to wait until January of 1937—the end of his probationary period—and then to demonstrate that Harrison had kept clear of communist sym-

pathy since 1932. He assured me that nothing could be
suggested which could be called fellow-traveling, even
remotely. Froebel threatened for a while to institute a
new suit, in favor of Will #2, but nothing came of his
threat.

The final test was in the form of a hearing. Harrison and I appeared at the Baltimore courthouse early
in January; Judge Lasker read the terms of Will #8 and
declared that if no one present could offer evidence of
such sympathies as were therein interdicted, he was prepared to declare the matter settled and to order the will
executed. Froebel then appeared, much to my surprise,
and announced that he had such evidence, enough to
warrant the reversal of bequests provided for by our
will, and was ready to offer it to the court.

"You told me there wasn't anything," I reminded
Harrison, who had turned white.

"I swear there isn't!" he whispered back, but nevertheless he began perspiring and trembling a little. I
sat back to see what Froebel had cooked up.

"What will you attempt to prove?" the Judge
asked him.

"That as recently as last year, your honor, while his
poor father was in the grave—perhaps speeded there
(who knows?) by his son's regrettable irresponsibility—
that just last year, your honor, this son, who is now so
eager to take from his mother what is rightfully hers,
was aiding and abetting actively, with large gifts of
money, that doctrine against which his father's entire
life was such an eloquent argument; confident, I doubt
not, that he could conceal his surreptitious Bolshevism
until such time as he was in a position to devote the
whole of the Mack estate toward overthrowing the way
of life that made its accumulation possible!"

Froebel was a past master of the detached noun
clause: judge and spectators were stirred.

"For heaven's sake!" Harrison whispered. "You
don't think he means my Spanish donations!"

"If you were silly enough to make any, then I
daresay he does," I replied, appalled anew at Harrison's
innocence.

And indeed, the "Spanish donations" were precisely what Froebel had in mind. He offered in evidence photostated checks, four of them, for one thousand dollars each, made out to an American subscription agency representing the Spanish Loyalist government. They were dated March 10, May 19, September 2, and October 7, and all were signed *Harrison A. Mack, Jr.*

Judge Lasker examined the photostats and frowned. "Did you write these checks?" he asked Harrison, passing the pictures to him.

"Of course!" Harrison yelled. "What the hell's that—"

"Order!" suggested the Judge. "Aren't you aware that the Loyalist movement is run by the Communist Party? Directed from the Kremlin?"

"Aw, come on!" Harrison pleaded, until I poked him and he sat down.

"May I point out," Froebel continued blandly, "that not only is a gift to the Loyalists in essence a gift to Moscow, but this particular subscription agency is a Party organization under FBI surveillance. A man may donate to the Loyalists through honest, if vague, liberalism, I daresay; but one doesn't send checks to this subscription outfit unless one is sympathetic with the Comintern. Young Mr. Mack, like too many of our idle aristocrats, is, I fear, a blue blood with a Red heart."

I believe it was this final metaphor that won Froebel the judgment. I saw the newspaper people virtually doff their hats in tribute, and scribble the immortal words for the next editions of their papers. Even the Judge smiled benignly upon the trope: I could see that it struck him square in the prejudices, and found a welcome there.

There was some further discussion, but no one listened closely; everyone was repeating to himself, with a self-satisfied smile, that too many young aristocrats are blue bloods with Red hearts. *Blue bloods with Red hearts!* How could mere justice cope with poetry? Men, I think, are ever attracted to the *bon mot* rather than the *mot juste*, and judges, no less than other men, are often moved by considerations more aesthetic than judicial. Even I was not a little impressed, and regretted only that we had no jury to be overwhelmed by such a purple plum from the groves of advocacy. *A blue blood with a Red heart!* How brandish reasonableness against music? Should I hope to tip the scales with puny logic, when Froebel had Parnassus in his pan? In vain might I warn Judge Lasker that, through the press, all America was watching, and Europe as well, for his decision.

"My client, a lover of freedom and human dignity," I declared, "made his contributions to the oppressed Loyalists as a moral obligation, proper to every good American, to fight those Rebels who would crush the independence of the human spirit, and trample liberty under hobnailed boots! How can you charge him with advocating anarchy and violent overthrow, when in a single year he gives four thousand dollars to support the Spanish Government against those who would overthrow it?"

And on I went for some minutes, trying to make capital out of the Spanish confusion, wherein the radicals were the *status quo* and the reactionaries the rebels. It was an admirable bit of casuistry, but I knew my cause was lost. Only Froebel, I think, had ears for my rhetoric; the rest of the room was filled with *blue bloods with Red hearts.*

And Judge Lasker, as I think I mentioned, was famously conservative. Though by no means a fascist himself—he was probably uncommitted in the Spanish revolution—he epitomized the unthinking antagonism of his class toward anything pinker than the blue end of the spectrum: a familiar antagonism that used to infuriate me when, prior to 1924, I was interested in such things as social justice. When finally he ruled, he ruled in Froebel's favor.

"It does not matter whether there is a difference between the Moscow and Madrid varieties of communism," he declared, "or whether the Court or anyone else approves or disapproves of the defendant's gifts or the cause for which they were intended. The fact is that the subscription agency involved is a communist organization under government surveillance, and a gift to that agency is a gift to communism. There can be no question of the donor's sympathy with what the agency represented, and what it represented was communism. The will before me provides that should such sympathy be demonstrated, as it has been here, the terms of the document are to be reversed. The Court here orders such a reversal."

Well, we were poor again. Harrison went weak, and when I offered him a cigar he came near to vomiting.

"It's incredible!" he croaked, actually perspiring from the shock of it.

"Do you give up?" I asked him. "Or shall I appeal?"

He clutched at the hope. "Can we appeal?"

"Sure," I said. "Don't you see how unlogical Lasker's reasoning is?"

"Unlogical! It was so logical it overwhelmed me!"

"Not at all. He said the subscription agency was sympathetic to communism. You give money to the agency; therefore you're sympathetic to communism. It's like saying that if you give money to a Salvation Army girl who happens to be a vegetarian you're sympathetic to vegetarians. The communists support the Loyalists; you support the Loyalists; therefore you're a communist."

Harrison was tremendously relieved, but so weak he could scarcely stand. He laughed shortly.

"Well! That puts us back in the race, doesn't it? Ha, I'd thought there for a while—Christ, Toddy, you've saved my ass again! Damned judge! We've got it now, boy!"

I shook my head, and he went white again.

"What the hell's wrong?"

"I'll appeal," I said, "but we'll lose again, I guess."

"How's that? Lose again!" He laughed, and sucked in his breath.

"Forget about the logic," I said. "Nobody really cares about the logic. They make up their minds by their prejudices about Spain. I think you'd have lost here even without Froebel's metaphor. I'd have to talk Lasker into liberalism to win the case."

I went on to explain that of the seven judges of the Court of Appeals who would review the decision, three were Republicans with a pronounced anti-liberal bias, two were fairly liberal Democrats, one was a reactionary "Southern Democrat," more anti-liberal than the Republicans, and the seventh, an unenthusiastic Democrat, was relatively unbiased.

"I know them all," I said. "Abrams, Moore, and Stevens, the Republicans, will vote against you. Forrester, the Southern Democrat, would vote for you if it were a party issue, but it's not; he'll go along with the Republicans. Stedman and Barnes, the liberals, will go along with you, and I think Haddaway will too, because he likes me and because he dislikes Lasker's bad logic."

"But hell, that's four to three!" Harrison cried. "That means I lose!"

"As I said."

"How about the Maryland Supreme Court?"

"That's too much to predict," I said. "I don't know that they've declared themselves on Spain, and I don't know them personally. But they've affirmed almost every important verdict of the Court of Appeals in three years."

Harrison was crushed. "It's unjust!"

I smiled. "You know how these things are."

"Aw, but what the hell!" He shook his head, tapped his feet impatiently, pursed his lips, sighed in spasms. I expected him to faint, but he held on tightly, though he could scarcely talk. The truth was, of course, that it is one thing—an easy thing—to give what Cardinal Newman calls "notional" assent to a proposition such as "There is no justice"; quite another and more difficult matter to give it "real" assent, to learn it stingingly, to the heart, through involvement. I remember hoping that Harrison was strong enough at least to be educated by his expensive loss.

I appealed the judgment of the Court.

"Just to leave the door open," I explained. "I might think of something."

That evening, before I left Baltimore with Harrison, we had dinner at Bill Froebel's club, as his guests. I praised his inspiration, and he my logic-twisting. Harrison was morose, and although he drank heavily, he refused to join in the conversation. He couldn't drive home. On the way, he would clutch my arm and groan, "Three million bucks, Toddy!"

I looked coldly at him.

"Hell, man," he protested, "I know what you're thinking, but you should know me better. I don't want the money like another man might, just to go crazy on. Think what we could do on three million bucks, the three of us!"

It was the first time since Jane and I had resumed our affair in 1935 that Harrison had spoken again of "the three of us," as he had used to do.

"A million apiece?" I asked. "Or a joint account?"

Harrison felt the bristles and flinched, and all the way home he felt constrained to pretend that the loss of three million dollars touched his philosophical heart not at all. I watched the effort from the corner of my eye, and marveled sadly at his disorientation.

Finally he broke down, as we were crossing the Choptank River bridge, pulling into Cambridge. The water was white-capped and cold-looking. Dead ahead, at the end of the boulevard that the bridge ran onto, Morton's Marvelous Tomatoes, Inc., spread its red neon banner across the sky, and I smiled. The town lights ran in a flat string along the water's edge, from Hambrooks Bar Lighthouse, flashing on the right, to the Macks' house in East Cambridge, its ground-floor windows still lit, where Jane was waiting.

"I give up, Toddy," he said tersely. "I'm no philosopher. I can't say I wouldn't have been happy at one time without the money—I *did* get myself disinherited a few times, you know. But once it came so close and seemed so sure—"

"What is it?" I demanded.

"Ah, Christ—Janie and I had plans." He choked on

his plans. "How the hell can I say it? I just don't feel like living any more."

"You *what?*" I sneered. "What'll you do—hang yourself in the cellar? There's a twentypenny nail right there, in a joist—you'll find it. It's already been broken in. And I know an undertaker who can turn black faces white again."

"All right, all right," Harrison said. "I don't care what you think. I said I'm no philosopher."

"Forget about philosophy," I said. "You don't lack philosophy; you lack guts. I suppose you're going to ask me to marry Jane afterwards, so the two of us can remember you? You're wallowing, Harrison. It's swinish."

"I'm weak, Toddy," he said. "I can't help it. Don't think I'm not ashamed of it."

"Then cut it out."

"You can't just cut it out," Harrison protested, and I sensed that he was growing stronger. "I'm past believing that people can change."

"You don't want to cut it out."

"Sure I do. It doesn't matter whether I do or not; I can't do it. I'm weak in some ways, Toddy. You don't understand that."

I flicked my cigarette out of the ventilator in a shower of sparks. We were off the bridge then, coasting along the dual highway in the Macks' big automobile.

"I know what weakness is. But you make your own difficulties, Harrison. It's hard because you never thought of it as easy. Listen. An act of will is the easiest thing there is—so easy it's laughable how people make mountains of it."

Harrison had by this time actually put aside the idea of his loss and was following the thought.

"You know better," he said. "You can't discount psychology."

"I'm not saying anything about psychology," I maintained. "Psychology doesn't interest me. We act as if we could choose, and so we can, in effect. All you have to do to be strong is stop being weak."

"Impossible."

"You never tried it."

Nor, alas, did he want to just then: I could see that plainly enough. We went into the house for a last drink. Jane had heard the news, of course, by telephone, and she cried awhile. I told her flatly that I had no sympathy for either of them while they behaved like that.

"What would *you* do, damn it!" she cried impatiently.

I laughed. "I've never lost three million bucks," I said, "but I'll tell you what I did once, after Dad hanged himself for losing a few thousand."

I told them then, for the first time, the story of my adventures with Col. Henry Morton—which story, reader, I'll pause to tell you, too, sooner or later, but not just now. I had decided that I didn't want Harrison to brood over his money: he wasn't ready to be strong of his own choosing yet, apparently, and so I opened the way toward turning him into a cynic, in emulation of me. He was ripe for it anyhow, it seemed to me, and even the one story might do the trick.

There's little need for weakness, reader: you are freer, perhaps, than you'd be comfortable knowing.

As I left, Jane asked me: "You don't have anything up your sleeve, Toddy?"

"I shan't commit myself," I said. "But Harrison might as well believe he's out three million bucks, at least for a while."

"What will he do?" she asked anxiously. "Did he say anything to you coming home?"

"He'll either grow stronger or hang himself," I predicted. "If he grows stronger it won't matter to him whether he gets the money or not, really, and then I wouldn't mind seeing him get it. If he kills himself over it, I'll be just as glad he's dead, frankly. Sissies make me uncomfortable. That goes for you, too. You're not ready for three million bucks yet. You don't deserve it."

Then I left. I suppose if *I* ever lost three million dollars I'd holler like a stuck hero. Or perhaps not: one really can't tell until the thing is upon one.

Well, the will case dropped out of the papers then; the Court of Appeals wouldn't hear the appeal for at least six months, though I doubted that they'd wait much longer than that. In the meantime, Lizzie Mack, Harrison's mother, couldn't use up the old man's estate (except for running expenses for the house), though it was temporarily hers.

I conducted, during the next few months, a rather intensive investigation into the characters of the appellate court judges—my findings confirmed my original estimate of the situation. As far as one with much information could guess, the decision would be four to three for Lizzie if the hearing were held when tentatively scheduled.

And if it weren't? I considered that question, sitting in my office, staring at my staring-wall opposite the desk. What advantage was there in delay, if any? And how could one delay the appeal? The advantage was negative: that is, I was certain of defeat if there were no delay; if there were any, I might very possibly still be defeated, but there would be more time for something to turn up. So, I suppose, a condemned man snatches at a day's reprieve, still hoping for a god on wires to fetch him off, and on the very gibbet, his neck roped, pleads eye-to-sky for the saving car. Who knows? Perhaps, hooded and dropped, he yet awaits in a second's agony for God's hands on him, till the noose cracks neck and hope in one sick snap. To be sure, ours was but a matter of money, but the principle was the same. By September the Loyalists might be winning, or it might become dangerous over here to like the fascists, the way Hitler was behaving. By October Franco might win, and the poor crushed Loyalists be pitied, then when they were no longer a threat. Anything could happen to swing one more vote our way. November was an off-year election month: perhaps some party issue would ally John Forrester, the reactionary Democrat, with his more liberal colleagues. Perhaps—

I smiled, moved my feet off the desk, and went to the file. I looked up each of the judges, checking the length of their incumbencies and the number of years in office remaining to each.

"Ah, Freddie Barnes, you old whoremonger," I cooed; "so you're up to the post again this year, are you?"

That fact mattered little, since Roosevelt was going great guns and Barnes was a popular figure in Maryland: he'd be re-elected without difficulty. Of the other Democrats, Forrester had two years to go, Haddaway had four, and Stedman had six. I checked the Republicans: Abrams had two years yet; Stevens, six; Moore—

"Well, well, well!" I grinned. "You rascal, Rollo! Time to run again, eh?"

Mrs. Lake, at my request, spent the rest of her afternoon telephoning various Baltimorians for me, some eminent and some shady, some honest and some flexible, some friendly and some employable. By quitting time I was one of perhaps seven people who knew as a fact, beyond puny speculation, that Judge Rollo Moore, despite the backing of Maryland republicanism, was going to lose his coming election by a well-insured margin to Joseph Singer, who, bless his heart, was a chronic if somewhat fuzzy liberal—a man after Harrison's own heart.

We would win, by God, almost certainly, if we could hold off the appeal until November! No, until January of 1938, after the new officeholders had been sworn in. Nearly a year! I racked my brain, in my thorough but unenthusiastic way, to think of some stalling maneuver, but of the few I could imagine, none was satisfactory. What I needed was something diverting, something tenuous and intricate, that I could go on complicating indefinitely, if need be. Nothing crude would do: my maneuver, whatever it was, must be subtle even if its motives were clear to the professional eye, or else I should lose the respect, and possibly the vote, of men like Judge Haddaway, for instance, whose decisions were more often influenced by such things as the symmetry and logical elegance of a brief than by more mundane considerations like the appellant's politics.

Ah, nonsense, there was nothing. The months passed; it was spring; August and judgment would soon be upon us. Harrison sweated but kept silent. Jane wept a little, and sometimes failed to come to my room when I expected her, but kept silent. They were learning; they were strengthening, or else they were naïve enough to have some canine faith in me. At least they kept silent about it, though I often caught them looking at me intently, at supper or wherever. In fact, they often stared at me, and sometimes didn't even notice when I noticed them.

As for me, I stared at my wall. I have in my office, opposite the desk, a fine staring-wall, a wall that I keep scrupulously clear for staring purposes, and I stared at it. I stared at it through February, March, April, and May, and through the first week of June, without reading on its empty surface a single idea.

Then, on the very hot June 17th of 1937, our Mrs. Lake, who is as a rule a model of decorum, came sweating decorously into my office with a paper cup of iced coffee for me, set it decorously on my desk, accepted my thanks, dropped a handkerchief on the floor as she turned to leave, bent decorously down to retrieve it, and most undaintily—oh, most indecorously,—broke wind, virtually in my coffee.

"Oh, *excuse* me!" she gasped, and blushed, and fled. But ah, the fart hung heavy in the humid air, long past the lady's flight. It hung, it lolled, it wisped; it miscegenated with the smoke of my cigar, caressed the beading oil on the skin of my nose, lay obscenely on the flat of my desk, among my briefs and papers. It was everywhere, but I had learned, even then, to live with nature and my fellow animals. I didn't flinch; I didn't move. Through its dense invisible presence I regarded my oracular wall, and this time fruitfully.

"By God, now!" I cried.

I heard a small sound in the outer office.

"Mrs. Lake!" I rushed to my door. "Where's all the crap?"

"Oh, Mr. Andrews!" she wailed, and buried her face in her arms. Harry Bishop and Jimmy Andrews peered skeptically from their doorways.

"No!" I said, patting Mrs. Lake furiously on the head. "No, I mean old man Mack's pickle jars. Where've they been all this time? Where does Lizzie keep them?"

"I don't know," Mrs. Lake sniffed, wiping her eyes.

"What was it?" I hurried back to my file, began pushing things around, and finally found the inventory of the Mack estate. "One hundred twenty-nine bottles of it, in the wine cellar!"

"Well," remarked Mr. Bishop, and returned to his work. Jimmy Andrews hung around to see what was up.

"Call 'Stacia," I said to Mrs. Lake. "No, hell no, don't. I'll run up to Baltimore." I looked at my watch. "Will you run me to the bus, Jim? I bet I can catch the four o'clock."

"Sure," Jimmy said. He drove insanely; I made the bus with two minutes to spare, and was soon off to Baltimore.

Eustacia Callader was an old Negro servant in the Mack household, whom I'd met during the course of the litigation. She had virtually raised Harrison Junior and was quietly on our side in the contest over the estate, though she grasped little of the controversy. She it was whom I sought now. Arriving in Baltimore four hours later, I stopped in a drugstore to buy envelopes and stamps, and then took a taxi out to Ruxton, getting out at the driveway of the Mack house. The sun had just set, and I actually hid myself on the grounds in the rear of the house—it was all quite theatrical—and waited, I suppose, for 'Stacia to come out of the kitchen for something. An unlikely plan, but then my whole scheme, my suspicion, was unlikely: when the great Negro woman did, as a matter of fact, come out just forty-five minutes later, en route to the garbage cans down by the big garage, I took her appearance as a good omen. Following her out of earshot of the house, I approached her.

"Lord 'a mercy, Mister Andrews!" she chuckled

enormously. "What y'all doin' up here? Come see Lizzie?"

" 'Stacia, listen," I whispered urgently. "I've got a five-buck question." I gave her the five, and she giggled helplessly.

"Where does Lizzie keep the old man's fertilizer?" I asked. "Is it still in the wine cellar?"

"De fertilize'?" 'Stacia chortled. "What fertilize'?" She laughed so hard that I knew she didn't understand.

"The crap, 'Stacia," I demanded. "How does Lizzie feel about all those bottles of crap?"

"Oh, *dat's* what you mean de fertilize'!"

"A hundred and twenty-nine jars of it," I said. "Used to be in the wine cellar. Are they still there?"

When 'Stacia regained control of her risibility, she admitted that she didn't know, but she promised to find out and tell me. I gave her a buss on the cheek and took up lodgings in a clump of forsythia bushes near the garbage cans, while 'Stacia returned to the house to question the other servants who lived in. I was prepared, if it should prove necessary, to bribe somebody heavily to destroy those pickle jars for me secretly, but I didn't look forward to taking that step, since it opened the way for blackmail. Still, it seemed highly unlikely to me that Mrs. Mack had ordered them removed herself, although it was exactly that possibility which had occurred to me on the occasion of Mrs. Lake's *faux pas*.

I was pleasantly surprised, then, when three hours later—it was after midnight—'Stacia lumbered back with the announcement that though the bottles were indeed still in the wine cellar, Mrs. Mack had observed last week to R. J. Collier, the gimpy, dusty old fellow who tended the gardens, that the seals on the jars were apparently not airtight, and had mentioned the possibility of someday disposing of the collection. Indeed, 'Stacia verified that with the coming of hot weather the jars had begun to smell noticeably, and that the odor was creeping up occasionally to the ground floor. Two days before, R. J. Collier had taken it upon himself to

pile the whole stack into the far corner of the wine
cellar and to cover it with a wet tarpaulin, hoping
thereby to check the bouquet, but his experiment had
yielded no apparent results. Mrs. Mack was growing
annoyed. R. J. Collier had, that very day, broached the
suggestion that his late employer's singular remains be
put to work around the flower gardens—the zinnia
beds, especially, could use the nourishment, he declared. All the servants considered the suggestion more
touching than tactless, and I, too, sensed a seed of
poetry in the gardener's practicality. But Lizzie had
remained noncommittal.

"Listen, 'Stacia," I said, "you mustn't say a word
about the pickle jars, or about me being here. I'm going
to give you ten dollars, honey—"

"Hoo, Mister Andrews!"

"—here, ten bucks. Now I want you to keep a
close watch on those jars. Make sure you know everything that Liz or R. J. Collier or anybody else does to
them. Look. I'm giving you all these envelopes with
stamps on them. They're addressed to me, so keep
them hidden, and there's paper inside. Now, then,
every time even one of those bottles is moved from
where it is now, you write to me and tell me. Understand?"

'Stacia giggled and shook and grunted, but I was
fairly sure she understood.

"For Christ's sake don't say a word," I cautioned
her again. "If everything turns out right, Harrison will
give you a brand new car. A yellow roadster, he'll buy
you. Okay?"

'Stacia could scarcely stand for laughing. But she
stuck the envelopes deep between her endless bosoms
and rumbled off to the house, shaking her head at my
derangement. I walked out to the road and hiked two
miles to a telephone. Next day I was back in my office,
smoking cigars and staring at my wall. I didn't bother
to tell Harrison anything about my trip—perhaps nothing would come of it after all.

And except for the infrequent parries with
Charley Parks, the attorney next door, over our auto-

mobile suit—you'll recall I mentioned it earlier?—I had done nothing else, no work at all on any case, since then: nearly a week. I was waiting for 'Stacia's letter, and thinking steadily about possible alternative plans of action. I'd decided to sit thus until July 1. If nothing had happened to the jars by then, I'd take the risk of bribing R. J. Collier to destroy some of them.

Then, this morning, there was 'Stacia's letter, one of the self-addressed envelopes I'd given her. It could contain anything from nonsense to the key to three million dollars, and it was merely as a disciplinary exercise that I'd postponed reading it until after I'd read the other letters and the handbill, and had called Marvin Rose. But I shan't exact such discipline from you, reader. Here is the letter:

> *Mr. Andrew. Mrs. Mack, has put pickle jars in grenhouse. R. J. Coler, has put on zinas. Eustacia M. Callader. R. J. Coler, has put 72 bottles on zinas. Eustacia M. Callader.*

I put the letter in the dossier with the other documents pertaining to the Mack will case, returned the dossier to the file, and locked the filing cabinets. For nearly two hours I stared at my wall, and then I left the office to stroll uptown for my appointment with Marvin.

A good morning's work, readers: I opened a few letters and put one in the file. An excellent morning's work for one's last morning on earth, I should say.

My friend Harrison is three million dollars richer for it.

xi an instructive, if sophisticated, observation

The thermometer outside the offices of the daily *Banner* read eighty-nine degrees when I walked past it on my way uptown. Few people were on the streets. At the curb in front of a large funeral parlor a black hearse was parked, its loading door closed, and several mourners, along with the black-suited employees of the establishment, stood quietly about in the yard. As I approached, an aged Chesapeake Bay retriever bitch loped from a hydrangea bush out onto the sidewalk and up onto the undertaker's porch, followed closely by a prancing, sniffing young mongrel setter. I saw the Chesapeake Bay dog stop to shake herself in front of the door; the setter clambered upon her at once, his long tongue lolling. Just then the door opened and the pallbearers came out with a casket. Their path was blocked by the dogs. Some of the bearers smiled guiltily; an employee caught the setter on his haunches with an unfuneral kick. The bitch trundled off the porch, her lover still half on her, and took up a position in the middle of the sidewalk, near the hearse. The pair then resumed their amours in the glaring sun, to the embarrassment of the company, who pretended not to notice them while the hearse's door was opened and the casket gently loaded aboard.

I smiled and walked on. Nature, coincidence, can be a heavy-handed symbolizer. She seems at times fairly to club one over the head with significances such as this clumsy "life-in-the-face-of-death" scenario, so obvious that it was embarrassing. One is constantly being confronted with a sun that bursts from behind the clouds just as the home team takes the ball; ominous rumblings of thunder when one is brooding desultorily at home; magnificent dawns on days when one has resolved to mend one's ways; hurricanes that demolish a bad man's house and leave his good neighbor's untouched, or vice-versa; Race Streets marked SLOW; Cemetery Avenues marked ONE WAY. The man whose perceptions are not so rudimentary, whose palate is attuned to subtler dishes, can only smile uncomfortably and walk away, reminding himself that good taste is a human invention.

But it's not easy to keep one's patience in the face of the world's abundant ingenuousness. For instance, when I came to the corner of High and Poplar Streets and stopped to chat awhile with Capt. Osborn and two of his cronies, installed on their loafers' bench in front of George Melvin's store, I had to put up with a prominent MEN WORKING sign near an open manhole in the street before them; a senile clock in the store window, which, like the store and the old men, had ceased to mark the passage of time; a movie-theater poster directly behind Capt. Osborn's head, advertising a double bill—*Life Begins at Forty* and *Captains Courageous;* a pigeon perched restlessly on a NO PARKING sign—I could go on for a page. Really, to resist the temptation to use such ponderous, ready-made symbols taxes one's integrity, and I'm certain that if I were writing stories for my bread and butter, my resistance would weaken. I recall once reading a story that ended with the hero dead on the floor—was he a suicide or a homicide?—beneath a cash register announcing: THIS REGISTERS THE AMOUNT OF YOUR PURCHASE. The machine, as one familiar with life's elephantine ironies might have anticipated, registered zero, and I for one take it as a mark of the author's lack of acumen that he couldn't ignore that cash register, or make it read $4.37 or some other meaningless figure. It's too easy otherwise, like using clichés.

So, reader, should you ever find yourself writing about the world, take care not to nibble at the many tempting symbols she sets squarely in your path, or you'll be baited into saying things you don't really mean, and offending the people you want most to entertain. Develop, if you can, the technique of the pallbearers and myself: smile, to be sure—for fucking dogs are truly funny—but walk on and say nothing, as though you hadn't noticed.

xii   a chorus of oysters

Socially, as well as economically, Capt. Osborn and his colleagues of the loafers' bench were exclusively consumers. They ate food, wore clothing, and smoked cigars, but they produced nothing. They sat immobile on their antique bench like a row of crusty oysters and ingested with their eyes everything that passed, but they did not participate. The life of Cambridge passed by and through them like sea water through an oyster's gills: they strained from it what nutrition they wanted as it passed, digesting people and events with a snort or a comment, but they never moved from their position. They were a chorus of ancient oysters, stolidly regarding the fish that swam through their ken. Their infrequent voices were slow, nasal, high-pitched, and senile.

A bright blue roadster, for example, would roar by.

"Eee, there rides young Mowb Henly!" one would observe.

" 'E's a hot one," another would add. "Ol' Mowb's boy. Can't do nothin' with that youngster."

"No, *sir*," a third would agree.

"Eee, ol' Mowb's boy!" the first would repeat, rumbling his way up to a wet cackle of mirth and expectoration.

" 'E's bad as 'is ol' man," the second would remark.

"Ye know what they say," would crow the third. *"Like father, like son."*

The first would choke and strangle then, his red

rheumy eyes a-twinkle, his red cracked face all grin-
ning, the small saliva spilling over his brown teeth and
thin red lips, and begin the refrain again:

"Eee! Humph! *Hawk!* Sploo! Ol'—*thoo!* Thff! Ol'—
Hawk! Thff! *Thoo!* Ol' Mowb Henly! *Thooie!*"

I had a few minutes to spare, so I took a seat at
the shady end of the bench—the old men liked the sun
—and listened to their hoary music for a while.
Presently the loaded hearse drove by from the funeral
parlor, two cars with lighted headlights following behind. The procession paused at the intersection and
then moved on through the red light, heading for
Greenlawn Cemetery, out toward the country club.

"Whose funeral?" I asked.

"Why, that's Clarence Wampler's wife, ain't it, Osborn?" offered my neighbor, watching the hearse move
off.

"Yep," assented Capt. Osborn. "Died Monday
night."

"That the Henry Street one, come from Golden
Hill?" asked the third.

"Naw, that's *Lewis* Wampler's wife yer thinkin'
of," Capt. Osborn declared. "Yer thinkin' of ol' Jenny
Fairwell."

"Ol' Jenny?" the first cackled. "Ol' Jenny?"

"Ol' Jenny," Capt. Osborn grinned, stretching his
leg. "There was a hot one."

"Ol' Jenny!" the first snuffled happily.

"This here's *Clarence* Wampler's wife," Capt. Osborn explained. "Lived on Ross Street, down by the
creek."

"Sure," the first said. "I b'lieve she was a Canlon,
weren't she?"

"Now let's see," Capt. Osborn mused. "She was the
oldest Canlon girl—must of been Louise Mae."

"Louise Mae Canlon. Hell, she weren't so durned
old, was she?"

"Louise Mae Canlon," Capt. Osborn repeated.
"She was the oldest—ol' Cap'n Will Canlon's girls,
down to Golden Hill. Louise Mae Canlon must of been
twenty when Clarence Wampler married 'er. I remem-

ber that was the year ol' Cap'n Canlon lost 'is schooner in the ice—I was just startin' out with my own boat that season, the *June Phillips*, I bought 'er off ol' man George Phillips, down to Fishin' Creek. That'd be 'bout 1885, I s'pect."

"Cap'n Canlon's schooner?" asked the third old fellow, who had remained silent. "Ye mean the *Samuel T. Brice?*"

"Naw, that was 'is ol' boat," Capt. Osborn declared. "I b'lieve the *Samuel T. Brice* burned up one time, tied up to Long Dock in Baltimore. This was Cap'n Will's *new* boat—what was 'er name? *LaVerne Canlon?* After 'is wife. Well, sir, Cap'n Will hadn't no more'n put 'er in the water, spankin' new, ever' line and whipstitch, 'fore we had that big freeze-up in the Bay, and be durned if 'e didn't git froze up in 'er, and the ice wrecked 'er. Weren't no icebreakers them days."

"No, sir," the others agreed.

"I durn near lost the *June Phillips* that winter, out off Sharp's Island. Durn water was icin' up so fast ye could watch it skim over, ever' time the wind let off. Then the breeze would puff up and we'd go a-scrunchin' a little farther. I had a extra-heavy chain for a bobstay, thank the Lord; I'd told Walter Jones to hang a big one on 'er when 'e was fittin' 'er out, and I mean I didn't know which would win, us or the ice. Thank the good Lord that breeze was up, kept us a-scrunchin' right through, don't no bobstay in the world would of cut that ice, I'm tellin' ye."

"Eee!" chuckled the first. "Don't freeze up no more like that!"

"Ol' Cap'n Jamie Snyder—you remember Cap'n Jamie? Cap'n Jamie Snyder says to me, 'e saw Walter Jones a-hangin' that big chain bobstay on the *June Phillips*, up in 'is yard, 'e says to me, 'Osborn,' 'e says, 'yer goin' to need six darkies in yer dinghy,' 'e says, 'jest to keep 'er sailin' trim!' Well, sir, I says to Cap'n Jamie, 'Cap'n Jamie, it looks like ice to me, this winter,' I says, 'and I'd a sight rather ship six darkies in my dinghy, than have to git out and walk home!' "

"Eee!"

"Yes, sir!"

"Well, sir, I didn't think no more about it," Capt. Osborn went on. "Then come that big ice, and the *June Phillips* come a-scrunchin' home from Sharp's Island— took us till past dark—with that big bobstay jest a-chewin' that ice like a lean hog corncobs, and a good load o' oysters piled in the bow to give 'er weight. Next day I seen Cap'n Jamie down to the creek, lookin' where the ice had ground the paint off the *June Phillips*'s cutwater, all round that chain, and a-shakin' 'is head. 'Osborn,' 'e says, when 'e saw me watchin' 'im, 'I didn't think nothin' at the time,' 'e says, 'but I got to admit yer one up on me.' 'How's that?' I says. 'Why,' 'e says, 'don't ye know I left the *B. John Gore* fast in the ice yesterday, right off Horn Point, stuck like a minner in a gill net? Didn't I walk ever' step o' the way from the *B. John Gore* to Sim Riley's farmhouse, to git a horse, jest like ye said? I'm eatin' humble pie, Osborn,' 'e said. Then be durn if 'e didn't laugh it off and buy me a drink. That was ol' Cap'n Jamie fer ye!"

"Ol' Cap'n Jamie!"

"Eee! *Thoo!*"

Poor Louise Mae Canlon Wampler: the oysters would, perhaps, sing of her another day.

I rose to leave, and then the same dogs that had done honor to the late Mrs. Wampler came trotting down to the loafers' bench. The retriever waddled up to Capt. Osborn for an ear-scratching. The setter, ears back, tongue lolling, panted behind and attempted in his ardor to enter her from the side.

"Hoo there, feller!" wheezed one old man. "That ain't no way!"

"Pshaw!" snorted another, embarrassed. "Look at 'em, won't ye? Pecker's a-winkin' like the Cedar Point Light! Git on, there!"

"Don't spoil 'is fun," Capt. Osborn scolded with a grin. "'E'll git old soon enough, or a car'll hit 'im. Let 'im take it as it comes."

"Hee hee hee!"

"Aw pshaw! Hawk! *Thoo!*"

Capt. Osborn even assisted the setter a trifle with his foot, shoving the dog's haunches down to where his efforts might be rewarded. The setter set to with a will, while Capt. Osborn fondly scratched the retriever's ear and the oysters snickered.

I chuckled too, and would have stayed to watch, but it was almost eleven-fifteen. I chuckled all the way up Poplar Street toward Marvin Rose's office, thinking of animals *in coito* and of what had occurred in my bedroom on my seventeenth birthday. Behind my back I heard the oysters busily ingesting Cambridge:

"Hee!"

"Pshaw!"

"Thoo!"

xiii a mirror up to life

My mother having died when I was seven years old, I grew up under the inconsistent tutelage of my father and a succession of maids and housekeepers. My father always expressed concern over my welfare and proper guidance, but from either necessity or disinclination he seldom gave me a great deal of personal attention. As for the maids and housekeepers, some liked me and some didn't, but all had their own affairs to mind while Dad was working, and so I was left to myself much of the time.

I was almost never an ill-behaved child. I was quiet, but not uncommunicative; reserved, but not reclusive; energetic at times, but seldom enthusiastic. There were few restrictions on my behavior, nor were many needed. I was (and am) temperamentally disposed of observing rules—my desires seldom fell without their pale. And because I so rarely gave him cause for concern, my father was incurious about my activities.

Therefore, when I really wanted to do something of which I was certain he wouldn't approve, it was not difficult for me to do it.

My sex life, reader, up to my seventeenth year, was so unspectacular as to be unworthy of mention. I did all the things that young anthropoids delight in while growing up; my high-school amours were limited to hot, open-mouthed kisses and much risqué conversation—until my *alliance* with Miss Betty June Gunter.

Betty June, at age seventeen, was a thin, almost

scrawny little thing, most ungainly and sharp in the face, with good eyes, crooked teeth, coarse blonde hair, fine skin, and no hips or breasts to speak of. She was not considered unattractive in my set, though socially she was certainly of an inferior caste. Betty June was a poor student but a spirited girl, and there was a sharpness in her speech that bespoke a mind livelier than those of a number of more scholarly girls in our class. Besides—and this was her chief attraction—Betty June was sophisticated, worldly, informed, in a way that none of the thoroughly respectable girls of my acquaintance could approach. Her father was dead, and her mother—one wasn't sure what to think about her mother. The girl had little to do with her classmates, especially with the other girls, although there were a few notable exceptions: one or two girls of the most respectable sort claimed her as their close friend. We boys lusted after her with our eyes and our speech, of course, but before her cool, experienced manner we were clumsy and abashed. She regarded the lot of us as puppies, I'm sure.

The relationship between Betty June and me commenced when she fell in love with one Smitty Herrin, a twenty-seven-year-old bachelor who lived two houses from me. Smitty ignored her existence, she was devoted to him, and she got the habit that winter of spending much time in and about my house, hoping that Smitty would notice her. I was delighted. Betty June told me all her troubles—and they were dramatic, *real* troubles! Woman had never loved man, it seemed to me, as she loved Smitty, and yet he ignored her. She wouldn't have cared what he did to her—he might beat her and curse her (a thrilling notion to a seventeen-year-old!)—if only he'd acknowledge her devotion, but he ignored her. She would even have suffered torture for him (together we dreamed up the tortures she'd be willing to suffer, considering each soberly); would even have died for him (we discussed, in detail, various unpleasant deaths) for the merest crumb of reciprocal passion. But Smitty remained oblivious. I was violently sympathetic, and helping her articulate her grievances I discovered that I could converse more easily and naturally with her than with anyone in my experience: there was no stultifying embarrassment, as there was with other girls, nor was there the necessity to impress that falsified all my communication with my male companions. Moreover, the things Betty June discussed were of a new and thrilling order—I felt mature and wise and confident, discussing them, and I found myself able to think more liberally, compassionately, and judiciously than I'd ever thought before.

In fact, reader, I should say that it was at just this point that I lost my innocence. Of what concern is it that eventually I made love to her? But Betty June, thin skinny Betty, she broke the seal of my mind, which had been before her coming an idle enough instrument; took from me my spiritual virginity, which is childishness and naïveté, and opened my eyes to the world of men and women—and this gently, and with warmth. A lucky virgin, I, to fall into those meager arms and pathetic problems; what she took from me, I lost with pleasure.

She came to the house nearly every afternoon, after school, and stayed until the housekeeper came to prepare supper. On Saturdays she often spent the whole day with me. We would sit alone, either in the living room or in Dad's study—I preferred the study—and I would fix drinks for us, often lacing them with rum or whiskey filched from the butler's pantry. And we talked and talked and talked, easily, sympathetically, wedding her experience with my articulation. I could feel myself expanding, maturing in the bath of her lean life, flexing the muscles of my rationality and my understanding. I've no real way of knowing how Betty June felt—whether she sensed the growing power in me or regarded me merely as a harmless colt.

There came times, alas, when, colt no more, I felt every inch a stone-horse! and regarded her leanness, perched on the couch, with nostrils all but quivering. Those were embarrassing times. I suspected that, should I ever approach her, our peculiar *rapport* would vanish. Besides—the chasm yawned, the mystery—what if she were to submit?

"Your ice is melting," Betty June would observe, and I would hide myself in my drink.

Up to this point—late winter, perhaps February—I had remained fairly objective about the matter. I understood that Betty June was in love with Smitty; that she found in me only a sort of spiritual brother; that both she and Smitty were people whom at bottom, I did not really respect; that, finally, one of her chief attractions was her *possibility*: the tantalizing fact that unlike most of the girls in my set, Betty June was experienced, and that it was therefore not *entirely* impossible that—

How many aching, perspiring nights I placed on the altar of that possibility!

One afternoon she came over to where I sat in Dad's leather study chair, to light my cigarette. She held the match expertly, and while I drew on the cigarette she ran her free hand playfully through my hair. I caught her arm instantly; she laughed and fell into my lap. I took the cigarette from my mouth and crushed her lips with a violent kiss. She grew skittish, playful, but she didn't move away, and I kissed her again and again, passionately. I could scarcely believe my good fortune; I couldn't speak. Betty June still laughed softly, and kissed back—no girl had done that to me!—and pinched, and nuzzled, and caught my ears, nose, and eyebrows gently in her teeth. I began pawing her flat chest clumsily, sure I'd be slapped, but she stretched and made no objection. Incredible! I had a field day. At three-thirty she left me to marvel at my good luck.

From that day on our relationship was of a different sort. She still regarded me as harmless, I'm certain, but now we played instead of talking. It was beautiful sport; every afternoon ended with my transgressing the boundaries she'd tacitly drawn, pleading with her to surrender to me—confident in the knowledge that she would not. Then she would leave.

How my opinion changed! My objectivity was

peeled off with her chemise and tossed unwanted into the corner. I came to loathe Smitty; to rail at him inwardly—for Betty June allowed not a word of criticism; to lay elaborate plans for his ruin. I wept furiously whenever she spoke of her love for him, and she pressed my wet face to her small breast. I regarded *my* love—it had never been voiced—as a thing inviolable, out of reach; a hot, virginal intercourse of souls. I went about looking wan and distracted, brooding, melancholy. My friends kept a respectful distance; none, I think, knew of Betty June's visits. I regarded us as lost souls, condemned by the Fates (Clotho, Lachesis, and Atropos—I remember looking them up, and weeping at the justice of their names) never to consummate our love, separated by prior commitments and by barriers of position and caste (be sure I never mentioned *this* to her!), *et cetera, et cetera.*

Thus until March 2, 1917—my seventeenth birthday. I wasn't expecting Betty June until that afternoon, and I had decided to spend the morning—it must have been a holiday—knocking down the weathered frame of my unfinished boat, which still stood rotting in the back yard. But no sooner had Dad gone to court, and the housekeeper to her sister's place, as she always did, than Betty June came running into the house, weeping crazily. I held her tightly, and when she refused to calm herself I shook her by the shoulders—it seemed a manly thing to do, and it worked. She still sobbed and whimpered, but less violently.

"What's the matter with you?" I demanded, so frightened by her emotion that I actually felt ill, and my knees trembled.

"Smitty's married!" she cried.

"What?"

She nodded, sniffing and shuddering. "He's been married secretly to Mona Johnston for a year," she said, "and all that time I was—"

"Shut up!" I commanded. "Don't even say it!" I had decided to be strong.

"Now he's got her in trouble, and her folks are making them announce it."

"Good for them!" I said toughly. "Serves the bastard right!"

"No!" Betty June loosed fresh tears. "Now he's enlisted in the Army, because he can't stand Mona any more! He'll go overseas, Toddy! I'll never see him again!"

She threatened to break down completely.

"Tough luck!" I sneered, very proud of my new strength.

Betty June ran into the study and collapsed on the leather couch. I sniffed, strode into the butler's pantry, and took a good pull of bourbon, right from the bottle. It scalded to my stomach, set my blood on fire. I gave Betty June a few minutes to cry (and to wonder what I was doing); then I took another swig of bourbon, choked on it, replaced the bottle, and went to the study, walking with precision. Betty June, her eyes red, looked up at me dubiously.

I said nothing (couldn't have if I'd wanted to). I sat carefully on the edge of the couch and with one wrench opened her blouse. I was in no mood for trifling!

"Don't rip it," Betty June whimpered, recovering her composure.

"That's your problem," I growled, and gave her a bruising kiss. "If you don't want 'em ripped, take 'em off yourself."

She sat up at once and slipped off her blouse and chemise. I stood up and watched impassively.

"You quitting there?" I demanded sarcastically, as a matter of form.

Betty June regarded me for a moment with a new expression on her face. Then she stood up, and unbuttoning her placket, let her long skirt fall to the floor. Quickly she stripped off her petticoat, and without the least hesitation, her shoes, stockings, and bloomers, and stood before me nude. I very nearly swooned. Luckily I had the presence of mind to embrace her at once, so that I was out of range of her eyes.

"Take me upstairs," she whispered.

I was petrified, now that the opportunity was at

hand. Take her upstairs! My mind raced for honorable excuses.

"Suppose somebody comes home?" I croaked.

"I'll run to the bathroom," she said. Obviously she was no novice at this sort of thing. "Come on, get my clothes." She broke away from me and ran, all pink skin, to the stairs. I retrieved her clothing and followed after, scared to death; soon, in my bedroom, cluttered like a museum with the relics of my boyhood, she received that boyhood happily, and kissed me, as I chose to think, for making her its custodian. I should have kissed her, for no hot bump of a boy ever had defter instruction. I have been uncommonly lucky with women, surely through no virtue of my own.

What follows is indiscreet, but it is the point of the story.

A seventeen-year-old boy is insatiable. His lust is a tall weed, which crushed repeatedly under the mower springs up again, green and unbowed. He is easily aroused and quickly satisfied, and easily aroused again. New to the manners of the business, I cried like a baby, bleated like a goat, roared like a lion. The time came, the lesson, when I was stallion indeed. . . .

And then I looked into the mirror on my dresser, beside us—an unusually large mirror, that gave back our images full-length and life-size—and there we were: Betty June's face buried in the pillow, her scrawny little buttocks thrust skywards; me gangly as a whippet and braying like an ass. I exploded with laughter!

"What's the matter?" Betty June asked sharply.

I tossed and rolled and roared with laughter.

"I don't see anything funny!"

I couldn't answer. I couldn't comfort the nervous tears that ran from her, though I swear I tried. I couldn't help her at all, or myself. I bellowed and snorted with laughter, long after Betty June had fumed out of my bed, out of my room, out of my house, for the last time. I laughed through lunch, to Dad's amusement (and subsequent irritation). I laughed that night when I undressed.

I have said that my experience in the Argonne, not

very long afterwards, was the second of two unforgettable demonstrations of my animality. This was the first. Nothing, to me, is so consistently, profoundly, earth-shakingly funny as we animals in the act of mating. Reader, if you are young and would live on love; if in the flights of intercourse you feel that you and your beloved are models for a Phidias—then don't include among the trappings of your love-nest a good plate mirror. For a mirror can reflect only what it sees, and what it sees is funny.

Well. I never laughed at poor Betty June again, because a few days after my birthday I enlisted in the Army. Smitty was killed; I was not. Mona Johnston married someone else. Betty June, I learned upon my return from service, had become a prostitute during the war, first in Cambridge, and then—when after the Armistice it was no longer patriotic to sleep with soldiers—in Baltimore. When I next saw her, it was under entirely different circumstances. I've not heard anything from her for years.

Think me heartless—I could wish I were—but even as I write this now, thirty-seven years later, though my heart goes out to pitiful Betty, generous Betty, nevertheless I can't expunge that mirror from my mind; I think of it and must smile. To see a pair of crabs, of dogs, of people—even lovely, graceful Jane—I can't finish, reader, can't hold my pen fast to the line: I am convulsed; I am weeping tears of laughter on the very page!

xiv bottles, needles, knives

A good habit to acquire, if you are interested in disciplining your strength, is the habit of habit-breaking. For one thing, to change your habits deliberately on occasion prevents you from being entirely consistent (I believe I explained the virtues of limited inconsistency earlier); for another, it prevents your becoming any more a vassal than you have to. Do you smoke? Stop smoking for a few years. Do you part your hair on the left? Try not parting it at all. Do you sleep on your left side, to the right of your wife? Sleep on your stomach, on her left. You have hundreds of habits: of dress, of manner, of speech, of eating, of thought, of aesthetic taste, of moral conduct. Break them now and then, deliberately, and institute new ones in their places for a while. It will slow you up sometimes, but you'll tend to grow strong and feel free. To be sure, don't break *all* your habits. Leave some untouched forever; otherwise you'll be consistent.

In deciding to see Marvin Rose for a physical examination I was accomplishing two things at once: the appointment was extraordinary, and that fact gave an element of inconsistency to my last day on earth, which I'd decided to live routinely. At the same time, I was breaking a thirteen-year-old habit of not seeing doctors.

Marvin Rose had last attended me in 1924, when he prescribed for my infected prostate. At the time, I had just enrolled in law school and he was interning at the Johns Hopkins Hospital; we had been fraternity brothers as undergraduates at the University, and were dependable, if not intimate, friends. It was a terrible morning that I went to him—drunken, bloody, half-conscious, aching—where he worked in the outpatient department of the old brown hive. He washed me up, gave me some kind of pill to swallow, perhaps even administered a needle. What he said, finally, was, "Stay here for a few days, Toddy."

I intended to refuse, but it seems I fainted; when I was conscious again I was hospitalized, and within a few hours, upon my being examined—painfully!—the infection was discovered. Although I wasn't aware of it at the time, Marvin's words had terminated a phase of my life, for upon my discharge from the hospital a month later, I was an entirely different person. I had stumbled in a drunken animal; I walked out a saint. The story is neither religious nor long.

Of the noises in my life, one of the loudest in my memory is the tiny popping puncture of my bayonet in the German sergeant's neck—that sergeant with whom I choose to think my soul had lain for a while. Were I ever so foolish as to try, I'm sure I could close my eyes and hear that puncture as distinctly now as I heard it then, and the soft slide of my metal into his throat. To a noise like that, thirty-six years is a blink of the eye.

Of the human voices I have heard, one of the very clearest in my memory is the gravelly, somnolent Missouri voice of Capt. John Frisbee, the Army doctor who examined me after a heart attack just prior to my discharge. Here are his very words:

"Ah sweah, Cawpr'l, if that isn't endocahditis yew got! How in the heyell did yew git in the Ahmy, boy? Yew too young to have a haht attack, now ahn't yew?"

He shook his head, examined me again to make sure, and then wrote his report, which he explained to me as gently as his naturally blunt manner would permit.

"The endocahditis isn't so bad, son; that's what clubbed yew fingahs, and it should of kept yew a civilian. It won't git no worse. The bad thing is that yew liable to have a myocahdial infahction—and that can very likely kill yew. Might be any second; might be a yeah from now; might be nevah. But yew just as well know 'bout it. Ah don't subscrahb to this secrecy hoss-m'nure, d'yew?"

Can you understand at once—I neither can nor will explain it—that I was relieved? To say that the puncture had deranged me would be too crude, but—well, I was relieved, that's all, to learn that every minute I lived might be my last.

My first impulse, after discharge, was to rush home as quickly as possible, in order to say farewell to Dad and my town before I fell dead. Every time the train slowed for a crossing I squirmed and fidgeted, sure I'd never reach Cambridge alive. Dad welcomed me warmly, and seemed so happy to have me safely home that I hadn't the courage to tell him the tragic news at once—though of course I mustn't wait too long, or my sudden death might surprise him, coming unprepared-for. I decided to gamble on a week, during which time I idled nervously about the big house, unable to concentrate on anything.

But at the week's end, when one night Dad called me into his study, and I resolved to tell him at once, he forestalled me by speaking first.

"Cheer up, Toddy," he laughed—I must have looked glum. "I didn't call you in to scold you, like I used to when your mother was alive! What I've got on my mind is serious, but it isn't solemn."

He was feeling affectionate. He handed me a cigar, and I sat on the leather couch and smoked it.

"Todd, the first thing I want you to do, if it's all right with you, is take a vacation—from now till fall. Don't feel obliged to stay here unless you feel like it—go anywhere you want to. For spending money you've got a pretty good wad in Liberty bonds that I banked for you while you were away."

I listened, hoping my heart would last until he finished, so that I could explain.

"Then when September comes, son, nothing could make me happier than if you'd go to school." He grinned. "I shan't specify Johns Hopkins, but I must say that that's where the bright men are coming from, lately. Then, if you *really* want to humor me, study law. And do it right, in a law school; not in an office like I did. But again, I shan't even specify the law. I do want you to go to school, though, son—after a vacation. See if you can spend your whole bank account by September!"

I must say that at that moment I felt wonderful about my father. His concern for me, the (for him) remarkable diplomacy of his approach, his generosity— all these, I see now, were ordinary sentiments, not unusual in themselves; but then I was a very ordinary sort of young man, too, at the time, and the sentiments, if commonplace, were nonetheless uncommonly strong. My ailing heart felt lodged in my throat; I couldn't speak.

Seeing my hesitation, Dad busied himself attending to his cigar. His smile perhaps set a little, but it did not disappear.

"Don't answer," he said then. "Don't say anything one way or the other, yet."

"No," I protested, "no, it's—"

"Not a word," Dad insisted, sure of himself again. "What a crude fellow I am, calling you in here without a word of notice and springing a whole life's plan on you! A fine son you'd be, come to think of it, if you ever agreed to anything that drastic without a little thought first!" His spirits were high again. "Get out now," he ordered cheerfully. "Go get a little tight or something, like a veteran's supposed to. I shan't listen to a word you say about this at least until tomorrow, if not next week. Go on, now, *git!*" And he buried his attention in pretended business on his desk.

Well, I worried for a day or so—and he did too, poor fellow, thinking I didn't like his proposal—and finally decided that, since I was after all still alive, and might be for several months, I might as well leave Dad happy by enrolling in college: he would have the satisfaction of knowing he'd done all a father could do for me. Besides, why tell him about my heart? Why make both suffer, when there was no help for it?

"I'm going to Hopkins, Dad," I announced one morning at breakfast, "and then to Maryland Law School, if it's all right with you. And I don't know if this is right or not to ask, but I'd like it if when I get out I could eventually set up here in town, like you did, maybe as a junior partner or something."

Dad didn't say a word. He was so happy his eyes watered, and he had to fold his napkin and get up from the breakfast table. I was certainly glad I'd said what I said.

So I went to Johns Hopkins, enrolled in the pre-law curriculum. At Dad's suggestion I joined a fraternity—Beta Alpha Order, a Southern outfit—and lived in the fraternity house. I must say that if one has to go to college under the conditions I went under, the early twenties was an excellent time to go. It seemed to me that nearly all of my fraternity brothers expected, like myself, to fall dead any moment, for they lived each day as though it were to be their last. Their way of life suited my feelings exactly, and I soon made myself one of them. We stayed drunk for days at a time. We set fire to the men's rooms in night clubs, ignited smudge pots in the streets, installed cows in unexpected places. We brawled and fought, made nuisances of ourselves, spent nights in jail sobering up. We kept women in the house overnight, in violation of University and chapter rules—night-club strippers, prostitutes, strange ladies, college girls—and we paid fines for it; some of us were justifiably expelled from the University. We went on adulterous weekend trips to Washington and New York, beach parties at Beaver Dam and Betterton, and once a fantastic bullfrog hunt in the Dorchester Marshes south of Cambridge. We fell from speeding automobiles, and were hospitalized; occasionally even fought honest-to-goodness duels, and were hospitalized. One of us died in an automobile crash, drunk. Two of us were obliged to marry girls inadvertently made pregnant. Three of us were withdrawn from the University by irate parents. One of us committed suicide with sleeping pills and was discovered at the autopsy to be syphilitic. Three of us turned into chronic alcoholics. Perhaps a dozen of us were dismissed from school for failing courses.

Does this sound like a lampoon of student life in the early twenties? It is, indeed, a thing easily lampooned, but remember that the lampoons didn't appear out of the air: they were written mostly by men who lived through just this sort of life. It reads like a lampoon to me, too—but that's how it was.

One thing more, which perhaps distinguished my crowd from similarly exuberant groups of undergraduates at other colleges at the time: those of us who didn't flunk out got an education—it is difficult to remain long at Hopkins and escape education. It was we who followed the real tradition of the chapter and, to some extent, of the University: *studentensleben*, in the manner of the old German universities. We drank hard, caroused hard, studied hard, and slept little. We crammed for examinations, drank black coffee, chewed cigarettes, took benzedrine—and read books, quizzed each other for days, and read more books, and asked more questions. The ones who failed were not really a part of us: the goal was to drink the most whiskey, fornicate the most girls, get the least sleep, and make the highest grades. I for one am thankful that studying was part of the sport, because otherwise I shouldn't have bothered with it, knowing I'd not live to take my bachelor's degree. To be sure, most of us remembered nothing two days after the final examinations; but some of us did. It was the professors, the fine, independent minds of Johns Hopkins—the maturity, the absence of restrictions, the very air of Homewood, that nourished the seeds of reason in our ruined bodies; the disinterested wisdom that refused even to see our ridiculous persons in the lecture halls; that talked, as it were, to itself, and seemed scarcely to care when some of us began to listen passionately.

I lived through 1920, through 1921, through 1922, through 1923. In the summers I lived on at the fraternity house and worked as a stonemason, a brush salesman, a factory laborer, a lifeguard at one of the city pools, a tutor of history, even, and once actually a ditchdigger. To my great surprise I was alive on commencement day, if not entirely sober, and lived to walk off Gilman Terrace with my diploma—pale, weak, educated. I had lost twenty pounds, countless prejudices, much provincialism, my chastity (what had remained of it), and my religion. I had gained a capacity for liquor and work; an ability to take beatings; a familiarity with card games, high society, and whorehouses; a taste for art and Marxism; and a habit of thinking that would ultimately lead me at least beyond the latter. My college years are as interesting, to me, as my time in the Army, but no more of them than what I've mentioned is relevant here.

Because at summer's end I was still alive and had to have something to do, I went ahead with my program and began reading the law at the University of Maryland Law School, in downtown Baltimore. I no longer lived in the fraternity house—in an adolescently idealistic moment I had proposed amending the Order's constitution to admit Jews and Negroes, and had brought the righteous wrath of Beta Alpha upon my head. Instead, I had a marvelous fourth-floor room in an ancient row house—it must once have been palatial—on Monument Street, very near Hopkins Hospital: a room suggested to me by Marvin Rose. My neighbors and companions were medical students; the atmosphere was intense, electric with work, exhausting—more deadly serious than before, perhaps (for we were no longer undergraduates), but not more sober. With Marvin I rode in ambulances on night duty, learned first aid, hardened my stomach to carnage that equaled Argonne's, made love to certain nurses and strange female patients, and drank.

I read Justices Holmes and Cardozo, and the Spanish and Italian legal philosophers; I studied criminal law, torts, wills, legal Latin. With the medical students, achievement, competence, even brilliance, were still part of the sport: I drove myself, drank much, read much, slept little. When I was discharged from the Army I'd weighed 180 pounds; on commencement day at Hopkins I weighed 160; by the end of my first year at law school I was down to 145.

"Less work for the pallbearers," I told myself—for no one else suspected my Damocletian heart.

One night in mid-December of 1924 (I believe it was the last night before the Christmas holiday at both the law school and the medical school), Marvin and some of his colleagues proposed going out on the town, and since I happened to have thirty dollars, I agreed. I was the more eager to drink because all that day I'd had strange, sharp pains in my lower abdomen—too low for appendicitis. Walking hadn't soothed them, nor had lying down, and so I looked forward to a pleasant general anesthesia.

"Dinner," Marvin announced, and six of us took two cabs to Miller Brothers' for crab imperial. I ached all through the meal.

"Drink," he announced later, and we took a bus out to a speakeasy near the hospital, one patronized by the medical students, and got somewhat drunk. I shifted and squirmed with pain.

"*Divertissement!*" announced someone a few hours later—we were five, then, because Marvin had to go on duty in the outpatient department for the rest of the night—and the whole party adjourned to a house of joy that someone else had heard of on North Calvert Street, about halfway to the University.

We rode out in a cab. Someone put something in the one whiskey bottle from which most of us drank—I'm no toxicologist, and so I can't say what it was. When we disembarked we were loud, rough, and on the verge of helplessness. Twice in the next half hour I nearly fainted, not from liquor but from the fiery pains in my abdomen. I could scarcely wait to get a woman, for apart from the blessing of lying down, I had an inebriate notion that sex might relieve the pain.

Someone must have done my selecting for me; I'm sure I neither saw nor cared which of the girls I went upstairs with.

But "Toddy!" one of my companions hollered from down a hallway, just as my girl and I were entering a bedroom. "Hol' on!"

"No," I called back politely.

"Hol' on!" my colleague hollered again, and came lurching down the hall, pulling a girl behind him. "I got a lady here knows you from 'way back, boy."

"Oh," I said, and went into the room where my girl was waiting.

"*Oh* nothing!" the medical student cried, striding in behind me. "Why take a total stranger when right here's an ol' buddy? I'm swappin' with you."

The new girl was apologizing to my girl for being dragged in.

"You guys better get straightened out quick," my girl snapped, "or I'm callin' Cozy to bounce you."

I fell on the bed, dizzy almost to vomiting. I felt as though a hot needle, a hot bayonet, were piercing—my liver? My spleen?

Then I was standing in the center of the room, holding onto a bedpost for support, and Betty June Gunter, not a day older than she had been in 1917, was sitting on the bed, holding a cigarette in her hand, dangling a slipper from one foot, smiling mockingly at me.

I could see now; in fact I felt much more sober, but I was certainly suffering to the point of delirium.

"Glad to see you, Toddy," Betty June said sarcastically.

"I'm not going to talk, if you don't mind," I said carefully. "We'd never get it all said, and if it's all the same to you, I—"

What happened was that I collapsed then. After that Betty June had slipped off her one-piece whore's dress and I was holding her. If six years of prostitution had changed her at all, I couldn't see how. I remember wishing I were entirely sober and painless so that I could appreciate the grotesque coincidence of my meeting her, and also talk to her coherently. As far as I can tell, I was passing out every few minutes from my pain. At one point she asked me, "Do you hurt, Toddy boy?"

"I'm damn near dead," I admitted.

Then she was leaning over me, rubbing my chest and arms with rubbing alcohol.

"What the hell."

"Service of the house," she grinned.

There was a tremendous racket outside in the hall

and downstairs. I believe my medical colleagues were destroying the whorehouse.

My original plan for relief occurred to me, but it was apparently out of the question: the pain unmanned me. I was perspiring.

Now Betty June was sitting perched at my feet, and was massaging my legs with the alcohol. Her business had not improved her bustline, I observed, but neither had it hardened her good eyes. I wished I were sober so that I could judge better how she felt about me. She certainly appeared affectionate enough. What an incredible coincidence! I wondered whether she knew Smitty was dead.

"You know Smitty's dead," I remarked.

Her expression, a puckered smile, didn't change. Her eyes followed her hands, rubbing my legs.

What I finally said—rather loudly, for the noise outside the door was incessant—was, "Damn it, honey, I owe you an apology. I wish this pain weren't so bad, I'd do things right for you, no laughing. That time in my room back home, I swear, I—"

That was when, still without any change of expression at all, Betty June emptied the whole bottle of rubbing alcohol in the worst possible place.

I hollered and leaped from the bed; I clutched myself and rolled on the floor. Stupendous pain! The two together were inconceivable! To make things worse, Betty June fell upon me, still smiling. She struck at me with the alcohol bottle, coolly, putting all her small strength into each blow, and although I was able to parry nearly every assault, the crack of the bottle on my arm or elbow was punishment enough. I pushed and kicked her away, but to stand up was beyond my power. I felt on fire.

Betty June had got the bottle broken by this time, and came at me with the jagged neck of it. I rolled away and struck at her, but it was a losing fight. Every parry cost me a slash on the arm, across the knuckles, in the palm of my hand. When I finally got a grip on her right wrist, she kicked and bit. What I wanted to do, what I tried to do, was break her arm, if possible, to slow her up. That's what I was attempting when the room filled with people.

"Cozy!" Betty June cried.

There was a din. I didn't dare let go of Betty June's arm, although I was too weak to break it. Much blood was on us both. I felt like going to sleep; I had the strongest impulse to say, "Let's be friends," and go to sleep on her poor thin arm, there on the floor. *Why isn't the whole thing a sailboat?* I remember wondering through the pain that was crucifying me; then I could let go of everything, tiller and sheets, and the boat would luff up into the wind and hang in stays, and I could sleep.

Cozy must have been a competent bouncer. I daresay he rabbit-punched me, considering the circumstances and the additional pain in the back of my neck when I woke up next, but I didn't even feel the blow when it fell. Cozy had stuffed me into the back seat of somebody's parked automobile, on the floor. I had my shirt and trousers and shoes on, loosely, but no underwear, necktie, stockings, coat, or overcoat. Three-inch adhesive tape had been rolled roughly around my slashed arm—Cozy's employer hadn't wanted me to die near the premises—and since no major blood vessels had been severed, the bleeding had virtually stopped, but not before daubing my clothes. My neck throbbed; I still burned, though not quite so severely—horrible few minutes!—and the mysterious original pain continued undiminished.

I crawled out of the car after a while. I still had my wristwatch: it was four in the morning. What part of town was I in? I kept close to the wall of row houses along the street, both to steady myself and to shelter myself from the cold, and walked to the corner gas lamp. As is usual in the poorer neighborhoods, the street signs around the lamp were broken off. I turned the corner and walked numbly for an infinity of uninhabited city blocks, all fronted with infinities of faceless, featureless, identical row houses and nightmare lines of marble steps like snaggled teeth. Then came the second coincidence of the evening: I had been walking in a lightless alleyway, quiet and black as a far cranny of the universe; I half-fell around a corner, and was on Monument Street—civilized, brightly lighted, filled with automobiles and streetcars even at four o'clock. The brown Victorian pile of Hopkins Hospital stood just across the street, disgorging frequent ambulances into the city and swallowing others. A flurry of lights and a succession of strong smells, and presently I was sitting in a hard chair in a corridor of the hospital. There was much glare; soft hustlings of cars, stretchers, nurses, orderlies; muffled clinkings of instruments and glass; laughter in the distance; activity, busyness, all around my hard chair where I sat holding my head tightly. Everybody was awake in the hospital; I felt so safe I wanted to vomit.

Marvin Rose was saying, "Stay here for a few days, Toddy."

Then I was in the ward—had slept for a long time and was in little pain—and when I opened my eyes a lean nurse was holding my left arm. Before I could explain to her whatever it was that I felt explosively needed explaining, her needle had made quite the wrong small popping puncture (more felt than heard, to be sure) in the white underskin of my forearm, and I fainted another time.

Few things, I venture, are more uncomfortable to a man than a needle biopsy. The horrid instrument opened the secret of my pain to the doctor who attended me. A severely infected prostate—most unusual in a twenty-four-year-old man. And my health was generally broken down. I remained in the ward for a month, with little to do but think.

Here are the things I thought about, lying long hours immobile with closed eyes: my imminent, instant death; the futility, for me, of plans and goals; the tight smile on Betty June's lips (she hadn't laughed); the sound of punctured skin. I thought at times coherently, at times dizzily, moving from one subject to the next and starting over again. I would not attempt to sort the causes from the effects in my month's thinking, but when I was finally discharged I had decided with my whole being that I was "out of it"; that the pursuits, the goals, the enthusiasms of the world of men were not mine. My stance had been wrong, I concluded: the fact with which I had to live was not to be escaped in whiskey and violence, not even in work. What I must do, I reasoned, is keep it squarely before me all the time; live with it soberly, looking it straight in the eye. There was more to my new attitude, but it was a matter of the rearrangement of abstractions, not important here. The visible effects on my behavior were primarily these: I still drank, but no longer got drunk. I smoked, but not nervously. I took women to bed only in the rare cases when it was they who assumed the initiative, and then I was thorough but dispassionate. I studied and worked hard and steadily, but no longer intensely. I talked less. I began in earnest what was to be a long process of assuming hard control over myself: the substitution of small, specific strengths for small, specific weaknesses, regarding the latter with the same unresentful disfavor with which one regards a speck of dust on one's coat sleeve, before plucking it quietly off. I unconsciously began to regard my fellow men variously as more or less pacific animals among whom it was generally safe to walk (so long as one observed certain tacitly assumed rules), or as a colony of more or less quiet lunatics among whom it was generally safe to live (so long as one humored, at least outwardly, certain aspects of their madness).

There have been other changes in my attitude during my life, but none altered my outward behavior and manner so markedly as this one. I was uninvolved; I was unmoved; I was a saint. I was, so I believed then, in the position of those South American butterflies who, themselves defenseless, mimic outwardly the more numerous species among which they live: appropriately, the so-called "nauseous" Danaïs, whose bad taste and smell render them relatively safe. At least when walking their streets, I had to pretend to be like all the other butterflies—but at heart I knew I was of another species, perhaps a less nauseous one.

I continued, therefore, my study of law, as part of

the mimicry; at Marvin's prescription I began taking a capsule of diethylstilbestrol every day; and I awaited more quietly the moment of death. In my good time I meditated, disinterestedly, that tight, puckered smile on the face of the female human being who had intended to kill me. And, for the next thirteen years, though the prostate continued to give me frequent pain, I ceased to share that pain with physicians. Who ever heard of a saint's crying for a doctor?

"Well, well, well!" Marvin shouted (in 1937) when I stepped into his office. He rubbed his hands gleefully. "Coming home to die, are you? What'll it be, Todd? What the hell, you pregnant?"

"A plain old physical examination, Marv," I said.

"Going to buy some insurance, man? I'll lie for you. Hell, boy, I'll euthanaze you."

"None of your business. Come on, examine."

But we smoked a cigar first, and Marvin reminisced about Baltimore. When he got around to examining me, I said:

"Will you go along with me on something, Marvin?"

"Where's the body? What'd you do, Todd?"

"Examine me to your heart's content," I said, "but I don't want you to say a word about anything you see or find; don't even change expression."

"I won't even examine you if you say so, you big sissy. I'll call Shirley in here and let her look at you."

"Just write it all down," I smiled, "and either mail it to me or drop it off at the hotel. The point is that I don't want to know anything at all, at least until tomorrow. Okay?"

Marvin grinned: "You're the doctor."

He then went through the examining routine, talking all the while he checked my height, weight, eyes, ears, nose, throat, and teeth. Then I stripped to the waist, and with stethoscope, watch and sphygmomanometer he checked my heart, my pulse, and my blood pressure, keeping the expressionless face I'd asked for. Then he tapped my chest and back, listening for congestion, and felt my vertebrae. Finally I removed trousers and underwear, and he tapped my knee, testing for locomotor ataxia, felt for hernias, and looked for hemorrhoids and flat feet, all without any alteration of expression.

"How about a blood test and a urinalysis?" he asked.

I produced a urine specimen, but declined the blood test.

"How's the old prostate? Been keeping her empty?"

"No trouble," I said.

"Sure raised hell that one time, didn't it? I swear I wanted to cut her out for you, Toddy; you wouldn't have had another twinge. But that screwball Hodges—remember him? the resident?—he was having a feud with O'Donnell, the surgeon, that year, over politics, and wasn't letting anybody get cut. Goddamn Hodges! I swear he'd have tried to amputate a leg with his damn internal medicine! What a bunch!" He made some notes on an examination form and slipped it into an envelope. "Here y'are, lad, the whole sad story. How about a little old needle biopsy? Have a look at the old infection. Make you dance and holler."

"Let it go," I said, and began dressing.

"No needle? How am I supposed to know what's what? How about an X ray, raise your bill a few bucks?"

"Drop the paper off any time after today," I said, accepting from Marvin another light for my cigar, which had gone out. "Please keep everything under your hat, Marv."

"I don't blame you," Marvin said, walking me to the door with his arm across my shoulders. "I'd be ashamed, too." We shook hands. "Well, hell, Toddy. Don't wait so long next time. And listen, if the old prostate commences to hurt you, I'll cut it out. You ought to keep check."

I smiled and shook my head.

"What do you say? Come down to the hospital Monday for an X ray, and I can take her right out, clean as a whistle."

"Wait till Monday," I said. "But don't hold your breath."

We said goodbye, and Marvin went back to lie on the examination table for a nap. He was (I'm late saying it) a beefy little man with sparse blond hair, flushed skin, and tiny red veins in his cheeks. His arms and hands were so full of meat that it seemed as if the skin of them were ready to burst, like overboiled frankfurters. It would be pleasant to be able to go on and say of Marvin's great hands that, awkward as they appeared, the moment they were slipped into surgeon's gloves they assumed the deftness and delicate strength of a violinist's. This is the sort of thing one usually hears. But the truth is that those clumsy-looking hands, once slipped into surgical gloves, remained rather clumsy, depending as they did from slightly clumsy arms and ultimately from a somewhat clumsy brain. The truth is that the magnificent Hopkins does not infallibly produce faultless medicine men; the truth, alas, is that in fact I should be markedly reluctant, even were I not opposed to it on principle, to allow my excellent friend Marvin to incise me with his not-altogether-unerring knives. The fact of affection needn't preclude objectivity.

xv that puckered smile

One doesn't move on without giving that tight smile, Betty June's puckered smile, some further attention. Mere drunkenness and pain are no excuse for my not having realized, until she was upon me with the bottle, that I had done to Betty June a thing warranting murder at her hands (I am, by the way, reasonably confident that it *was* Betty June in the Calvert Street whorehouse, although I was certainly drunk). She wanted to kill me, I see now, for having laughed that time in my bedroom.

Here's how I understand it: that morning in 1917 she had learned that Smitty Herrin, to whom she had unreservedly humbled herself, had all the while been married to Mona Johnston, from Henry Street, and had made Mona pregnant. In desperation, Betty June had come to me and had attempted—unconsciously, I daresay—to reassert her wounded ego by humbling me with the gift of her body, a lean receptacle for my innocence. But in the throes of intercourse I had laughed, so violently as to unman myself, and couldn't even stanch her injured tears for very helplessness. She had assumed that I was laughing at her, at some ridiculousness of her, although this was not *particularly* true. And then—what? Smitty and I both enlisted, he was killed, and she became a prostitute. Ordinarily, perhaps, it would have been possible for her to rationalize her behavior, first as a patriotic gesture and later as gaining a livelihood from "the oldest profession"—but she had my laughter in her ears to remind her, every time she unhooked her one-piece gown for a new customer, that there was something ludicrous about her and about what she was doing. For many sorts of people, and Betty June is one of them, this suspicion would be nearly intolerable. So: seven years later, when she's doubtless so deeply enmired in the business and all its attendant vices that she can't very well escape, seven years later I show up party-drunk at her whorehouse—looking prosperous and smug to her, no doubt—accept her as my whore without a word, and only later, after permitting her to massage my body, refer with vague regret to the time I laughed at her.

Don't you agree that this is probably how it was? I can't account otherwise for her murderousness (yet I must say, though I can scarcely explain it, that if I hadn't *mentioned* the matter, I believe Betty June would have gone through with the intercourse I had paid for). The remarkable thing, it seems to me, is not at all that she wanted to kill me—even simple shame at being thus discovered could account for that—but that I failed to realize it at once; that I missed the obvious implication of that puckered smile.

And this is what I wanted to say, because I consider it fairly important (hell, even urgently important) to the understanding of this whole story: quite frequently, things that are obvious to other people aren't even apparent to me. The fact doesn't especially bother me, except when it leads to my not jumping clear of dangerous animals like poor Betty. The only likely explanation I can imagine is that out of any situation I can usually interpret a number of possible significances, often conflicting, sometimes contradictory. Why, for instance, could it not have been that Betty June, after seven years of prostitution and various unfortunate experiences, had come to see, as I did, the essential grotesqueness of the whole business—the very four-letter verb for which is wittily onomatopoeic—and upon encountering me had decided to demonstrate her agreement by a rousing good copulation, at which we'd both laugh long and loud? Or, less dramatically, why could it not have been that she'd forgotten the affair in my bedroom, and was smiling merely at my drunkenness, or in anticipation of scorching me with isopropyl alcohol? Or, less kindly, that observing my helplessness she was smiling at the thought of earning seven dollars for giving me nothing more voluptuous than a rubdown? I'm not especially defending myself: very possibly another person would have seen factors in the situation that would preclude all these alternatives; or, possibly, another person wouldn't have imagined these alternatives in the first place. I honestly believe that to most men (and to any woman) Betty June's intentions would have been obvious. To me they were not.

On the other hand, things that are clear to me are sometimes incomprehensible to others—which fact occasions this chapter, if not the whole book.

xvi the judge's lunch

Harrison and I were in the habit of lunching at a confectionery store on Race Street, beside the old opera house. It was run by an orphan's court judge, an engaging fellow who refused, for purely aesthetic reasons, to serve hot platters: he disliked the smells of cooking in his store. This integrity alone would have attracted me to the place; but the proprietor had a host of such opinions; like me, he was in the habit of giving sound, unorthodox, and not infrequently *post facto* reasons for his behavior, which reasons he was wont to articulate at length to his regular customers in a loud voice, for he was slightly deaf.

It was to this place that I walked after leaving Marvin. Race Street was afire with dusty sunlight, and few people were out. A number of unclean children were playing tag on the wide cracked steps of the opera house, swinging over and under the brown brass rail that led up to the shuttered box office. On both inner walls of the arcaded façade, crusty with weathered architectural gingerbread, were plastered posters advertising *Adam's Original & Unparalleled Floating Opera*.

Not until I'd actually entered the confectioner's—until the Judge, small, dapper, bald, and boutonniered, greeted me and I remarked politely that he looked like a million dollars—did I remember that, should I choose, I was in a position to make my friend Harrison worth nearly three million. It may seem incredible that such a thing could simply slip one's mind, but it very nearly did. I believe that if the Judge hadn't prompted my remark, I'd have forgotten the matter entirely, perhaps until too late. And I was glad I remembered it.

You see, although Eustacia's information assured me that I could win the case (all that was necessary was to secure from Equity an order holding up the appeal until the missing portions were accounted for. The thing could be complicated indefinitely, and after the coming elections, when Joe Singer had replaced Rollo Moore on the appellate court bench, I was confident that the Circuit Court judgment would be reversed)—although the thing was in my hands, by no means did it neces-sarily follow that I would do anything about it. Very possibly I would decide to keep the new information secret, let it die that day with me instead of giving it to young Jimmy Andrews or Mr. Bishop to work with after my death. For one thing, remember that I was a fairly thoroughgoing cynic at the time, especially concerning money; also—nothing cynical about this—I believed Har-rison was undeserving of the money unless he overcame his former weakness. It was my opinion that in order for him to be worthy of the inheritance, he had to demon-strate a strength of character that would make the loss of it unimportant: a pretty lofty opinion for a cynic. At any rate, I decided not to mention Eustacia's letter right away.

I was a few minutes late; Harrison was waiting for me, talking to the Judge. We went back to our table.

"Janie dropped out to the plant just before I drove in," he said. "What are you needling her for?"

"Needling her?"

"That note you sent her this morning," Harrison said mildly. "You know what I'm talking about."

"I do now," I smiled. "I'd forgotten." I gave my order to the girl who came to our table; Harrison had already ordered. "I wasn't entirely joking, Harrison. Cap'n Osborn's got a couple more years, at the most, be-fore he dies. Suppose you were in his place: wouldn't you like a fine send-off like Janie? Hell, he couldn't do anything to her. Are you angry?"

"I wasn't before," Harrison grinned, "because I thought you were just being nasty. But if you're *serious* about her showing herself to the old buzzard, I probably ought to get mad."

I held a light for his cigar. He was doing fine so far.

"Well, if you want to," I laughed. "But Janie handled it pretty brightly, I think. Did she tell you about *her* note?"

"No."

"She said she'd do what I asked if I'd agree to let Marvin Rose look at me, to see why I'm such a pansy. Her very words."

Harrison chuckled, a little relieved. "Fair enough," he said. "What did she mean, *pansy?* Or shouldn't I ask?"

"You may ask, but a little more softly next time. The fact is, I spent most of last night looking out my window, and the rest of the time reading a book."

Harrison looked concerned. "You getting senile?"

"Quitting while I'm still ahead, maybe." I smiled. "As a matter of fact, I don't think Marvin found anything especially wrong with me, at least not below the belt. I was just up there."

Harrison's peace of mind vanished. "You did what she said?"

"Yep."

The girl brought our lunches: a bacon and tomato sandwich and iced tea for Harrison, and a chopped olive and Swiss cheese on rye for me, with iced coffee.

"Well, what now?" Harrison asked. "I don't know what to say. You sure do change your mind about things."

I shrugged. "It's not your problem; it's Jane's. Cap'n Osborn won't know the difference either way."

Harrison started to object, but then he changed his mind and bit into his sandwich instead.

"All right," he said, talking with his mouth full. "I won't worry about it."

"Good man."

Harrison then changed the subject and talked idly about a possible strike of his cucumber picklers. His mouth was still full, and there were three little flecks of mayonnaise on his lower lip. As he spoke, an occasional crumb blew over to me. I admired two things: the casual bad manners that one often encounters in finely bred animals like Harrison, and the fact that his description of the labor difficulties in his plant suggested neither a pro-union bias from his Marxist days nor an anti-union bias from his present position. He was interested in the situation, but rather cynical toward both the union leaders, who were making him out to be a slave driver, and his own administrative staff, who advocated firing the lot of them and hiring "new niggers" in their places. It seemed to me that cynicism, although he was not entirely at home with it yet, became him a great deal more than had his earlier saintliness. I listened with some interest, regarding his still-handsome face (he was forty-three, I guess, and Jane in her early thirties) and the little drops of mayonnaise, which he finally licked away.

We finished our sandwiches and smoked for a while, enjoying our drinks. The Judge's store wasn't air-conditioned, but he had three big old ceiling fans, and the place was light and cool.

"Oh, by the way," Harrison said, "Jane wasn't in when your secretary called this morning, but the maid took the message, and then apparently you were out when Jane called back. She says she'll drop Jeannine off at your office at three, if that's not too early. She's coming uptown to the hairdresser's around then."

I was a little disturbed, not at the change of hours (I had planned to take Jeannine to see the showboat at four), but because my instructions to Mrs. Lake—to call Jane—were the second thing I'd forgotten in a few hours. No, come to think of it, I'd had *three* lapses of memory: Eustacia's letter, my note to Jane, and my request to Mrs. Lake. This was a serious matter, for it could be taken as a sign of nervousness, of apprehension at my decision to destroy myself that day. I was of course not indifferent toward the resolution, but my feeling was more one of pleasure at having found the final solution to my problem than one of commonplace fear. And, pleasure or fear, I marked it an indication of imperfect control to be so touched by my feeling as to make unusual slips of memory on what I'd decided was to be a quite usual day.

"I thought I'd take her down to see the showboat when it pulls in," I said. "How's her tonsils?"

"All right, I guess. Anyhow it wasn't tonsillitis. Marvin came out and looked at her throat yesterday, and said it didn't look like he'd have to take them out, unless we wanted him to go ahead and get it over with. It was her throat that was infected, and her tonsils just swelled up on general principles. I don't know what Jane's decided. Both of us had tonsillitis when we were kids."

"Better leave them in," I suggested. "Mine used to swell up every now and then, whenever I had a sore throat, but it never amounted to anything."

There was a certain tactlessness in this remark, as I'll explain presently, and I made it for that reason, with nonchalance. Harrison took the cigar from his mouth and studied its ash.

"I don't know," he said.

"Marvin's a little quick with the knife. Once when I was in law school and he was interning, he was all set to make a eunuch out of me."

Harrison replaced the cigar in his mouth and drew on it as we got up from the table.

"That would've been too bad," he observed, and put a quarter down for the girl. Then he fetched his straw and mine, and we walked through the front of the store. Have I described Harrison? Not being a writer by trade, I sometimes neglect these details. He was heavy—weighed perhaps two hundred pounds—and still well-built, though he showed signs of going to fat from lack of exercise. His features, which had been chiseled when I first knew him, had begun to round off a little, and his cheeks and belly no longer looked hard, as they had when he played much tennis and rode horses. He still had a good head of tightly curled blond hair, contrasting nicely with a complexion as much flushed as sunburned (I daresay his blood pressure registered somewhere between mine and Marvin's), and his eyes, teeth, and arms were excellent.

Very wealthy-looking fellow, Harrison, and very clean and handsome. The thin, consumptive communist would justifiably loathe him, but the properly nourished parlor communist would be made uncomfortable by his charm. Those particular aspects of Harrison relevant to this story have made him look less engaging than he really was—I can't dwell on him, of course, for it's not his story. Let me repeat, if I've mentioned it before, that he was by no means either a fool or a weakling. He was a reasonable, generous, affable, alert fellow. I might even say that if this were a rational universe and if I could be any person I chose, I should not choose to be Todd Andrews at all. I should choose to be very much like my friend Harrison Mack.

"How's the pickle business, Todd?" the Judge called to me as we stepped out on the sidewalk, where he spent much of his time watching the town. He referred, of course, to the disputed will, which case he had followed with great interest. "You gentlemen in the money yet?"

Ordinarily I'd have enjoyed explaining the new development to him, for although he was not professionally trained, his mind was quick and sure, and he'd have appreciated the maneuver. But of course I could not.

"Nothing new, Judge," I said loudly. "Depends on how the war goes, maybe."

"Well, I doubt it'll go good for the Loyalists," he declared. "They've been holding their own lately, but it can't keep up. They've got the Russians, but Mr. Franco, he's got the Germans, and like it or not, the German's a better soldier than the Russian is. The German might be dumb, but he's dumb like a smart dog. Old Russian, he's dumb like an ox."

Harrison was fidgeting to leave. For my part, I was interested enough in the Judge's prognostications, for he knew how to read newspapers, and read five or six a day. It was, in fact, the Judge who had first predicted to me that Rollo Moore wouldn't be re-elected, and I'd have gone ahead with my plans on the strength of his judgment even had I not been able to confirm it in certain Baltimore Republican circles.

"You think Franco's in, then?"

"I think it'll take him a couple of years yet to wind it up," the Judge said. "By that time the whole shebang might blow."

"Well," Harrison fidgeted.

I said goodbye to the Judge—after all, I probably would not see him again, and he was one of my favorite citizens—and walked with Harrison as far as his car, which was parked on Poplar Street.

"Will you come for cocktails tonight?" he asked as he slipped behind the wheel.

I leaned down and talked to him through the window on my side. "Much obliged."

Harrison put the Cadillac in gear.

"*Don't feel obligated*," he smiled ruefully. "Any time after four."

He slid away down the brick street, which shimmered now in the very hot sun. I walked toward the hotel for my nap, feeling fine about Harrison. There was no need for haste in making my decision, but the lunchtime had done his cause much good indeed.

xvii   the end of the outline

Climatologically, this day of which I write was rare for
Dorchester County, rare for the Eastern Shore, where
the same ubiquitous waters that moderate the temper-
atures—the ocean, the Bay, the infinite estuaries,
creeks, coves, guts, marshes, and inlets—also make
them uncomfortable. This day, on the contrary, was
excessively warm (the temperature as I walked to the
hotel must have reached 95), but extremely dry. I was
wearing shirt, suit, underwear, and hat, and there was
no shade on Poplar Street, but my body was dry as a
white bone in the desert, and I was entirely comfortable. It was a day when one would have liked to sit
alone on a high dune by the ocean—the Atlantic beach
is often just this dry, given a land breeze—in air as hot
and salty as Earth's commencement, the drought of
precreation before the damp of procreation; to sit a
dried and salted sterile saint, Saint Todd of the Beach,
and watch voracious gulls dissect the stranded carcass-
es of sandy skates and sharks, bleached and brined to
stenchlessness. The locust trees by People's Trust were
dusty, and mast-truck high in the High Street poplars,
locusts rasped and whirred a parched dirge for my last
high noon. It was a lovely day for suicide. One felt that
one would hardly bleed into such aridity; more probably a knife in the neck would be kissed with a desiccant
hiss of mere dry air.

Turning the corner of Poplar, High, and Locust
Streets, I found the loafers' bench empty: the old men
were home to nap. The Choptank sparkled at the foot

of the boulevard. *Adam's Original & Unparalleled Floating Opera* posters graced every business window on the empty streets from the Judge's place to the hotel, red, white, and blue, as though the town had been set for Independence Day and then everyone—men, women, dogs, and pallbearers—had gone to a parade somewhere else.

The hotel lobby was light and cool; a small chat with Jerry Hogey, and then I went to my room. Are you so curious as to follow me down the hall to the men's room? If you aren't (I shall be only a minute), read while you wait the story of my resumption of the affair with Jane Mack. Look back into Chapter III, and you'll find that near the end of it I reproduced an outline of the events that I imagined led up to my seduction by the Macks. In the final section of that outline I listed what I considered to be the four possible courses that my relationship with them could take after I'd broken it off by an act that, judged in the very terms that I objected to, they must regard as an insult. Now of these four courses, either I or IV (that is, permanent disaffection or the resumption of a qualified affection, one of the qualifications being a suspension of the affair) seemed the most probable to me after the incident in my office with Dorothy Miner, which terminated the friendship.

However, I was reckoning without two things, neither of which I could reasonably have been expected to predict.

In the first place, just a few weeks after the Macks had severed relations with me, Jane learned, upon being examined by Marvin Rose for chronic nausea, that she was pregnant. Moreover, she was probably three months pregnant: it was possible for her not to guess it herself only because she had always been irregular. As soon as Marvin looked at her, he said, "You're pregnant," and it instantly seemed so obvious to her (she swore later that her tummy filled out the moment he spoke the word) that she became a little hysterical at not having recognized it herself. Marvin gave her a sedative. Jane hurried home and could scarcely wait to tell Harrison when he came in from work, she was so delighted. But when he walked into the house and she opened her mouth to tell him, it suddenly occurred to her that she was *three months* pregnant, not three weeks or three days; she remembered me, burst into tears, and nearly fainted. When finally she was able to explain things to Harrison, he couldn't say a word.

The pregnancy was pretty miserable for both of them (I learned this later, of course). It would have been simple enough to arrange an abortion, but it happened that they really wanted a child, and had tried unsuccessfully for several years to have one. They both wished, too late, that Jane had been more diligent in using precautions with me, but the fact was that she hadn't; it is a mark of Harrison's saintliness that not once did he suggest a reproach for her carelessness, and a mark of Jane's that she owned up to it in the first place. Being intelligent people, they were able to talk about the matter frankly, and they tried hard to articulate their sentiments, to decide how they really felt about it.

"Look at it this way," Harrison's most frequent argument ran; "suppose I was sterile—wouldn't we sooner or later probably adopt a kid? Or suppose you'd been married before and had a kid—wouldn't we still love it after you married me? Now, this is better than adoption, because you're going to be the real mother either way. And it's better than a previous marriage, because there's a good chance I'm the real father. After all, I slept with you more than Andrews did."

That was a pretty good argument, I thought, but Harrison never could put enough conviction into his voice, and that last sentence, whether intended to do so or not, usually brought Jane to tears.

"That's all true," was her typical reply, "but no amount of reasoning can get around the fact that if I hadn't made love to Todd in the first place—or if I'd only kept my stupid head and been careful—then either I wouldn't be pregnant or we'd know you're the father." This said with her fine head in her hands, her excellent shoulders shaking.

Harrison then, quite calmly (but not kissing the sable hair or stroking the shoulders): "What the hell, hon, a fact's a fact. It was my idea as much as yours. We shouldn't have taken the step if we can't stand up to the consequences."

"But we didn't think of this!" Jane would wail.

And Harrison would shrug. "People get pregnant."

And so on. A lousy pregnancy. To make it worse, Jane was ill for most of the remaining six months. She could keep nothing on her stomach, and on several occasions required uncomfortable glucose injections to stave off malnutrition. At the same time, though, her illness had the virtue of keeping her weight down. I saw her just once, in her ninth month, from a short distance away, and she was so beautiful that I suffered a rare twinge of regret and real longing, no less intense for its being short-lived. And her moderate size eased her delivery: on October 2, 1933, in the Cambridge Memorial Hospital, after only three hours of labor, she gave birth to a six-pound ten-ounce girl, whom she named Jeannine Paulsen (Jane's maiden name) Mack.

Harrison and Jane had, understandably, been not a little fearful of the day when they must actually bring their baby home; when it would be committed totally into their hands and they would be expected to love and care for it. The care was no problem—there were bottles, formulas, and trained nurses—but they feared that the love might simply not be forthcoming. Jane especially feared this about Harrison, and Harrison about himself. But as it happened they quickly took to their daughter—she was an engaging child, luckily, right from her infancy—and found it easy to be affectionate parents. Perhaps their knowledge of the danger of any other reaction sufficed to open the buds of love in their hearts. They breathed more easily (the baby obviously doing her best to protect her own interests, contrived to resemble neither Harrison nor me to any embarrassing degree) and wondered what they'd worried so much about.

"I swear," Harrison volunteered, "if somebody

should prove to me, right this minute, that Todd was Jeannine's father, I wouldn't love her a bit less for it."

"Oh, I'm sure he's not," Jane scoffed (you understand that I heard all this later). "But I don't think I would, either. She's beautiful."

But the important statement, for this story, Harrison made sometime in the spring of 1934, about a year after I'd insulted them.

"You know," he said, "you may not agree with this, because I know how much you dislike him, but I sometimes think that that business with Todd was partly our fault, too."

"*Our* fault!"

"I mean, what the hell, we put him on the spot, when you got in bed with him; he might not even have wanted to, you know—not because he didn't want you, but because he might have thought it would hurt our marriage. But if he'd refused, we'd have been insulted, wouldn't we? And, in fact, if he hadn't done it on our terms, we'd have been insulted, I think."

"Still, he had no business telling us he was a virgin," Jane insisted.

"But you can't deny we were pleased when he did," Harrison replied. "That proves we were expecting too much of him. And we certainly had no right to expect him not to make love to other women. What the hell, he's a bachelor."

"But he was supposed to be in love with me."

"You're in love with me, too," Harrison smiled, "but you made love to Todd. You understand."

Jane sulked.

"We expected too much. We should've known him better."

"Well maybe you're right," Jane said. "But he certainly had no right to break it off like he did, with that damned colored girl!"

Harrison grinned. "I guess he's unprejudiced. To tell the truth, the more I think about that, the more I believe he was just ad-libbing. That girl didn't know what was up any more than I did."

Jane pouted for a while, but after the ice had been

broken they talked more freely about me, and less bitterly. Gradually it got to be assumed that they'd really been too demanding (a piece of objectivity that still appalls me), and that to some extent I'd been justified in showing my claws.

The next step was for Jane to say, "Hell, I forgive him; I just don't want anything to do with him any more."

And for Harrison to say, "I still like Todd all right; it's just that I can't get enthusiastic about seeing him any more. I don't bear him any grudge."

Jeannine grew and grew, and discreetly began to look like her mother.

The second thing that I hadn't predicted was that on January 10, 1935, Harrison Mack Senior would die, leaving seventeen testamentary instruments for his wife, son, and nurses to play games with. But he did, as surely as sweet Jane got herself impregnated, and as irremediably. No one needed to suggest to Harrison that he needed professional assistance, either; he consulted a lawyer a lot more quickly than Jane had consulted a physician, and the firm that he retained was Andrews, Bishop, & Andrews. The obvious necessity for legal counsel, the disturbance over his father's death, the excitement over the big estate—all these made his move seem quite natural, so that if there was anything in it of an overt act to reinstate our friendship, the overtness was effectively camouflaged, and one needn't even think of it.

There were, one can imagine, dozens of details in the litigation that required discussion, strategies to be worked out, conferences to be held: many more than could be conveniently fitted into my leisurely office schedule. It was inevitable, then, that Harrison and I should occasionally utilize our lunch hours for the purpose; even that he should eventually invite me, with aplomb, to come for late cocktails one evening, and that I, with commensurate grace, should accept.

Of that evening—at first somewhat strained, since it was my first meeting with Jane in more than two years—just one incident will do here: the Macks had

put Jeannine to bed early, thinking thereby to keep
discomfort at a minimum, and with the assistance of
Gilbey's gin and Sherbrook rye, the three of us had
contrived to reach a condition of mellow, if tacit, mutual forgiveness. We all felt relieved that the nonsense of
the past two years was done, though nothing was said
about it directly; our good spirits were reflected in the
unusual amount of liquor consumed, in the fact that
whatever legal matters had provided the excuse for our
meeting never got discussed, and (most significantly)
by the fact that when Jeannine, who had a slight cold,
began to fret in her crib, Jane, despite a private resolve
to the contrary, said spontaneously: "Come on, Toddy,
you haven't met this little Mack! Come upstairs and be
introduced."

She realized her slip as soon as it was out, and
added at once, without changing her tone or expression, "Harrison will do the honors, won't you, honey?"

The three of us went to the nursery, where Jeannine—a blonde little charmer whom I must say I'd be
delighted to learn I'd fathered—stood up sleepily in
her crib and grinned at her parents, shyly, because I
was there.

"Jeannine," Harrison said, "this is Toddy. Can you
say *Toddy?*"

Jeannine could not, or would not.

"Would you like to kiss Toddy good night, honey?"
Jane asked her. Jeannine hung her head, but looked up
at me from under her eyebrows and chortled. When I
kissed her hair—as soft as silk thread, and fragrant
with baby soap—she dived into the mattress and
buried her giggles in the blanket.

Jane had crossed the room to adjust the window,
and Harrison and I stood side by side at the crib, where
Jeannine was already on the verge of sleep. A number
of obvious thoughts were in the air of the nursery—it
was like a scene arranged by a heavy-handed director—
and I, for one, was embarrassed when Jane, after her
excellent and immediate good taste of a few minutes
before, now came up behind us and grasped both our
arms while we looked at the little girl. *Our little girl,*

the tableau simpered, underlining the pronoun. Ah, reader, the thing was gross, sentimental; and yet I was moved, for with the Macks these sentiments are sincere. They are simply full of love, for themselves, for each other, for me.

We went back downstairs, soberly, but Harrison, sensitive by then to such solemnities, at once poured a round of cocktails and we were soon gay again, restored to grace. The evening was a success; I returned often; and soon, but for the two quiet years that sometimes hung heavy over our conversation, we spoke together as easily as ever.

Had the friendship remained at this stage of reconstruction, I should have asked for nothing more. I was content to see the Macks outgrow their unbecoming jealousy, which was as dangerous to their own relationship as it was inconsistent with their previous behavior. Nor did I see how things could tactfully become any more intimate, after my rebuff of 1933. But on the night of July 31, 1935, while I was sitting at my window reading a book for my *Inquiry* (somebody's critique of Adam Smith's economics, I do believe), there was a small knock on my door, the knob rattled, and Jane stepped in, wearing shorts.

"Hi," she said, standing just inside the closed door.

"Hello." I closed my book, threw my cigar stub out the window, and got up to give her the chair. "Sit down."

"All right." She grinned quickly and came over to the window, where I was sitting on the sill, but she forgot to sit down. I didn't want any nonsense this time—for her sake, not because I objected to nonsense on principle—and so I kept my eyes on her face, not to make it any easier for her. She mostly looked down at the street.

"We've been for a boat ride," she said. When I didn't answer, she looked at me irritably and began to fidget.

"You have to understand everything at once," she declared. "I'm not able to talk about anything just now."

"That's impossible," I said. "I can understand everything at once in about three different ways."

"You're not helping me. You're not saying any of the right things." She laughed.

I didn't smile. "That's only because I don't know what you want to hear, Jane. You should know I'll say anything I think you want to hear."

Her smile disappeared, and she regarded the dark Post Office across the street and fiddled with the curtain pull.

"That was a hard lesson, Toddy."

"I wasn't teaching anybody anything," I said sharply. "What do you think I am? I was just getting clear."

She fiddled with the cord.

"Let me ask you," I said. "Do I love you?"

"No."

"Now let's get that straight. I don't want to hurt you all."

"You don't love me and I don't love you."

This was getting as theatrical as the other. I gave it up. For ten minutes more Jane stared at the Post Office. I honestly couldn't guess what would come of it. After a few minutes, though I didn't intend any such thing, my mind—never very impressed by this sort of dramatics—wandered to other things: to the seventeen wills, to Bill Froebel, to the critique of Adam Smith. And it startled me, for I'd honestly forgotten for an instant that she was there, when Jane spun around from the window and said, "Let's get in bed, Todd." Without looking at me, she walked to the bed, unfastened her shorts and halter, and lay down, and very shortly after that I joined her.

So. Nothing remains to be told of the affair, except that after its resumption it was conducted in a manner more satisfactory to me. No schedules, no demands, no jealousy, no fictions—all was spontaneity and candor. I think that my increasingly frequent impotency after that time (by 1936, about every fourth attempt at intercourse was a failure; by 1937, about every other attempt) would have led me to call off the thing for good in time anyway, even had I not resolved on this day to kill myself. But by 1937 I could contemplate with equanimity the prospect of terminating our affair, for it left, from my point of view, nothing to be desired. Jane Mack is the finest woman I've ever slept with. Since the morning of the day at hand, when she last left my rented bed, I have desired nothing from women. She satisfied me.

Now, if you'll excuse me, I shall sleep.

xviii   a matter of life or death

Although it was my custom to nap for an hour every day, on the day I intended to be my last I was waked almost as soon as my eyes were closed, by an urgent knock on my door.

"Come on in," I called, and pulled a robe on over my underwear.

There was no response for several moments, and I had begun to decide that my unknown caller had gone away, when I heard two or three footsteps in the hall and then another knock.

"Yes, come on in," I repeated, still tying my robe.

Another pause. I started toward the door, but it opened just before I reached it, and Mister Haecker, taut as a piano wire, stepped inside.

"Sit down, Mister Haecker!" I exclaimed, for he looked ready to faint. His smile was thin and broken like the smiles of army recruits hearing heavy artillery for the first time, and his face was white. I took his arm firmly and led him to the chair. "Let me get you a drop of rye, Mister Haecker." My first thought was that the old fellow was ill and had come to me for help.

"No thank you, Todd," he managed to say. His voice I can describe only as a prim croak. He perched on the edge of the chair as daintily as a canary on its swing, and his hands clutched his knees.

"Is anything wrong, sir?" He looked a bit better now, but still none too stable.

"No," he said shortly, closing his eyes and shaking his head. "No. I just—came in to talk to you, Todd." He looked directly at me then for the first time, and gave me a quick, sick smile. I can recall smiling at my father in just that way once at some amusement park—Tolchester, perhaps—when he put me on a carrousel much too large, loud, and rapid for my tastes, and expected me to enjoy it as everyone else did. "Are you busy?"

"Busy loafing," I said, and sat on the edge of the bed. "What's on your mind, sir?" I offered him a cigarette, which he refused with a quick shake of his head, and then I lit one myself for a change.

"I daresay you'll think me foolish, son," he began, in a tone that I at once recognized as false—a deep, head-of-the-clan tone. "A garrulous old man, like many another."

"Not unless what you say is foolish," I said flatly.

Mister Haecker blushed—a surprising thing in a man seventy-nine years old. "It may well be," he laughed nervously.

I smiled. "You don't talk nonsense as a rule."

Mister Haecker sighed, but his sigh was not spontaneous as his blush had been. And he glanced at me sharply.

"It's a not uncommon thing for quite old men—men my age—to lose their perspective," he observed. "I'm aware of that fact, and I often wonder whether we are always being fair when we call it simply senility."

He paused, but I said nothing: I was waiting for him to finish tuning his piano.

"What I mean is, there are conditions of most people's old age, other than mental failure, that could lead to the same crankiness, if you like. Disease, for example, or poverty, or isolation. Don't you think?"

"It sounds reasonable to me," I agreed mildly.

Mister Haecker looked relieved. "Now, then," he said, "the thing I actually came down here for was this—" He clenched his lean fists on his knees and stared at them. "You must tell me frankly—I think you'll be honest with me—did you think the things I told Captain Osborn this morning were entirely silly? You said you didn't agree with me, I remember."

To myself I said "Ah," and regarded my visitor's face more carefully, for the first note on the piano had been sounded. To him I said, "This morning? Oh, you mean the 'growing old' business."

I'd hoped his question was merely rhetorical, an attempt to get himself going; but apparently he expected an answer, for he remained silent, a distracted look on his really quite distinguished face.

"Well, yes and no," I answered. "If the idea you're referring to is the one I'm thinking of, that old age is the glorious finale of life—the last of life for which the first was made, and all that—then I'd say yes, it's possible that Cicero wasn't just whistling in the graveyard. After all, a good Roman fell on his sword when things got too miserable; Cicero was famous and pretty well off in his old age, and probably got a toot out of being a public figure."

"I believe he deeply loved life," Mister Haecker remarked in another false tone, a ministerial one delivered with chin thrust out and head nodding gravely. "Every stage of it for its own peculiar virtues."

"And I think the notion probably works for a number of people who actually believe in a hereafter, or who are honestly content with their careers, or who are temperamentally stoical."

"I quite agree," Mister Haecker said. "But you said *yes* and *no*."

"That's right. I think it's silly to talk about what a man's attitude *should* be, toward a thing like old age and death. Even if you start with *If he wants to die content*, you'd find that different people are content with different things. Cap'n Osborn, for example, will die content, I think; he'll be having the time of his life cussing around his deathbed, and whipping his legs for turning cold."

Mister Haecker clucked his tongue. "And what about me? I quite respect your opinion, Todd, as you should know. I've often wished I were your age"—he smiled ruefully—"or you were mine, so we could discuss things more freely. Intellectual discussion, after all, is the real joy of the winter of life, when other pleasures have flown, as it were."

I spoke as gently as I could without defeating my purpose. "If I were used to feeling pity for people," I said, "I think I'd feel sorrier for you than for anyone in this hotel, sir."

Mister Haecker's eyes grew panicky—their first really honest expression. "Indeed?"

"Don't assault me when I say this," I smiled. "I'm not by any means the truth-at-any-price sort. But since you asked, I'll admit I consider your position the least enviable of anyone's in the Explorers' Club. Miss Holiday Hopkinson has been ready to die for so long, that when death actually gets to her it'll be an anticlimax. That could lead to hysteria, like the kid who studies diving from books all winter and then gets out on the high board and forgets everything he learned; but probably it won't. She'll die in her sleep, I'll bet. And Cap'n Osborn has known how he honestly feels about it too, for a long time, whenever he bothers to think about it, which is damned seldom. He'll just put up a whale of a tussle when the time comes. But the trouble with you, sir, if I may say so, is that you've tried to pretend you're enjoying yourself and looking forward to death as a grand finale, when actually you're not."

"Oh, that's not so!" Mister Haecker protested.

"There's nothing wrong with fooling yourself," I said soothingly. "Lots of times it's that or the insane asylum. But it doesn't work if it doesn't work. The trouble is that you're *not* fooling yourself; you know very well it's an act. What the hell's glorious about your old age? What's wrong with facing the fact that things are pretty bleak, and complaining like hell about it?"

When Mister Haecker slipped anger onto his face then, I began to weary of the colloquy and wish I were alone. Had he been sincerely angry I'd not have objected, but his anger was another of his wardrobe of masks.

"You're being quite frank, young man!" he cried.

"Forget I said anything, then." I sighed, and

stretched out on the bed in my robe and slippers. "All's for the best in the best of all possible worlds."

"I'm not angry at your impertinence," he went on, "but I must say I'm disappointed in your values. They're pretty commonplace, for you."

I said nothing, and wished I'd said nothing from the beginning. After all, he was seventy-nine; even with his excellent health, he couldn't be expected to live much more than ten years, and it was no special concern of mine whether he enjoyed them or not.

"Of course my career in the public schools wasn't spectacular, if you judge it by promotions and the like," he pouted. "And I shan't deny that I'd be happier if my wife were alive, or if we'd had children—" He was watching himself being strong. He even paused before continuing in a firm voice, "—but she's not, and we didn't. Do you want me to go around in mourning, begging for pity? My friend Cicero has something to say about that, too: '*In times like these, theirs is far from being the worst fate to whom it has been given to exchange life for a painless death.*' And this: '*If she had not died now, she would yet have had to die a few years hence, for she was mortal born.*' What has happened has happened."

Was there any reason to bother pointing out to him how directly his first quotation contradicted his whole position? I flipped my cigarette out the open window.

"Of all my acquaintances," Mister Haecker went on determinedly, "I'd have expected you to be the first to recognize the happiness a mature man can get from a solitary old age, if he doesn't act childish about it. After all the hustle and bustle, one is finally able to live in the company of his thoughts, and contemplate the beauty of God's works. Isn't that what all the philosophers wanted? I can understand Osborn not realizing it; good a chap as he is, the poor fellow hasn't had the opportunity to educate himself. But *you* certainly must be aware that the life of solitary contemplation is the best—after all, you're alone, too."

"I do precious little contemplating," I said. "And if

I wanted to, I could chuck the whole thing tomorrow
and get married. The point is, I'm here by choice. Also,
I can't quote you the lines," I added, "but your pal
Cicero wasn't so enthusiastic about the contemplative
life. He said somewhere that if a man could ascend into
heaven all by himself and see the workings of the
universe and so forth, the sight wouldn't give him
much pleasure; but it would be the finest thing in the
world if he had somebody to describe it to. I'm not
saying I believe any of this—I think all these generali-
zations are asinine. But you're changing texts every few
minutes."

Another mask: Mister Haecker got up from the
chair and assumed an injured tone. "I see I'm keeping
you from your nap," he said. "It took some courage for
one my age to discuss these things with a young man. I
thought you'd be interested in them."

"You're begging the question with that attitude," I
said, sitting up. "If there *was* any question. You asked
me how I felt about it."

"Well how *do* you feel?" he cried. "What do you
want a man to do who doesn't have anything to live
for? It's either pretend to be content, like a man, or go
around wailing and weeping like a child."

"I don't care what anyone does," I said. "It makes
no difference to me, on principle, whether you're happy or not. I'm no humanitarian. I only said I pitied
you; I wouldn't want to be in your shoes. But I don't
agree that the alternatives you just mentioned are the
only ones."

"What else is there?" Mister Haecker cried. He was
getting worked up again, and his eyes, honest now,
showed despair through any mask he donned. "Maybe
you recommend suicide?" He laughed explosively. "Is
that the other alternative?"

"It was for Cicero's crowd," I said. "Let me tell you
something. Unless a man subscribes to some religion
that doesn't allow it, the question of whether or not to
commit suicide is the first question he has to answer
before he can work things out for himself. This applies
only to people who want to live rationally, of course.

Most people never realize that there's a question in the first place, and I don't see any particular reason why they should have it pointed out to them. I'm telling you because you asked me."

"Well, I'm not a religious man," Mister Haecker declared, "but I think that's reason enough not to kill myself. If death is the absolute end, then you're better off alive under any circumstances."

"That doesn't follow. If death is the end, then it's neutral. Which is better, to be unhappy or to be neutral? It would be different if you could look forward to something better in the near future. I wouldn't commit suicide, for instance, just because the Yankees lost a ball game."

Mister Haecker stood rigid and pale, refusing to be entertained.

"You advise me to kill myself," he said stiffly.

"Not at all. I didn't say everybody *should* work out a rationale. But if you do, then you must answer the suicide question for yourself before you start, obviously. If you want to make sense, I've learned, you should never use the word *should* or *ought* until after you've used the word *if*."

"Then if I want to live rationally, I should kill myself?" he asked, his voice a thin laugh.

"You should only think about the question," I repeated. *"Whether 'tis better in the mind to suffer ..."*

"Of course, Hamlet was either insane or pretending to be," Mister Haecker remembered triumphantly.

"You're evading the question."

"How about you?" he snickered. "Have you thought about it? I see you're still alive. Why is that?"

I smiled. "I promise I'll think about it after supper tonight, and let you know tomorrow what I decide. You do the same, and we'll compare notes and chip in for either a box of cigars or a pistol, as the case may be. But don't forget," I added seriously, "to consider every objection to suicide that you can think of. If you decide *not* to kill yourself, you can always change your mind later, but the other decision is hard to correct."

Again Mister Haecker refused to be entertained.

"It's a question of values," he observed, "and life itself has a value, under any circumstances. There is an absolute value to human life that won't be denied."

"I deny it," I said. Mister Haecker smiled grimly and went to the door. His eyes were still honest; he could no nothing with the fear in them, although he covered the rest of his features with a visionary false-face when he turned at the door and said, "Life, the simple fact of life, is good, young man. Life has intrinsic value."

I was licking a cigar.

"Nothing has intrinsic value," I remarked, as coolly as though I'd known it for years, when in fact that fundamental notion had just occurred to me, between licks. Mister Haecker closed the door, and I wondered why he'd come to see me; what exactly he'd had on his mind. If it had been some sort of confession, my reaction had driven him behind his masks. No matter: if now in protest against my ideas he actually began to believe his own, that was no concern of mine.

xix   a premise to swallow

Quantitative changes suddenly become qualitative changes. From all of Marxism, which I once thought attractive enough, I find only this dictum remaining in the realm of my opinions. Water grows colder and colder and colder, and suddenly it's ice. The day grows darker and darker, and suddenly it's night. Man ages and ages, and suddenly he's dead. Differences in degree lead to differences in kind.

When Mister Haecker had gone (Where? Up to his room, for another day of solitary confinement in the contemplative life), I donned my trousers, shirt, coat, and straw, and walked back through the great dry heat to the office. The sky was brilliant blue, the water likewise, a darker shade. Everything was still: only a few cars moved along High Street; no boats were visible on the river; the flag at Long Wharf hung limply against its staff. Everything was baking in the enormous heat, which nevertheless drew not a bead of perspiration from my skin.

What was on my mind, as I walked, was the grand proposition that had occurred to me while I was licking my cigar: that absolutely nothing has intrinsic value. Now that the idea was articulated in my head, it seemed to me ridiculous that I hadn't seen it years ago. All my life I'd been deciding that specific things had no intrinsic value—that things like money, honesty, strength, love, information, wisdom, even life, are not valuable in themselves, but only with reference to certain ends—and yet I'd never considered generaliz-

ing from those specific instances. But one instance was
added to another, and another to that, and suddenly
the total realization was effected—*nothing* is intrinsically valuable; the value of everything is attributed to
it, assigned to it, from outside, by people.

I must confess to feeling in my tranquil way some
real excitement at the idea. Need I repeat that I am
not a thinker? That technical philosophy is not my cup
of tea? Doubtless (as I later learned) this idea was not
original with me, but it was completely new to me, and
I delighted in it like a child turned loose in the endless
out-of-doors, full of scornful pity for those inside.
Nothing is valuable in itself. Not even truth; not even
this truth. I am not a philosopher, except after the fact;
but I am a mean rationalizer, and once the world has
forced me into a new position, I can philosophize (or
rationalize) like two Kants, like seven Philadelphia
lawyers. Beginning with my new conclusions, I can
work out first-rate premises.

On this morning, for example, I had opened my
eyes with the knowledge that I would this day destroy
myself (a conclusion in itself demonstrating Marx's dictum); here the day was but half spent, and already
premises were springing to my mind, to justify on
philosophical grounds what had been a purely personal
decision. The argument was staggering. Enough now to
establish this first premise: nothing is intrinsically valuable.

If you are no philosopher either, reader, take a
good comfortable time to swallow that proposition—I
daresay it will stick in some throats. If you can stomach
it, why then you've done enough for one chapter and so
have I.

xx calliope music

My prose is a plodding, graceless thing, and I've no comprehension of stylistic tricks. Nevertheless I must begin this chapter in two voices, because it requires two separate introductions delivered simultaneously.

It's not so difficult, is it, to read two columns at the same time? I'll commence by saying the same thing with both voices, so, until you've got the knack, and then separate them ever so gradually until you're used to keeping two distinct narrative voices in your head at the same time.

Ready? Well: when I re-entered my office the clock in the tower of the Municipal Building was just striking two, and as if by a prearranged signal, at the same moment the raucous voice of a stream calliope came whistling in off the river: *Adam's Original & Unparalleled Floating Opera*, one could guess, had just passed Hambrooks Bar Light and was heading up the channel to the bell buoy and thence to Long Wharf. For the thou-

It's not so difficult, is it, to read two columns at the same time? I'll commence by saying the same thing with both voices, so, until you've got the knack, and then part them very carefully until it's no trouble for you to follow both sets of ideas simultaneously and accurately.

Ready? Well: you'll recall that chapter before last I declared to Mister Haecker that anyone who wishes to order his life in terms of a rationale must first of all answer for himself Hamlet's question, the question of suicide. I would add further that if he wants my respect, his choice to live must be based on firmer ground than Hamlet's—that "conscience does make cowards of us all": that to choose suicide is to exchange unknown evils sandth time I blushed at the clumsy ironies of coincidence, for it happened that just as I drew from my files the nearly completed brief of a litigation involving a slight injury to the left foot of perhaps the richest man in Cambridge—who stood to be some fifteen thousand dollars richer if my client lost the case—the calliope broke into "Oh, Dem Golden Slippers," and a few minutes later, when I was reflecting on the difficulties my client would have in scraping together that sum, the melody changed to "What You Gon' Do When De Rent Comes 'Round?"

In fact, even to think of the name *Adam's Original & Unparalleled Floating Opera* —its completely unsubtle significance—when I had before me the extraordinary case of *Morton* v. *Butler*, was the greatest of accidental ironies: never did there exist such an unparalleled floating opera as the law in its less efficient moments, and seldom had the law such inefficient moments as those during which it involved itself—nay, diffused, dissipated, lost itself—in *Morton* v. *Butler*. Hamlet listed "the law's delay" as one of the things that could drive a man to suicide. That I don't accept the Prince's list, your starboard eye has already observed; that neither Morton

for known ones. This position (like Montaigne's argument against revolution) is, as the Prince admits, simply cowardly, not reasonable. On the other hand, if one chooses to die, for mercy's sake let this choice be more reasonably founded than Hamlet's, too—merely escaping "the slings and arrows of outrageous fortune" is as cowardly as is fearing dreams beyond the grave. Don't think I'm an indiscriminating promoter of suicides: I merely hold that those who would live reasonably should have reasons for remaining alive. Reasonable enough?

But I cannot accept bad luck as sufficient reason for anyone's suicide, including my father's. Indeed, it was the absence, in my opinion, of any valid reason for his hanging himself that turned me into a cynic after his death, though I had, no doubt, the seeds of cynicism in me all along. It was a sudden qualitative change, the impingement of the world onto my philosophy.

Before I tell you more about my reaction to Dad's death, and about the little adventure that followed it, let me review very briefly the case on which I spent my afternoon hour's work—what I meant to be my final hour's work as a lawyer. It will serve as an introduction to Col. Henry Morton, who nor Butler accepted this particular annoyance as suicidal is evidenced by their both still walking the earth. Let me review the case, a bump on the log of my story:

plays a role in the little adventure, and at the same time keep you from assuming that I simply loafed all afternoon, when in fact I did some fruitful wall-staring. Here's a resume of the case, a bump on the log of my story:

Morton v. *Butler*, by June of 1937, was a litigation almost six years old, and at the time of this story the litigants hadn't yet even begun to try the case on its merits, but were still enmeshed, via their attorneys, in procedural disputes. Col. Henry Morton, the packer of Morton's Marvelous Tomatoes, along with his wife, was the plaintiff, and was represented by Charley Parks, my neighbor and poker partner. I represented the defendant, Mr. William T. Butler, an investment broker who happened to run the New-Deal wing of the local Democratic machine, the other, conservative, wing of which was run by Col. Morton.

What happened was simple. On October 31, 1931, Mr. Butler was driving his Cadillac sedan down Court Lane, just outside my office, and Col. Morton's only son, Allan (for whom the Colonel had a great, if overprotective, affection), was driving *his* Cadillac sedan down Gay Street, which meets Court Lane at the creek. Col. and Mrs. Morton were passengers in their son's car. The two cars met at the bottom of the hill. Butler had to make a right turn up Gay Street, and young Morton a left turn up Court Lane. Both drivers signaled their turns, and each saw the other's signal. Then (from what I gather privately) both drivers executed poor turns simultaneously, Butler turning too wide and Allan Morton too short. The automobiles collided, and both were damaged slightly. Also, Mrs. Morton broke her spectacles and scratched her face on the lenses, and the Colonel wrenched the tendons of his left foot. The drivers got out; Butler and the limping Colonel shook hands, as rival candidates for the same office might.

"Well, Bill!" the Colonel bellowed heartily. "Can't you drive that machine?"

"Not on the same street with that boy of yours!" Butler guffawed back. The two men chortled and chuckled, slapped each other on the shoulders, and then parted, having tacitly agreed that the injuries didn't seem serious, and that among responsible gentlemen such private affairs didn't go to court. Next day, Butler sent Mrs. Morton a fifteen-dollar spray of mixed flowers, and the Colonel sent Butler a quart of Haig & Haig.

Had it not been for Franklin Roosevelt, the affair might have ended there. But Roosevelt was elected in 1932, initiated the New Deal just afterwards, and in the summer of 1933 sailed up the Choptank to Cambridge, to dedicate the just-completed Harrington Bridge across that river. Both factions of the party were enthusiastic: when it was announced that the President would not come ashore, but would broadcast his dedication from the presidential yacht *Potomac*, anchored out by the bell buoy, Col. Morton took it upon himself to have razed the old freight house that stood on Long Wharf, declaring it to be a natural place of concealment for assassins with high-powered rifles. The city council nodded, and the old structure came down. The Colonel then declared that no private vessels should be permitted to leave the creek or the yacht basin while the *Potomac* was at anchor—the scene otherwise would be disrespectfully cluttered. The mayor made such a resolution, and the yacht club followed suit. Surely a magnanimous solicitude for an anti-New Dealer! But of the citizens of Cambridge, thousands of whom respectfully lined the bulkheads to see the *Potomac* and listen to the President's amplified voice, only one was invited aboard: "Old Bill" Butler, of the Butler Democrats.

One month later, for no stated reason, Mr. Butler dropped into my office and described to me his automobile accident of nearly two years before.

"I'll want you to handle it if anything comes up, honey," he chuckled (it was his habit always to speak with a chuckle, whether the thing he said was funny or not).

And not long after that (it was, in fact, on October 13, 1933, just two weeks before the statute of limitations would have run out), Charley Parks called me to say that he was filing suit against Butler for Col. and Mrs. Morton, who claimed personal injuries, and for Allan Morton, who claimed damages of $75.00 for repairs to and $600 for alleged depreciation in the value of his Cadillac. The injury claims of the Colonel and his wife totaled nearly $15,000; their hospital and medical expenses amounted to a total of $854.26, and in addition they claimed $14,000 for pain and suffering (in the case of the Colonel) and mental anguish (resulting from Evelyn Morton's permanent, if faint, disfigurement and the Colonel's perpetual limp). I guessed at once that even had Mr. Roosevelt remained in Washington, Butler's retaining me as his counsel would have been sufficient reason for the Colonel to decide, belatedly, to press the case, for as you shall see directly, between the Mortons and myself there was small love lost. I worked out my strategy at once.

Now, although Charley and I have on occasion enjoyed long sessions of legal hair-splitting over beer and seven-card stud, at no time did we ever say in so many words that we were making game out of *Morton v. Butler*. Nevertheless, here is what happened in the remaining two months of 1933: On November 20, the three plaintiffs filed their official complaint, charging that the collision had been due to Butler's negligence in that he took the corner at an excessive rate of speed; that he failed to have his car under proper and adequate control; and that he was guilty of other acts of commission and omission. On December 15, I filed for Butler a petition for severance of Allan Morton's action from that of the other plaintiffs. On December 29, the Circuit Court dismissed the petition. I went to Butler's New Year's Eve party and drank sloe gin.

1934: On January 9, I filed a petition to set aside the court order of December 29, which had dismissed my original petition. On April 26, the court set aside

that order and granted the severance we wanted.
Then, on May 4, I obtained a writ to join Allan Morton
as an additional defendant, along with Butler, in the
severed suit of Col. and Mrs. Morton, and filed a
complaint against him—substantially identical to his
complaint against Butler. On June 18, Charley Parks
answered for Allan, pleading in new matter the statute
of limitations, which of course had run out nearly eight
months ago. On August 8, Butler replied to the new
matter. On October 26, Charley filed a motion, in
Allan's name, for a judgment on the proceedings relative to Butler's complaint. On December 29, exactly a
year since the dismissal of my original petition for
severance, the court dismissed my complaint against
young Morton, and on New Year's Eve, far from com-
mitting suicide (as Hamlet would have done by this
time), I got drunk at Butler's party, on vodka sours.

1935: On January 10 (while Harrison Mack Senior,
by the way, was dying in his bed in Ruxton), I peti-
tioned for permission to file an amended complaint for
Butler. On January 18, the court granted its permission, and I filed an amended complaint against Allan
Morton, averring that his parents, in their complaint
against Butler, had charged that their $15,000 injuries
were due solely to Butler's negligence; that Butler was
prepared to serve a copy of that very complaint against
their son; that Butler admitted neither in whole nor in
part their charges; that Allan had been negligent in the
operation of *his* Cadillac; that only the actual trial
would determine whether Allan's own negligence had
been the sole or a major contributing cause of the
accident, but that it was one or the other; that Butler
desired to be able to protect his right of contribution in
the event the court found him to have been jointly or
concurrently negligent with Allan; and that therefore
Allan was jointly liable with Butler upon the causes of
action declared upon by Col. and Mrs. Morton. On
February 6, Allan—or rather, Charley—filed his answer
along with new matter again pleading the statute of
limitations. On April 8, the court, while not ruling on
the accuracy of Butler's charges, dismissed my amend-

ed complaint on five grounds, all as sensible and excep-
tionable as are the grounds for any such ruling. Charley
and I played poker a few times in March and April,
and then on May 1 a stipulation of counsel was filed,
agreeing to my filing a second amended complaint for
Butler against Allan, and I filed the new complaint, a
document differing from its predecessors only in its
rhetoric. On May 21, Charley filed Allan's answer, with
new matter as before. On October 21, the court dismissed the second amended complaint on the same
grounds as before, and on November 12 entered orders
in each of the two cases separately to the same effect.
By this time I was well enmeshed in the Mack will
case, but nevertheless, as Charley grinned and Butler
chuckled, I took the Circuit Court's order to the Court
of Appeals on November 13. That New Year's Eve I
drank Sherbrook rye, first with the Macks in their club
cellar, then with Butler in his club cellar, and finally
with Jane in my room, but did not get drunk.

1936: The Mack will case was now involved in its
own glorious intricacies, but I found time on March 17
to argue in the Maryland Court of Appeals for reversal
of the Circuit Court's order. The question, for both
courts, was whether, since the statute of limitations
prevented our joining young Morton as an additional
defendant on grounds of sole liability, we had averred
in our amended complaint facts sufficient to warrant a
finding of joint or concurrent liability, and the Court of
Appeals agreed (on December 4) that we did not. But
they quite reasonably allowed me to appeal to the
Maryland Supreme Court their affirmation of the Circuit Court's order, so that the procedural question might
be finally determined. That New Year's Eve, as I recall,
I drank alone in my room.

1937: Now I had never agreed with the two lower
courts that what they thought was the question was
really the question. And so, on April 26, I argued to the
Supreme Court that the *real* issue was whether a defendant in a tort action who, like Butler, was barred by
the statute of limitations from joining an additional
defendant (to whom he was also liable, you see) on

the grounds of sole liability, might yet preserve his
right of contribution by pleading joint or several liability *without* alleging facts admitting his own liability to
the plaintiff (Col. and Mrs. Morton). My position was
that if Butler, in order to establish Allan's joint liability,
were obliged, in addition to averring facts showing
Allan's negligence, to admit his *own* negligence, it
amounted to denying Butler's right to bring Allan on
the record at all, since any such admissions could be
placed in evidence and exploited by Col. Morton when
the case came to trial. Now, since in our amended
complaint we alleged facts establishing Allan's negligence, all we were pleading, actually, was that if,
when the thing ever came to trial, the jury should find
Butler to be negligent as the plaintiffs charged, then
Allan's negligence, as described in our complaint, was
also a contributing cause of the collision. The Supreme
Bench, reasonable fellows all, saw no justification for
not allowing such a plea, especially in the case of an
automobile collision, where it is always possible that
both drivers were at fault. On May 24, they rendered
their opinion, which reversed the order of the Court of
Appeals affirming the order of the Circuit Court dis-
missing our second amended complaint against the
additional defendant, and remanded the record to the
Circuit Court with a procedendo.

There was no appealing this judgment. Charley
set me up to a drink, and the suit was ready to be
tried. Col. Morton in effect suing his only-begotten son.
Bill Butler chuckled happily, for with Roosevelt so
firmly entrenched in the White House and in public
popularity as he was in 1937, the Morton wing of the
local Democratic party could ill afford any bad publicity.

I wish, reader, that I could at this point announce
some trump that I'd saved to play on this last day of
my career, when already I'd been able to settle, as far
as I was concerned, the Mack will case in favor of
Harrison. But the truth is that my interest in *Morton* v.
Butler ended with the Supreme Court's ruling, for that
terminated the procedural dispute. I didn't mind miss-

ing the actual trial, which would be dull enough whoever won. I had got out the record of the case on this last afternoon only because Bill Butler, according to a note Mrs. Lake had left on my desk, was coming to see me at two-fifteen.

At two-thirty he strode in, chuckling, a bald, beefy fellow with good eyes and bad teeth, carrying a shoe box.

"What do I owe you, Todd old cod?" he sang out. "What's my bill, hon?"

"You owe me your skin," I smiled. "Charley would have hanged you. You better wait till after the trial to pay me the rest of your bill, though."

"Ain't going to be any trial," Butler chuckled.

"Does the Colonel know that?"

"Oh hell yes indeedy," Butler chuckled. "He's the one thought of calling it off, honey. Called me yesterday, day before, gives me the old family squabble routine, old party harmony song and dance. Haw! Told me if I'd let some of his boys run on my ticket next year in the primary, he'd call off the suit."

"You didn't have to take any conditions."

Butler chuckled grandly. "I told him he could have sheriff and one county commissioner if he'd call his damn state cop off my ass. You know that cop Yarberry, that the Colonel got him his job? Every time I go over the new bridge that Yarberry is after me—Colonel's got him looking for me. I could tell you plenty on Yarberry and the Colonel, hon! Old Colonel don't care about one lousy county commissioner, but he sure does want sheriff, so he promises to curb his cop and drop the suit. I already sent Evelyn another bunch of flowers."

"Hell, you didn't have to give him a thing, Bill," I said again. "He'd never sue his boy."

"Haw!" Butler chuckled. "Tell you the facts, Todd, I didn't have a sonofabitch in the stable to put up for them jobs, that I would walk on the same side of the street with, so old Colonel would of got them anyhow. That's *principles*, boy! Give Roosevelt another go-round in '40, honey, and I'll elect you governor. How 'bout that?"

"No trial, then?"

"No trial," Butler chuckled. "Fetch in old Charley-horse from next door; we'll try the Colonel's whiskey."

He opened the shoe box and took out a fifth of Park & Tilford.

"Call up old Charleyhorse, Julia," he chuckled to Mrs. Lake. "Come on, there, Harry Bishop; come on, Jimmy boy. We're drinking the Colonel's whiskey!"

The calliope down at the wharf broke into "Out of the Wilderness." I blushed, replaced the bulky brief of *Morton* v. *Butler* in the file, and accepted a drink of Park & Tilford.

xxi coals to newcastle

When, as I said earlier, I came home from the office on the afternoon of February 2, 1930, and after searching the house for my father, finally found him in the cellar, one end of his belt spiked to a floor joist and the other fastened around his neck, there was not a smudge of dirt anywhere on him, though the cellar was dusty. His clothes were perfectly creased and free of wrinkles, and although his face was black and his eyes were popped, his hair was neatly and correctly combed. Except that the chair upon which Dad had stood was kicked over, everything in the cellar was in order.

The same could not be said of his estate. Indeed, as soon became apparent, there was no estate. It is such a commonplace story that I hesitate to tell it—and yet nothing was ever less true or pitiful for its being commonplace. Dad had had a sizable savings account; between the years 1925 and 1927 he increased it by investing in stocks. He didn't expect the boom to last, and so decided to make one big splash and quit. To make the splash he mortgaged all his property—a summer cottage and lot at Fenwick Island and one or two timber lots down the county—for as much as he could, and sank the whole wad on the market. In early 1929, when the speculative structure began to quiver, and every public official in the country began to assure us that the economy was fundamentally sound, Dad mortgaged the house and lot, borrowed on his life insurance, and contracted private notes from what few of his many friends were able to lend him money. All this, too, went on the market. No, not quite all: five thousand dollars he persuaded Harry Bishop to put in a safe-deposit box, in my name—suspecting, perhaps, that otherwise he'd not be able to resist plunging that, too.

Then the market collapsed. People were anxious enough to hire lawyers, all right, to collect debts, but they had no money to pay the lawyers with, and most debts had suddenly become uncollectable. Dad had payments falling due on at least four mortgages and countless loans, and no money to meet them with. Foreclosures threatened from all sides, lawsuits from every quarter. He would, it appeared, lose his summer cottage, his timber lots, the family home, the car, virtually everything he owned. His debts amounted to perhaps $35,000. He would have to sleep in the office, walk to court, wear his suits threadbare. Very possibly he would never reach again his former security or regain all his former respect. It was a hard pill to swallow. Instead of swallowing it anyway, he hanged himself.

Does one's father hang himself for a simple, stupid lack of money? And is one expected to set up again the chair one's father has kicked over in his strangling? Can one actually, with a kitchen knife, saw through the belt? Carry one's father up to the bed whereon one was conceived, and laying him on it, dig one's fingers into the black and ruptured flesh to release the dead neck from its collar? Reader, I still recall with shudders a summer day when I was five years old. My father (dressed in good clothes) was killing chickens in the back yard. He caught one, and holding it by the feet, laid it on the chopping block, a sawn stump; unruffled by the flailing wings, he raised the old ax, which he held close to the head, and with a soft stroke decapitated the hen. The head still lay on the stump, the little red eyes staring, the beak opening and shutting in soundless squawks. The body, once my father released it, flailed about the yard for thirty seconds and then died. I watched everything with great, uneasy absorption.

Dad picked up the chicken by its feet again.

"Will you take this in to Bessie, please?"

I held out my hand dumbly. Dad put the feet in my hand—cold, hard, dirty, stringy, scaly, dead yellow feet. I was ill then, reader, and if I think of those feet a minute longer I shall be ill now. But of this matter one *can* think, if queasily. Is one, then, expected to close the popping eyes of his father's corpse? Eyes the very veins of which are burst? Surely the dirt of the planet would cry the reason for it, the justification that would brook no questioning. I waited.

Of course there were debts. The Fenwick place; take it. The timber lots? To be sure. The house? The car? The insurance? Take them, take them. One doesn't concern oneself with trifles at one's father's grave, only with reasons. I waited.

Back at the office, Harry Bishop gave me the envelope from Dad. I took it eagerly, hoping it would contain the answer, but instead it merely had five thousand dollars in it. There was a note, too, which I must have suppressed—it's honestly, completely gone from my mind—because it said all the things I certainly didn't want to hear, in just the wrong language. Is five thousand dollars enough to pay for digging my fingers under that belt? It's not enough payment even for thinking about it! His debt to me was the last, but hardly the least debt my father escaped.

If I was demoralized by Dad's death, I was paralyzed by the five thousand dollars and the note. Certainly I sat in the office for thirty minutes with my jaw slack, staring at the bills as if I'd opened that precious last envelope and discovered inside a handful of dung, the color of a hanged man's cheeks. Five thousand dollars! After some time I replaced the crisp new thousand-dollar bills in their envelope, which was, after all, unstamped and unaddressed, and thought of all the people I knew.

The question became simple: Who was the richest man in Cambridge? Col. Henry Morton. I wrote on the envelope *Col. Henry Morton, c/o Morton's Marvelous Tomatoes, Inc., Cambridge, Maryland*, put a three-cent stamp in place, and snuffling like a hobbled race horse, dropped the envelope into a mailbox on my way to lunch. Next day I moved into the Dorset Hotel.

This was, I believe, in early March 1930. Very soon afterwards I received a call from the Colonel, whom I knew only slightly.

"Hello? Hello?" he shouted, as though it were not his custom to speak on telephones. "Is this Todd Andrews?"

"Yes, sir."

"Hello? Andrews? Andrews, what's this money I got from you in the mail?"

"It's a gift from me to you," I said.

"Andrews? You there, Andrews? What's going on, eh?"

"It's a gift," I repeated; "a gift."

"Huh? What? *Hello*? Andrews! Gift! *Hello*?"

"It's a gift," I repeated.

The day after that, the Colonel came to see me, striding unappointed into my office.

"Andrews? You Andrews? See here, young man, I don't know what you've got up your sleeve—"

"It was a gift," I explained; "that's all."

"A gift? You're crazy, son! Here, take it back, and no more foolishness!"

He did not wave anything at me—no bills under my nose.

"Of course not," I said. "It was just a gift."

"Gift? Well! Gift? What's up your sleeve, young man? What do you think I'm supposed to do?"

"Not a blessed thing, sir," I repeated. "It was a gift."

"I won't stand for tricks," the Colonel warned. "Here, take it back. No more!"

Again, he extended nothing toward me.

"I've never been obligated to any man," the Colonel said then, more calmly. "I shan't begin now."

"No obligation, sir," I insisted.

"Hmph! Whatever's on your mind, you might as well forget it. I can't be bought! If anybody was to ask me the secret of my success, I'd tell them I was never obligated to any man."

"I'd never try to obligate you, sir. It was just a gift."

"I'll teach you a lesson, son." The Colonel smiled, as though the idea had just dawned on him. "I'm going to keep half your money, and you shan't get a thing out of me in return."

"You must keep it all," I said. "I don't take back gifts."

"Hmph! You've got a lot to learn, boy. A lot to learn! Never obligate yourself to anybody."

"I shan't, sir."

"Hard times, Andrews!" the Colonel sputtered. "Bad times! Plant's laying off! A man doesn't throw his money away! What's on your mind? Eh? Eh?"

I shook my head. "Nothing, sir. No explanation."

The Colonel stood up suddenly to leave, looking grimly around my office and chewing his cigar.

"I'll teach you, boy," he said. "You'll wish you had it back!"

"No, sir."

He started out and then grinned back into the doorway.

"You'd've been better off using it to square some of your Dad's debts!" he declared and, satisfied that he'd demonstrated his independence, left. Mrs. Lake gasped at his remark.

Some time afterwards a letter came.

Dear Mr. Andrews:

By this time you are doubtless of a different mind concerning the transaction of some days ago. I am, however, a man of my word, and intend to carry out my resolution for your instruction.

Yours truly,
Henry W. Morton

I replied at once:

Dear Col. Morton:

I have not changed my mind at all. The matter to which you refer was not any sort of transaction, and you are not obliged to me in any way. It was a gift.

Yours truly,
Todd Andrews

Within the month, Morton's Marvelous Tomatoes, Inc., became involved in a contractual dispute with a small shipping concern that ferried some of the Colonel's canned goods to Baltimore. The evidence was all in favor of the shipping company (the suit was an intricate one, and I shan't describe it here), but the Colonel had never lost a litigation before, and so he determined to spend his way to justice. An executive from MMT, Inc., called on me and announced that the Colonel wanted Andrews, Bishop, & Andrews to handle his defense.

"Sure," I said. "I'm not interested myself, but Mr. Bishop can take the case."

"I believe the Colonel is anxious for you to handle it personally," the executive said (he was Wingate Collins, a kind of vice-president); "in fact, I'm sure he is. I heard him say so."

But I declined. The Colonel took his business to Charley Parks, and ultimately obtained justice in the Court of Appeals.

Then the drivers of the Morton Trucking Company, a subsidiary of the packing house, went on strike when the Colonel refused to allow the company union to affiliate with the CIO, and Norbert Adkins, of the union, asked our firm for legal counsel. Jimmy Andrews, who had just joined us, was itching for the job, and Mr. Bishop and I saw no reason why he shouldn't take it. But Wingate Collins gave us a reason.

"I'll tell you frankly," he said, "the Colonel doesn't want any of his friends to take that job. Your outfit would be pretty unpopular if you fellows took it. You know what I mean?"

"Cut it out, Wingate," I smiled. "You've been going to the movies too much."

"I'll tell you what," he said. "You stand to come into a good thing if you don't stick up for those strikers. The Colonel's been unhappy with Matson & Parks lately—just between us, of course—and he's looking around for another law firm to represent MMT officially. That's between six and eight thousand a year extra for the firm that gets it. The Colonel's taken a liking to you, Todd, I don't mind saying. He thinks you're a very promising fellow. And I'd bet my bottom dollar you'd get that job if you'll lay off these strikers. Hell, I know you would—off the record, now—I heard him say as much yesterday."

"I guess Jim wants to handle it, Wingate," I said. "You'd better talk to him."

"I already did," Wingate sniffed. "He says he wants the union thing, but it's up to you and Harry. Harry says he don't care one way or the other."

"I don't either," I said.

"Well, I frankly think you're a damn fool, if you'll excuse me for saying so!" Wingate said heatedly. "The Colonel'll have a tough time swallowing this, I declare!"

But apparently he swallowed it. Jimmy counseled the union in the arbitration that followed, and Matson & Parks, next door, counseled the company. It was finally decided that the union would remain "independent," and, solemnly, that the strikers would pay from their treasury for the damage to six trucks that they'd overturned during the strike.

During the next year or so, the Colonel approached me, either directly or through his vice-presidents, on ten different occasions with offers of business. I declined to handle any of them personally (they were routine affairs, if lucrative); some he took elsewhere, others he rather reluctantly allowed Mr. Bishop to handle. Whenever I encountered him on the street (he rarely walked), he clapped me on the shoulder, took my arm, invited me for dinner, invited me for cruises on his yacht, invited me to membership in the

Cambridge Yacht Club, the Elks, the Rotary, the Masons, the Odd Fellows (the Colonel was a joiner), and the country club (because I sometimes played golf, I was already a member). I declined his invitations politely. He fumed and stewed.

More offers for legal business came in from Morton's Marvelous Tomatoes.

"I'll say quite frankly," Wingate Collins said, "I think you're a damn fool. What you got against us? You fellows are passing up the chance of a lifetime. You got more money than you can use? I'll tell you the Christ truth, Todd, the Colonel's got ants in his pants about that money you sent him—off the cuff, now, understand. I told him you're just a damn fool, frankly, but he don't know you like I do. He can't understand it. He's got ants in his pants because he says he don't want to be obligated to any man. Now, then. You'd make him a lot easier to live with if you'd take some of this business he's throwing your way."

"The firm's not turning it down," I reminded him. "I'm just not interested personally."

"Hell, man, it's not like it's an outright gift to you!" Wingate cried. "He just wants to hire you, like anybody else might do. What you want to hold him by the tail for? Nobody else ever got him so het up before!"

"He's being childish," I said. "He knows he's not obligated to me. He even took the trouble to get it in writing."

Wingate told me frankly I was a damn fool.

Word got around town (I suspect through either Wingate or Mrs. Lake or Jimmy) about the five thousand dollars, and I was asked about it by a few extra-curious people.

"It was just a gift," I shrugged.

Most people, though, had already regarded me as rather eccentric, and so were pleased enough to have their suspicions confirmed. I heard through friends that one or two of Dad's creditors were disgruntled, but of course the money was mine, not Dad's, and so they could do nothing. Some cynics wondered what I was after.

On Christmas the Colonel sent me, via his chauffeur, a case of Harvey's Scotch. When he got it back two days later, via the Cambridge Cab Company, he came again in person to my office.

"Good morning, sir," I said. "What can I do for you?"

"You can quit this damn nonsense!" the Colonel said heartily. I offered him a cigar, which he refused almost violently. I waited for him to continue.

"Do you still mean to sit there and swear to God you gave me five thousand dollars out of a clear blue sky for nothing? With times as hard as they are?"

"It was a gift," I said.

"Don't think I don't know why your father committed suicide, young man," the Colonel said. "No offense intended; you know how these things get around."

"That's right."

The Colonel sighed impatiently and tapped his cane on the floor. "I don't get it," he said.

"There's nothing to get."

"Listen," he said, rather quietly. "This needn't go beyond the two of us. Wingate Collins—you know him? Good. Wingate Collins is my vice-president unofficially in charge of labor relations. Good man, Wingate, but he's doing a lousy job. Makes everybody mad, and he's supposed to make everybody happy. Union doesn't like him, office people don't like him, I don't like him. Great fellow, you know, but makes folks mad. Well, then. Wingate's going to retire soon—he don't know it yet—and I'm going to hire a labor relations man. Want a lawyer, somebody knows people. Take you half a day, five days. Five thousand a year, and you can keep your law practice on the side."

"Nope."

"Listen," the Colonel said. "This isn't any gift. I don't know anybody else I'd rather hire. I'm just glad I got to know you."

"Thanks," I said. "I don't want the job, sir, thank you just the same."

"Don't want it!" the Colonel cried. "Men are begging for work! Don't want it!"

"No, sir."

"*Yes!*" the Colonel shouted, forgetting himself. His face was red.

"Nope," I said again.

"Take your damn money back!" the Colonel cried, but waved no bills under my nose.

"Of course not."

The Colonel actually mopped his forehead with his handkerchief.

"How about the Scotch?"

"No thank you, sir," I said.

He rose to leave, shaken.

"I shall have a great many guests in on New Year's Eve," he said softly. "You'll get an invitation; Mrs. Morton has already sent them out. It's her first big affair, and she's heard of you but hasn't met you." The Colonel had remarried perhaps a year before, his first wife having died in 1926.

"Thank you," I said.

"You needn't take the trouble to send it back, as you did the Scotch. There's no need to insult Evelyn. Just throw it in your wastebasket."

I did indeed get the engraved invitation next day, and on New Year's Eve, having drunk four double highballs in my room after supper, I decided to drop in on the Colonel's party, thinking it consistent with my policy of incomplete consistency. At eleven o'clock I took a cab out to the Morton estate on Hambrooks Bay.

The party was in full swing when I arrived. Both wings of the great brick house were bright, and perhaps a hundred and fifty people milled around inside, in tuxedos and gowns. I wouldn't have thought that there were that many tuxedos in Dorchester County. A champagne fountain had been rigged up in the main living room, and a sparkling burgundy fountain in the library. The women were drinking mostly from these. On the summer porch three white-coated Negroes tended bar, and male guests stood two deep before them. A small orchestra was playing in the basement.

The butler took my coat and my invitation at the door, but before he could do anything with the latter, the Colonel caught sight of me from across the room, where he stood laughing with some vice-presidential-looking friends. He stared for a moment, took the cigar from his mouth, and then broke into a great smile.

"Well, well, *well!*" he roared, charging toward me with hand extended. "Andrews!" He could think of nothing to say, and so pumped my arm for a minute.

"Well, well, *well!*" he roared again.

"Looks like a pleasant party," I declared.

"Well!" the Colonel said. "Ha! Say, you must meet Evelyn. *Evelyn! Evelyn!*"

Evelyn appeared from the library, near at hand. She was perhaps forty—more than half the Colonel's age—and, perhaps because she'd borne no children, her figure was still slender, and the skin on her face fairly tight. She was much better-looking than her husband.

"Evelyn, this is young Andrews, Todd Andrews; the young lawyer, you know."

"How do you do, Mr. Andrews."

"Good evening," I said.

"My husband doubted that you'd do us the honor," Mrs. Morton smiled. I guessed that she was thoroughly enjoying her first big affair: her smile was a trifle liquorish.

"Ha!" the Colonel exclaimed, and still held fast to my arm, as though afraid I'd bolt. "He's an independent young man, all right! Well, what say to a drink, Andrews? A little Scotch, eh? Ha!"

"I thank you."

"I'll be seeing you in a moment, Mr. Andrews," Mrs. Morton said. "I certainly must get to know you while we've got you. Toodleoo!"

"Toodleoo," I said.

"You've made her very pleased by coming tonight," the Colonel confided as he marched me through the crowd to the summer porch. People turned to watch us go by.

Well, it was the first party of any size that I'd been

to since my saintly days prior to Dad's suicide, and I found myself reverting to that pose. As soon as I could escape the Colonel's introductions to people I already knew—there were only ten or twelve strangers at the party—I garnered two double Scotches from one of the Negroes (whom I also knew well) and retreated to the darkened basement, which had been cleared out for dancing. An auxiliary, one-tender bar had been set up across from the orchestra, and so I was able to drink uninterruptedly for some time, watching the players and the dancers. And, truth to tell, I got splendidly drunk on the Colonel's Scotch.

What followed I must tell in broken sequences, for that is how I remember it:

At midnight the place went to hell, as though every guest—there must have been two hundred then, or else all were in the basement—had decided simply to throw back his head and holler at the top of his lungs for several hours. The orchestra played on, but without audible effect, and people danced brokenly to no music. For a while someone was kissing me, and I proposed to whoever it was that we fling our glasses into the fireplace, as one should.

"There isn't any fireplace."

"Into the noise, then."

"You can't hit noise, silly."

"*Regardez*," I said, and threw mine at the drummer.

I did indeed dance a tango with Evelyn Morton. Nay, ten, a dozen tangos, without the encumbrances of music or prior experience. And in every ill-lit corner, as his wife clung to me, I saw the Colonel smiling redly, benignly, nodding his great head, flashing his gold teeth, his gold-headed cane.

Certainly there was a floor show of drunken wives of vice-presidents, to the horror of some husbands. A cancan line. Remarkable. I recall vividly the upflung leg, the fat veined thighs of the wife of Wingate Collins, that marked man. The roaring went on, no matter how many glasses one threw at the orchestra, who played in terror. There is a picture of the drummer shielding himself behind a great cymbal, apparently carried for that purpose; of my thin, elegant highball glass glittering through the air to splinter against the wall just off his starboard ear. No matter whom one attempted to dance with, it was Mrs. Morton—slender, graceful, unattractive, drunk—and the Colonel nodded.

Then there was a tendency to take cold showers in several of the upstairs bathrooms. These showers were taken by gluts of singing men. My group sang verses of "Mademoiselle from Armentières," and I recall even now the vibrancy of my baritone, but I don't remember getting wet at all until the entrance of wet Mrs. Morton. Standing outside the shower, we had sung the line declaring that Mademoiselle had not enjoyed herself for forty years, and then between the *hinkey* and the *dinkey* my choir vanished, as in a movie, and shimmering, dripping Mrs. Morton leaped like a damp naiad from behind the shower curtain, into my arms. Her dewy bosoms, none too firm, crushed into my shirt front; her dripping hair fell over her eyes; her teeth sank into my lapel, into my boutonniere; she ground herself against my trousers. We danced a magnificent *parley-voo*, stopping with a dip that dropped us to the tiles, tapped by the tip of the Colonel's cane. Mrs. Morton caught sight of the gold teeth glinting in the light from the bathroom bulb and swooned or died, sprawling pink and sprinkled like a blushing dugong hoist from the deep.

I picked myself up and straightened my wet bow tie. The Colonel grinned feverishly and tapped his cane (seven inches from his wife's wet head) as though conversing with her spirit by Morse Code.

"Mrs. Morton dances well," I said, bowing slightly to the Colonel as I stepped over Evelyn en route to the door. And then, parting, with what seemed to me a nice conjunction of wit and *savoir-faire*: "One might call her Morton's Most Marvelous Tomato, mightn't one? Good night, sir."

One was, in fact, tempted to add that it was a pity to see such a fresh tomato stewed, as it were, if not altogether canned—but one knew the line beyond which the prick of wit becomes the sting of insult, and so held one's tongue and exited gracefully.

In the new year that followed, the firm of Andrews, Bishop, & Andrews was not pressed to render its services to the Colonel, nor was I dunned with invitations to join clubs or lodges, nor confronted at every turn with invitations to parties and dinners at the Morton manor. Indeed, if there have been any parties at the Mortons' since that New Year's Eve, I've not heard of them. Jacob Matson, of Matson & Parks, became vice-president in charge of personnel for MMT, Inc., when Wingate Collins suddenly retired.

And on the rare occasions when I met Col. Morton on Race Street and tipped my hat in greeting, he flushed red, bared his gold teeth, and ignored me with the grim smile of one who is obligated in no way to any man.

xxii   a tour of the opera

At three o'clock, just after Bill Butler and Charley Parks had left my office, Jane Mack came in with her daughter. I heard Jane exchange greetings with Mrs. Lake, and then little Jeannine—three and a half years old now, and brown and lovely like her mother—came up to my desk and watched me shyly.

"Hi, Toddy," she said.

"Hi, baby."

"Honey, may I fix your pencil?"

"Sure." It was Jeannine's habit to sharpen pencils. I gave her a good long one, and she went happily to the sharpener and proceeded to grind away on it.

"Oh, my," Jane said, coming into my office, "she's happy now. How do you feel, Toddy? Any better?"

"Hello, Jane. I wasn't sick."

"Then why did you act so silly last night?" she asked, more softly, so that Mrs. Lake couldn't hear. She perched on the corner of my desk. She was wearing khaki shorts—unusual for that year—and a blue cotton blouse, and looked quite fresh and desirable.

I smiled. "I guess I just wasn't in the mood."

She smiled back and patted me on the head. "That's a stupid way to be," she said. "*I* was in the mood."

"*I* was, too," Jeannine declared from the pencil sharpener.

"Maybe I'm getting senile," I proposed. "Stamina was never my strong point, as you know."

"I know your strong point," Jane said. "Did you get my note?"

"I did."

"You sent me a dumb one, so I thought I'd send you a dumb one."

I smiled. "I don't know what Marvin found wrong with me. He'll bring the report around tonight, and we'll look at it next time you're up."

I had certainly expected some astonishment at this news, but Jane, unlike Harrison, didn't bat an eye.

"God knows it's time you went to doctor," she said. "Well—" She jumped off the desk. "I'll be seeing you later at the house, won't I? For a Manhattan? Try not to keep Jeannine right in the sun too long, if you can help it. She's got that bonnet, but it's awfully hot out."

"All right."

"I'll be done at the hairdresser's in an hour, if you want me to drop in and pick her up. If you're finished before then and she gets on your nerves, pop her in a cab and send her home. She likes that. And for God's sake buy her an ice-cream cone."

"All right."

" 'Bye now, honey." Jane kissed her daughter. "So long, Toddy."

" 'Bye, Mommy," Jeannine said.

"So long," I said, and she left. I was impressed: between the time in 1933 when I insulted her and the time in 1935 when we resumed our affair, Jane's personality had strengthened in some ways; for one thing, she was unpredictable. I wondered with quite sharp interest what she intended to do about my note, now that I'd fulfilled the conditions of hers—and when it occurred to me that I'd not be alive to find out, I experienced a small sensation of regret; the only such sensation I felt that day.

"Let's go see the showboat, honey," I suggested to Jeannine, who by this time was pushing the last fragment of the pencil into the sharpener.

"All right, honey," she said, and politely took my hand.

We went out into the bright sun and walked the

dry block to Long Wharf, where the showboat lay immensely along the bulkhead. Unlike its Mississippi counterparts, *Adam's Original & Unparalleled Floating Opera* was no architectural extravaganza of gilt and gingerbread. It was, by comparison with them, severely unadorned, for it had been built to withstand the tempestuous moods of Tangier Sound and the lower Bay, and even ventured into the Atlantic on occasion. The *Opera* itself was a long, narrow clapboard box mounted on a massive barge. On the bow was lettered S.S. *Thespian*, the vessel's registered name, but down both sides of the clapboards, in red letters three feet tall, was emblazoned its less modest trade name. A simple balcony affair graced either end of the theater, apparently for the employees' benefit, and lifelines ran down both sides. On the roof were ventilators, stovepipes, clotheslines, lifeboats, a trim little shed with window boxes and curtained windows, an improvised bandstand, and the steam calliope, now silent. The whole structure was braced against humping or buckling by a trusswork of piers and cables on both sides. Two tugboats moored alongside, the *Pamlico* and the *Albemarle*, provided the showboat's motive power.

"What's that, Toddy?" Jeannine asked excitedly.

"That's a showboat," I said. "Can you say showboat?"

"*Showboat.*"

"Would you like to go up close and see it?"

"All right."

Fortunately, for I'd forgotten my promise, some entrepreneur had set up a refreshment stand near the bulkhead, and so I was able to buy two vanilla ice-cream cones before we went up for a close look at the showboat. Not many people were curious enough to come out in the terrific heat; we had the spectacle pretty much to ourselves, and I set Jeannine up on a piling to get a good view.

As was her habit when excited, Jeannine slipped into the "Why?" routine.

"What's it for, Toddy honey?" she shouted, awed at the *Opera*'s size.

"It's a showboat, hon. People go on it and listen to music and watch the actors dance and act funny."

"Why?"

"Why what?" I asked. "Why do the actors act funny or why do the people like to watch them?"

"Why do the people?"

"The people like to go to the show because it makes them laugh. They like to laugh at the actors."

"Why?"

"They like to laugh, because laughing makes them happy. They like being happy, just like you."

"Why?"

Of course she wasn't the least bit interested in either her question or my answers, as questions or answers; she was simply excited over the monstrous showboat and wanted to hear me talk. I could have recited the alphabet in a knowing tone, and she'd have been satisfied.

"Why do they like being happy? That's the end of the line."

"Why do the actors?"

"Why do the actors act funny? They do that so the people will pay to come see them. They want to earn money."

"Why?"

"So they can eat. They like eating."

"Why?"

"You have to eat to stay alive. They like staying alive."

"Why?"

"That's the end of the line again," I said.

"Hey there!" cried a little man on the aft balcony. "Want to look 'er over? Go on up forrard, I'll show ye round."

"Want to go on the showboat?" I asked Jeannine.

"All right."

The little man met us at the gangplank and waved us aboard. He was tough-looking, wiry, leather-faced, with knotted hands and the eyes of a starling, and was dressed in wrinkled black trousers, an immaculate white shirt, and a yachting cap. Jeannine regarded him soberly while I shook hands.

"Are you Captain Adam?"

"That's a fact, sir. Jacob Adam. Bring yer little girl along now, I'll show ye the boat. Quite a boat, ain't she?"

"She is indeed."

"Quite a boat, sir," Capt. Adam agreed. "Thirty-one years old, and she's still sound as a dollar, if you know what I mean—" He tugged my arm and chortled. "Dollar ain't worth what it was in 1906!

"Quite a boat," he said again. "Had 'er built in Little Washington, North Carolina, in 1906, sir, and I had 'er built strong. Why, you set one o' them Miss'ssippi showboats down in the ocean for a minute, there wouldn't be a stick left fit to pick yer teeth with."

"Why?" Jeannine demanded, gaining courage.

"Did you use to run boats on the Mississippi?" I asked.

"No, sir, I don't mind tellin' ye," the Captain declared, "I never set foot on a boat in my life till I built the *Op'ry*. Not even a row-skiff; now, then. I run a two-car ten-cent vaudeville show all over the country, sir, from 1895 till 1905, and did so good I had to quit, 'cause ever'body I hired cut out to start a ten-cent show hisself. Next thing I knew there was so much competition I couldn't make the nut. I figured I'd set me up in something that takes a big wad to start with, so ever' Tom, Dick, and Harry with ten bucks and a lot o' brass can't squeeze in. I don't mind tellin' ye, I sunk sixty thousand dollars in this showboat, sir, in a time when dollars was dollars, I mean. But I wanted 'er tough, and I still got 'er."

"She looks plenty sturdy," I admitted. So far we hadn't moved from the gangplank: there is that in me which brings out old men's garrulity.

"She *is* sturdy, sir. Ye see them strakes along the sides there?" He pointed to the barge's side planking. "First time I saw them boards, they was trees. I walked around the Carolina woods for a year, sir, pickin' out my timber where it stood. Hundred-and-twenty-two-foot long and four inches thick, them strakes, and not a splice in 'em from stem to stern, nor a knot, either. And I got 'em drift-bolted ever' two feet with twenty-seven-inch bolts. That's for the ocean, sir! Thirty-two-foot planks across the bottom, beam to beam; not a splice. Cost me plenty, sir, but it was money well spent, let me tell *you*. One time in 1920 we was caught in a small squall in Tangier Sound, and they couldn't get a boat to us. I'm not lyin', sir, for fourteen hours the waves was breakin' over the *Op'ry*'s roof. Took Mrs. Adam's pansies right out o' the window box up there, but the *Op'ry* didn't spring a plank. That's what plannin' does, sir!"

Jeannine was jumping up and down; I moved toward the shuttered box office.

"Come on inside," the Captain invited. We entered the theater, dark and cool, and Capt. Adam provided us with a running commentary on what we were observing.

"Seats seven hundred," he said. "White folks down here and in the boxes, colored folks in the balcony."

Jeannine, happily, didn't ask why.

"Used to be, couldn't get a darkie on board," he went on. "Word got around we was baitin' 'em on to send back to Africa. (That there stage is nineteen foot across; hall's eighty foot long.) Used to carry a car on board, but the salt water ruined 'er, seemed like."

"Where's *your* house?" Jeannine demanded.

"Well, little lady, I live up on the roof."

"Why?"

"*Why?* Heh! She's a fresh one, ain't she? Well, sir, come on back here with me, I'll show ye the dressin' rooms and all."

We followed the Captain behind the stage, where a row of numbered doors ran along a short hallway.

"Good big dressin' rooms," Capt. Adam said proudly. "The actors live in 'em, too. Most ever'body's into town just now, sir."

"Why?" Jeannine murmured.

"Now come on down here." We were led down a companionway. "Here's the cook's quarters and the din-in' room—we're right under the stage now—and over there's the galley. Bottle-gas stove and a nine-hundred-pound icebox. That there door leads right out to the orchestra pit. What ye think of 'er?"

"Very impressive," I said.

"Whole shebang don't draw but fourteen inch o' water, by golly. I always say, 'You give me a good-size mud puddle, I'll give you a show!' Yes, sir. Six big ventilators up on the roof. Runnin' water in all the dressin' rooms. Plenty o' heat in the wintertime. See them pipes runnin' under the stage? Heat pipes, water pipes, acetylene pipes for the footlights."

"You don't use electricity?"

"I use it for the ventilators and lights too, when I can, but ye can't depend on it. Lots o' landings ain't electrified. Ye can give a show without ventilators, but not without lights. I carry two banks o' footlights, one electric and one acetylene."

I remarked that acetylene seemed a dangerous shipmate to me.

"No sirree!" Capt. Adam denied. "Never had a speck o' trouble. Got the tanks rigged outside, where a leak won't cause no trouble, and I just run it in through this little copper line here"—he indicated with his finger a small pipe leading through a valve, from which hung a sign reading DO NOT OPEN UNTIL READY TO LIGHT FOOTLIGHTS—"and out to the foots. The rig works fine. Don't ye worry, sir; ain't nothin' about this boat that ain't been thought out plenty careful. Got a tug bow and stern, so she rides steady in a seaway. Got our circuit figured so we hit fresh water twice a year, to kill off the moss and barnacles on the bottom. Start out from Elizabeth City, North Carolina (fresh-water town), soon's it gets warm, and play up along Albemarle Sound, Pamlico Sound, through the Dismal Swamp Canal, and up the Chesapeake far as Port Deposit, hittin' all the best landings on the way. That's fresh water up by Port Deposit, so we head back home with a clean bottom again. Saves me a haulin' out."

Jeannine had begun to swing back and forth on my hand. I thanked Capt. Adam for showing us around his craft, and he ushered us through a side door that led from the dining room, where we'd been standing, to the starboard quarter of the barge.

"Did you like the showboat?" I asked Jeannine.

"All right." Her face was flushed, and I thought it best to get her out of the sun.

We passed the refreshment stand, unoccupied except for the vendor himself.

"Toddy honey, will you buy me another ice-cream cone?"

"Why?"

"I want one, honey."

"Why?"

"I want one."

"*Why* do you want one?"

"I want one."

"But why? Tell me *why*."

"I want one."

She got one, and we strolled back to the office in all the heat and light.

xxiii so long, so long

Before we reached Court Lane, Jeannine's second ice-cream cone was dripping from brown chin and dimpled elbow, down her sundress and onto her sneakers. I paused under a great poplar tree to scrub her up a bit with my handkerchief. My head felt a little dizzy—whether from the sun or from Jeannine's questions, I couldn't say.

"Toddy, honey, I got to sit on the potty," she now remarked.

"Can you hold on a minute?" I grinned, hoping she wouldn't start asking *why*.

I picked her up and strode quickly up the sidewalk, expecting at any moment to have my coat sleeve moistened, but Jeannine chuckled and clung to my neck, her fat little arm over my mouth.

"Mmm, you smell like your mommy," I said.

This amused her. "You smell like my daddy," she countered.

"Ah."

We reached port safely, and Mrs. Lake took Jeannine to the lavatory. I spent the time writing a note to Jimmy Andrews, who stood not ten feet from me, and thinking about Jeannine, whose opinion it was that I smelled like her daddy. Possibly, of course, she was right: *I* could certainly smell some Andrews in her infant curiosity.

I finished the note (which informed Jimmy of the letter from Eustacia Callader and instructed him to institute proceedings against Harrison's mother for recovery of that part of the estate which she'd disposed of) and put it in my inside coat pocket. A few minutes later Jane came in, her hair cropped short, and we left to go to her place for cocktails. I didn't bother to straighten out my desk, to say a last goodbye to Mr. Bishop, Jimmy, or Mrs. Lake, or even to take a final look at my office, at my wonderful staring-wall. Why should I?

On the drive to East Cambridge, although I chatted amiably with Jane and Jeannine, I was filled with my plan, which had crystallized by then into its final form. If out of my meager vocabulary only the term *unenthusiastic excitement* comes anywhere near describing the feeling with which all my thoughts were suffused, you must resolve my meaning from that term's dissonance. There remained still no small measure of the excitement which had attended my first realization that I was ready to destroy myself; but, like all my major decisions of policy, that resolution had been a rapid one, the effect of external impingement upon whatever was my current mask—and as in those other cases, the resolution itself was only afterwards rationalized into some kind of coherent and arguable position. Though it is too much to expect that I should become solemn about it, certainly the direction of this day's rationalizing was an awesome one—yet full of the attractiveness of desolation, the charm of the abyss. A simple fact—that there are no ultimate reasons—and how chilling! I heard beyond it the whistle of the black winds of Chaos; my hackles rose, as if I had been breathed upon by a cold sigh from the pit.

It was four o'clock; the heat lingered at its greatest intensity. What Jane's car filled with as we drove over the creek bridge was not the black wind of Chaos, but the stench of the crabhouses, steaming up from small mountains of red carapaces and other nonedible parts of the crab thrown out in the sun by the pickers. It is a smell that grabs you—I've seen many a visitor retch while crossing the creek in summer—but like many another thing, it can be lived with: most of the natives aren't even aware of it, and I, for one, have learned to

inhale it deeply and savor it in my nostrils. I did so as
we drove off the bridge, and composed a mental note
for my *Inquiry*, as follows:

> Olfactory pleasures being no more absolute
> than other kinds of pleasures, one would do well
> to outgrow conventional odor-judgments. It is
> a meager standard that will call perverse that
> seeker of wisdom who, his toenails picked, must
> sniff his fingers in secret joy.

This meditation took its place beside my early
morning's reflection on Plato and the crabbers—a good
day for my *Inquiry!*—and I continued without inter-
ruption my conversation with Jane, who was as a matter of fact talking animatedly. She had announced, to
my surprise, that she and Harrison were planning a trip
to Italy for the fall.

"It's Harrison's idea," she said, "and I'm tickled to
death with it. He wants to stay till Christmas, but I'm
holding out for Easter. I was there one summer when I
was a kid, and it's all beautiful! I wish we could live
there."

I believe she kept glancing at me to judge my
reaction, but that belief might be simple vanity. At any
rate, I showed no reaction at all.

"Are you counting on the inheritance to travel
on?" I asked. "It's probably wiser not to."

She looked surprised. "I thought that was out of
the question. Isn't it? I'd given up hoping for that."

"I suspect you're doing the right thing."

"We're going on Harrison's salary. Hell, we can
afford it." She glanced at me again. "We might even
consider selling the house—if you don't mind."

"Why should I mind?"

"Well—" She shrugged her shoulders.

"Do you think Harrison will be able to swallow
Mussolini's boys?"

"Oh, this isn't a political tour," Jane smiled. "I'm
not even interested in politics, are you? I don't think
Harrison is any more, either, the way the Spanish

thing's going. He's getting cynical about political move-
ments, I believe. He's cynical about everything
nowadays, in fact, but in a sweet way. I think he got it
from you."

"Not the sweetness, certainly."

"Certainly not," Jane said, and patted my leg.
There was still some nervousness in her exuberance, or
so I thought at least: I smelled a plan in the air, now
that the crabhouses were out of range.

"When did you decide all this?" I asked cheerfully.
"About the trip and the house?"

"Oh, it was Harrison's idea," she said. "About the
trip. The house was my idea, because I want us to be
independent. I guess it sort of popped up about a week
ago. We haven't worked out any details. You don't
mind, do you, if we go?" She looked at Jeannine, who
was staring listlessly out the window. "You know what
I mean."

"Of course I don't mind."

"I'd love it! With the money from the house we
could stay there a year. Harrison can fix it with his job.
God, just think—*Italy!*"

"When did you get so hot on Italy?" I smiled.

"I've always been hot on Italy. Didn't I tell you?
Are you mad at me, Toddy?"

"No."

"You kind of acted like it."

We pulled up in front of the Mack house, and I
lifted Jeannine down to run to Harrison, who waved
from the porch.

"Were you offended by my note this morning?"
Jane persisted as we walked up the lawn. "I certainly
didn't think you'd take me up on going to Marvin, but
I'm glad you did."

"How about *my* note?" I asked. "Harrison seemed a
little concerned when I told him at lunchtime I'd been
to see Marvin, but you don't seem alarmed at all."

"Should I be alarmed? What about?"

By that time we were at the porch, and Jane
skipped up the steps, kissed Harrison lightly on the
forehead, and disappeared inside.

Usually we drank our Manhattans on the porch, but on this day it was much cooler in the living room. Harrison and I chatted for a few minutes about the weather, agreeing that the dull haze over the Bay prophesied a squall, and then we went inside.

"So you're going to Italy?" I remarked.

"Yes, it looks like it." Harrison fumbled at once for a cigarette in his shirt. "Did Janie tell you?"

"A minute ago. I think it's a fine idea, of course."

"Do you? Well, I wasn't so sure. It means selling the house and all—but you know how crazy Jane is about Italy, Fascists or not, and I'd like to see the place myself while there's still time. I suspect things are going to blow up over there sooner or later. Frankly, I wasn't sure how you'd feel about it," he added carefully.

"How *I'd* feel? What possible difference could it make if I objected? And I don't, at all."

"Well—"

Jane reappeared from the kitchen, and behind her came the maid with our cocktails. Jane sat down beside Harrison, on the couch; I was in an easy chair across the room, facing them.

"Well," Jane said brightly, smiling at her cocktail.

We all sipped.

"Will you be going to the showboat tonight?" Harrison asked me.

"Maybe so. I hadn't thought much about it."

"Jeannine was crazy about it this afternoon," Jane told Harrison, for my benefit. "She got two ice-cream cones, and the man took her and Todd all over the boat."

"Oh? Well," Harrison said.

"In fact, she got too excited—she's a little feverish. I called Marvin, and he says don't worry."

We sipped some more.

"Why not have supper with us?" Jane asked me. "It's just cold platters—sliced ham and potato salad."

I shrugged.

"I'll tell Louise." She jumped up and went into the

kitchen again. Harrison and I sipped and sipped, and after a while I lit a cigar.

"Don't be offended by what I'm going to say now, Toddy," Harrison began, and immediately, involuntarily, I smiled around my cigar: the pressure was off.

"You can't offend me," I declared.

"Well, here's the thing. You know very well we'd like to have you come along with us to Italy"—I made a quick gesture of negation—"but I figured you had your work, and besides, the fact is, I think Jane sort of planned this thing just for the two of us. Three, counting Jeannine. You know."

"Don't even speak of it."

"Well, that's not the thing. The thing is, of course Janie won't be around here for a year, maybe two years, you never can tell. Now—I don't know how I can say this without hurting you, Toddy—the truth is, I kind of think when we come back (I don't know when that'll be) what with Jeannine getting older and all— well, it might not look too good, you know what I mean, if Janie kept on going up to the hotel."

"I agree completely," I said at once.

"Hell, I guess you're insulted, Toddy. I don't want you to take it the wrong way. You know what I think of you. But hell—"

"Sure, man. No explanation."

"Well, I want to make certain you take it right," Harrison persisted, examining his empty glass closely.

Jane came in, glanced quickly at me, then at Harrison and took a seat midway between us. She absorbed herself in rubbing her brown knee.

"You don't need to explain anything," I insisted firmly. "As a matter of fact—"

"I'll tell you the honest truth, Toddy," Jane broke in (I believe it was the first time she'd ever interrupted me). "If it's all right with you, I'd like to call the thing off as of now. Do you mind?"

"I was just going to suggest it," I said. Jane smiled briefly at her knee. "I'd been thinking about it for some time."

"Well, let me see if I can explain it right," Jane

said, looking at me directly and pleasantly. "I'm not too good at expressing things."

"There's no need to say a word," I declared.

"Yes there is," she smiled. "I don't want to break it off unless you can understand everything."

"I understand everything."

"No, you don't," Jane said sweetly. I looked up in surprise. "If you'd understood everything, there wouldn't have been that trouble a few years ago."

"Whoa, now—" I protested.

"Let me see if I can say what I want to say, and then you can take it apart," she proposed. I grinned shortly at Harrison, who, however, didn't see me, engrossed as he was in his empty glass. "When Harrison and I got married we were as prudish as they come about extracurricular sex," Jane began. "I swore I could never look at another man, and Harrison swore he never even thought of another woman in a sexual way. Then as we got a little older we saw how dishonest that was—is that the right word?—yes, *dishonest*. I won't go into all that. Well, we decided there was nothing wrong with either of us making love to somebody else now and then, because we were absolutely sure of each other. I was very attracted to you as Harrison's friend, and as soon as we didn't have to be dishonest any more, I realized I'd like to make love to you. And except for the one bad spell, it worked out all right. It was mostly our fault, we realize, about that bad time."

"Oh, I don't know." I shrugged. This was all very embarrassing for Harrison and me.

"Well, anyhow, neither of us has any regrets that it happened."

"Or that you're calling it off," I smiled.

"Don't be bitter," Harrison said.

"I didn't mean it that way."

"You're right," Jane said. "We don't have to have any regrets about that either, if you understand why I'm doing it."

"Is it because of that note this morning?" I asked.

"The note? Oh, that stupid thing! I never did pay

any attention to that. I assumed you were upset about last night, for some reason or other. I sent you my note as a joke, to get even. Heavens no, that's silly! I hadn't even considered it. Here's the thing: I don't want you to think that Harrison and I are retreating in any way to our old standards."

I raised my eyebrows.

"I can't find the damned words—what I mean is, we were unsure of ourselves when we decided to try this extracurricular business, I guess that's why we were so demanding, come to think of it. We wanted reassurance that we hadn't made a mistake. God knows that's understandable enough!"

"I think that's probably why Janie thought she was in love with you," Harrison put in, "and why I thought that was a good thing."

I pursed my lips.

"That's right," Janie agreed, looking at her husband. "Then after we started up again, after Jeannine was born, everything was fine. We all understood each other, and nobody was kidding himself. Now, then. What I want to say is that it was kind of *necessary* before to be actually carrying on affairs, to prove to ourselves that we meant what we were talking about. But we don't feel it's necessary any more. I just feel stronger, is all. Harrison does, too. Do you understand anything I've said, Toddy?"

"I told you before, I understood everything before you said a word. I exude understanding. Didn't I say that the same thing exactly was on *my* mind? I was going to broach the subject this evening."

"He doesn't understand," Harrison observed to Jane. I turned to him at once, startled, but said nothing.

Jane sighed. "I can't make it any clearer."

The maid signaled silently from the dining room.

"Dinner's almost ready, if you want to wash up," Jane said. She got up and headed for the kitchen, paused, and came over and kissed me lightly on the mouth.

"You were wonderful a great many times," she said. "I hope this doesn't leave you with a bad taste."

I licked my lips. "Tasted fine." Jane laughed and went to help the maid, and Harrison and I went upstairs to wash.

"Did you find a buyer for the house yet?" I asked him.

"No, not yet. Matter of fact, the whole thing's been sort of tentative. All we knew for sure is that we wanted to go to Italy for a while. It's kind of crazy, I guess, but a small town can be right stultifying."

We talked for a while in the bathroom, but there was a coolness between us. And at dinner afterwards, the talk, though pleasant (even relieved), was devoid of warmth. Harrison and Jane seemed fused into one person, entirely self-sufficient. They should, it occurred to me, be permanently locked together, like the doubler crab or Plato's protohumans. I caught myself smiling inadvertently at my cold cuts all through the meal, as I thought of Jane's speech. And, I am obliged to add, I noticed several times that Harrison and Jane smiled at their cold cuts as well: for what reasons, I shan't presume to say.

A final observation: when, after dinner, I went upstairs to the bathroom before leaving the house; when, indeed, I stood there comfortably reflecting, an entirely unexpected emotion gripped me: I suddenly wavered in my resolution to die—was shaken, in fact, by reluctance. The reason was simply that my suicide would be interpreted by the Macks as evidence that their move had crushed me; that I was unable to endure life after their rebuff. And this interpretation would fill them with a deplorable proud pity. Happily, the faltering lasted only a moment. By the time I'd washed my hands, I had come to my senses; my new premises reasserted themselves with force. What difference did it make to me how they interpreted my death? Nothing, absolutely, made any difference. And, sane again, I was able to see a nice attraction in the idea that, at least partly by my own choosing, that last act would be robbed of its significance, would be interpreted in every way but the way I intended. This fact once realized, it seemed likely to me that here was a new significance, even more appropriate.

Passing down the hallway from the bathroom to the stairs, I happened to glance into my old bedroom, now a guest room, and my eye fell on a large mirror near the bed. I chuckled so hard that my eyes watered, and I walked jauntily down the stairs, more ready than ever to carry out my plan.

"Be seeing you around," Harrison called from the porch as I left; and Jane, too, added cheerful good-byes.

"So long, so long," I called back, just as cheerfully. Looking over my shoulder as I walked down the road, I saw them standing close beside each other, talking together as they watched me leave. Perhaps—I clucked my tongue—their arms were even encircling each other's waists. I waved, but they didn't see me.

I turned and headed back toward the hotel. I believe I might even have whistled something or other, for I was as unburdened at that moment as must have been Socrates when, Xanthippe at last departed, he was free to face without distraction the hemlock that lay at the end of his reasoning.

xxiv three million dollars

No; there was one final matter to be settled before I could call myself really free from distracting encumbrances. I had to decide what to do about Harrison's three million dollars.

I paused halfway across the creek bridge to think about it. In order to focus the problem, I took from my billfold the letter from Eustacia Callader, and from my coat pocket the note to Jimmy Andrews, and laid them both before me on the bridge railing. Either I must put Eustacia's letter in my writing desk, where Jimmy was instructed to find it, and drop the note to Jimmy in the mailbox, or else I must drop both documents into the creek below, where fat gray gulls fed lazily on perch killed by the pollution from the packing houses. The first course would result in Jimmy's filing suit for Harrison against Elizabeth Sweetman Mack, charging that, by allowing her gardener, R. J. Collier, to spread the contents of the seventy-two pickle jars on the ailing zinnias, she had disposed of a portion of the Mack estate which was no more hers to dispose of than the three million dollars. This suit would serve to postpone the hearing of my appeal of the Circuit Court's order (to execute the will in favor of Mrs. Mack) until after Joseph Singer had replaced Rollo Moore on the Court of Appeals bench. Then Jimmy would drop the suit and argue our appeal: for the reasons explained in Chapter X, the lower-court order would almost certainly be reversed, and Harrison would get the inheritance. If, on the other hand, I decided to drop both letters into the creek, then there was little chance that the appellate court would do anything except affirm the court order.

Now, you'll recall that in the morning I had decided that the basis for my decision was to be Harrison's and Jane's strength; specifically, whether they had the strength not to care, except superficially, whether they got the money or the manure. And I must say that the morning's note from Jane and my luncheon conversation with Harrison had both inclined me in their favor. By afternoon I had, although I didn't clearly realize it at the time, more or less resolved to let the deciding factor be Jane's response to my note of the early morning, now that I'd fulfilled the conditions of hers by going to see Marvin Rose. If she chose to make Capt. Osborn the happiest old satyr in the country, I'd make her the richest woman in the country; if she was as angry and insulted by my proposal as Harrison had been by the incident in my office in 1933, then I'd destroy the letters.

But Jane had nullified this basis by choosing a third course, one difficult to evaluate. She'd been neither angry nor insulted, nor had she felt obliged to carry out her end of the bargain. She'd simply laughed at the whole thing. Was this evidence of obtuseness, insincerity, or a real and formidable strength? In fact, I no longer knew how to feel about the Macks at all, whether their new resolutions manifested a commonplace sentimentality or a strange integrity. I had no feeling about them at all.

Consequently, after inhaling deeply the fetid air of the creek for several minutes, I chose a new basis for judgment: taking a nickel from my pocket, I flipped it, caught it, and slapped it down on the letters. Heads, I preserve them; tails, they go in the creek.

My hand uncovered the skinny-assed, curly-tailed old buffalo.

Despite which fact, I gathered up the letters, dropped one in the mailbox on the corner of Academy, Market, and Muse Streets, just off the creek bridge, and put the other in my desk when I reached the hotel. Harrison had survived a double chance: that the coin would demand the destruction of the letters, and that I would allow myself, a free agent, to be dictated to by a miserable nickel.

Then, let us say, I doubtless whistled some tune or other, unburdened as must have been Socrates when, *etc.*

xxv   the inquiry

It was a few minutes after six o'clock when I reached
my room, set my straw hat on the dresser top, and
prepared to put in a last evening's work on my *Inquiry*. I gathered around my writing desk the three peach
baskets and one cardboard box of notes and data, put
in a convenient place the empty beef-stew can my
ashtray, and began my night's work by transcribing
from memory the notes I'd made that day and filing
them at an appropriate depth in one of the peach
baskets. Then I sat back in the chair and stared at the
window for a while, deciding which aspect of the
project should receive my attention.

When the clock on the People's Trust building
chimed six-thirty (the Macks, as usual, had eaten early), I sat up, took a long ruled sheet of yellow legal
paper from one of the pads stacked on the desk, and
wrote on the top:

I. Nothing has intrinsic value.

Because I regarded this sentence for some minutes
before adding to it, and because staring and regarding
is duller to describe than to do, let me use the time to
explain as clearly as I can the nature and history of my
Inquiry and of the great project of which the *Inquiry*
itself is only one part.

The full title of the *Inquiry*, if it ever should reach
the stage of completion where a title would be appropriate, will be *An Inquiry into the Circumstances Sur-*

rounding the Self-Destruction of Thomas T. Andrews, of Cambridge, Maryland, on Ground-Hog Day, 1930 (More Especially into the Causes Therefor), or something of the sort. It is an attempt to learn why my father hanged himself, no more.

And no less—for it became apparent to me after a mere two years of questioning, searching, reading, and staring, that there is no will-o'-the-wisp so elusive as the cause of any human act. Easy enough to spend weeks poring over bank statements, budget books, letters from stockbrokers; to spend months examining newspaper files, stock-market reports, volumes on the theory and the history of economics; to spend years in careful, unhurried, apparently casual questioning of every person who had more than a superficial acquaintanceship with my father. All this is just more or less laborious research. But it is another thing to examine this information and see in it, so clearly that to question is out of the question, the *cause* of a human act.

In fact, it's impossible, for as Hume pointed out, causation is never more than an inference; and any inference involves at some point the leap from what we see to what we can't see. Very well. It's the purpose of my *Inquiry* to shorten as much as is humanly possible the distance over which I must leap; to gather every scrap of information that a human being might gather concerning the circumstances of my father's suicide. Say, if you wish, that the true reason for this investigation is my reluctance to admit that Dad hanged himself because he was afraid to face his creditors. Perhaps so (noble work has been accomplished for more questionable reasons), although consciously, at least, I have a different reason. At any rate, I am certainly prepared to admit that my observation of the data I collect is biased, and it's partly for that reason that even in 1937 I kept one peach basket reserved for notes on myself—it was into this basket that my two thoughts of the day, for example, were filed. It would be more accurate to say that my rejection of the stock-market losses as the cause of his suicide was the hypothesis with which I approached the *Inquiry*, the thesis that oriented my investigations.

You understand, do you, that the nature of my purpose—to make as short as possible the gap between fact and opinion—renders the *Inquiry* interminable? One could, of course, stop at some point and declare, "I have sufficient information to warrant the inference that the cause of Thomas T. Andrews' suicide was such-and-such." But my purpose is not really to leap the gap (which can be deep, however narrow), only to shorten it. So, the task is endless; I've never fooled myself about that. But the fact that it's endless doesn't mean that I can't work on other aspects of the grand project, even though the *completion* of those aspects depends ultimately on the leaping of the gap in my *Inquiry*. It doesn't follow that because a goal is unattainable, one shouldn't work toward its attainment. Besides, as I've observed elsewhere, processes continued for long enough tend to become ends in themselves, and if for no other reason, I should continue my researches simply in order to occupy pleasantly two hours after dinner.

But let's suppose that by some miracle it were given to me to know the unknowable, to *know* the cause or causes of Dad's suicide. My *Inquiry* would be complete. But my researches would not, for after supper on the day of that revelation I should draw to my desk a different peach basket—that one beside the lamp there—and after some minutes of wall-staring, resume work on a larger *Inquiry*, of which the abovementioned is at most a relevant chapter. And this *Inquiry*, had I world enough and time, might someday be entitled *An Inquiry into the Life of Thomas T. Andrews, of Cambridge, Maryland(1867–1930), Giving Especial Consideration to His Relations with His Son, Todd Andrews (1900–   )*. In other words, a complete study of my father's mind and life from his birth in the front bedroom of the Andrews house to his death in its cellar; from the umbilicus that tied him to his mother to the belt that hanged him from the floor joist.

A considerable task: it is my aim to learn all that can be learned of my father's life; to get the best possible insight into the workings of his mind. To do this I must, in addition to carrying out on a larger scale all the researches described in connection with the other *Inquiry*, perform extra labors as well—I must read, for example, all the books that I know my father read, looking for influences on his character and way of thinking. If one can compare infinities, this task is even more endless than the other.

I said a moment ago that the death-*Inquiry* was but a chapter in the life-*Inquiry*; in another sense, the study of Dad's life is only a necessary preliminary to the study of his death. And ultimately, I should say, they stand side by side, for they share a common purpose: what I really want to discover is the nature and extent of my father's contribution to our imperfect communication.

Imperfect communication: that's the problem. If you understand that (for to go into greater detail would enmesh us beyond hope of ever returning to the story), then it's time to pass on to the last document of all, of which my two colossal *Inquiries* combined are no more than important studies for one aspect: the *Letter to My Father*.

This document dates from the fall of 1920, when after my unsuccessful attempts to tell Dad about my uncertain heart, I enrolled in the University. I had resolved, you'll remember, not to tell him at all while I lived, because I believed that my death was imminent and that therefore I'd as well humor him during what remained of my life. Nevertheless I worried that I'd been unable to tell him when I wanted to, and (I was no cynic then) that the both of us would go to our graves without ever having understood each other.

And so I began to write a letter to my father, working on it in snatches during my four exhausting years at college. The letter was to be found by him after my death, and its original purpose was to explain what Dr. John Frisbee had told me about my heart.

But this purpose, though I never lost sight of it, was soon subsumed into a larger one: I set out to study myself, to discover why my communication with Dad had always been imperfect. I reviewed my whole life carefully, selecting and rejecting incidents for use in the letter. I spent a month, at least, attempting to explain to Dad why I'd never finished building my boat in the back yard. More than a year went to searching my muddy embrace with the German sergeant (with whom my communication had been pitifully imperfect) and to analyzing the effects on me of a certain particular popping noise. I worked, of course, irregularly, completing perhaps twenty pages of notes and one page of letter every month; seldom more than that. By the time I was installed in law school, the letter was perhaps fifty pages long, and I had a respectable stack of notes. I did not shy away from mentioning Betty June Gunter, even, although I realize now that those early attempts to understand our liaison were shallow. Especially between 1925 and 1927—the first of my saintly years—I worked with some diligence on the letter.

Then in 1927, when I set up practice in Cambridge, the letter and notes were packed into my trunk. I moved in with Dad and to my great pleasure found myself—or so I believed—closer to him than I'd ever been before. He was still garrulous and gruff by turns, but I thought I was beginning to understand him somewhat; at least I had hope that our communication was becoming less imperfect, and in this hope I abandoned the letter. I had, you see, always assumed that the source of the imperfection was in myself, and it seemed to me that perhaps as I matured (although I was twenty-seven then) my difficulty would vanish.

But Dad hanged himself, and rack my memory as I might until sleep was a red-eyed wish, I could find no adequate reason for his act. I realized then that I had been pursuing an impossible task since 1920: to understand an imperfect communication requires perfect knowledge of the party at each end, and I'd been studying only myself. When, in the course of moving into the Dorset Hotel, my letter and notes came to light, I put the pages of the letter on my new writing desk, dumped the notes into an empty suitcase (not until later did I begin to use peach baskets), and began work on it again. I saw at once that the next step was to open an inquiry into Dad's life, in order to understand the nature and extent of his contribution to our imperfect communication; and at the same time I saw the necessity of a special and separate inquiry into the circumstances surrounding his death, this inquiry to be in the nature of a control (for unless the suicide were explained, nothing was explained) and also perhaps a key (for should I find the answer to the question of his death, the whole problem might be solved by the same solution). Thus my two *Inquiries* were initiated; but they did not close off my work on the letter and the notes on myself.

You see, then, the purposes of the three peach baskets beside my desk in 1937: one represented the life-*Inquiry*, one the death-*Inquiry*, the third the less organized self-*Inquiry*. And the cardboard box (MORTON'S MARVELOUS TOMATOES) contained the drafts of the letter to my father. To be sure, he can never now receive it. If you don't see that this fact only demonstrates further the imperfection of my communication with him, and hence intensifies the need for the letter instead of eliminating it, then between you and me, too, the communication is less than perfect. But you shall have to investigate it: I've enough to do with the three baskets and the box beside me—four parallel projects, which, like parallel lines, will meet only in infinity.

On this particular evening, to be sure, their progress would cease, for the notes I took then I intended to be my last.

I. *Nothing has intrinsic value.*
II. *The reasons for which people attribute value to things are always ultimately irrational.*
III. *There is, therefore, no ultimate "reason" for valuing anything.*

By seven o'clock, these were the things I had written on my piece of paper, not knowing exactly which file would finally receive them. But I felt very strongly that this sequence of ideas, which represented my day's rationalizing, was of supreme importance to my *Inquiries* and my letter. In fact, when in the same list I entered the Roman numeral *IV*, without yet writing anything after it, I had a nostril-flaring sensation of the chase; I felt that some sort of answer was on the verge of being treed.

I called these ideas rationalizings, and so they were: the *post facto* justification, on logical grounds, of what had been an entirely personal, unlogical resolve. Such, you remember, had been the case with all my major mind-changes. My masks were each first assumed, then justified.

My heart, reader! My heart! You must comprehend quickly, if you are to comprehend at all, that those masks were not assumed to hide my face, but to hide my heart from my mind, and my mind from my heart. Understand it now, because I may not live to end the chapter! To be sure, each mask hid other things as well, as a falseface hides identity and personality as well as nose and mouth; but it was to hide my enigmatic heart that I became a rake, a saint, and then a cynic. For when one mask no longer served its purpose of disguise, another had perforce to take its place at once. I had been a not-very-extraordinary boy; then one day in 1919 while standing retreat I collapsed on the parade grounds at Fort Meade, Dr. Frisbee looked up from his stethoscope, and I began to eat, drink, and be merry at Johns Hopkins—my first mask. In 1924 Betty June Gunter slashed me with a broken bottle, a man named Cozy rabbit-punched me and threw me out of a Calvert Street brothel, Marvin Rose found a wicked infection in my prostate, and I became a saint— my second mask. In 1930 my father, with whom (thinking my saintliness was bringing on maturity) I had thought I was beginning to communicate, *inexplicably* hanged himself; I took the belt from his neck, mailed my legacy to Col. Morton, and became a cynic—my third mask. And each time, it did not take me long to come to believe that my current attitude was not only best for me, because it put me on some kind of terms with my heart, but best in itself, absolutely. Then, on the night of June 20 or 21, 1937—

But now you must know my last secret. In my life I have experienced emotion intensely on only five occasions, each time a different emotion. With Betty June in my bedroom I learned *mirth*; with myself in the Argonne I learned *fear*; with my father in the basement of our house I learned *frustration*; with Jane Mack in her summer cottage I learned *surprise*; with my heart, in my hotel room on the night before this last day, I learned *despair*, utter despair, a despair beyond wailing.

My despair began, not with my heart, but with two other parts of my body. Jane was in my room for the night, as you know. She had come in at perhaps ten o'clock; we'd had a drink and retired shortly afterwards. Jane had sat Turk-fashion on the bed for some time, plucking her eyebrows before we turned out the light, and I had stroked her idly while I lay beside her reading a book. We hadn't been talking at all. Then, taking my hand in hers to examine it, she said, "Did you ever ask Marvin about your fingers, Todd? My, they're ugly."

I jerked my hand away, blushing hotly. Had you forgotten that my fingers were clubbed? So had I, reader, and Jane's remark, though offered in a mild enough tone, stung me all out of proportion to my actual sensitivity about my fingers—perhaps because I'd been caressing her.

"Oh, I'm awfully sorry!" she said at once. "I didn't mean to insult you at all." She tried to kiss my fingers then, but I couldn't bear the thought. I kept them out of sight.

My subsequent failure at love-making no doubt grew out of that. For one thing, in her efforts to redeem herself Jane made all the advances, immediately, and I have rarely responded well in such situations. For another, the remark about my fingers made me irrationally disgusted with my whole skinny body, and disgust is a cold bedfellow for desire.

"Please tell me what's wrong, Toddy," Jane pleaded. "I really don't want to hurt you." (There was more to this than ordinary solicitude, as I realized next day when she announced the Italian trip.)

I assured her that I wasn't offended—after the first few minutes I really wasn't—but both her curiosity and her desire had to go unsatisfied. I got up, smoked a cigarette, went to bed, tossed and turned, sat up and read, drank another drink, and tossed and turned some more. Jane fell asleep, annoyance and injured pride still pouting from her lips. I kissed her very lightly on her frowning brow and got out of bed, resolved, since sleep was impossible, to work on the *Inquiry*.

My mood was black; I had little patience with my work. It is only in very weak moments like this that I call my project silly; I sat for an hour in the window, looking over at the Post Office and thinking how incomparably silly my thirteen years work was. How silly, for that matter, was my whole life during those thirteen years—one feeble mask after another!

Ah, there was a symptomatic thought: it was, I think, the first time I'd ever used the term *masks* in referring to what I'd always considered to be the stages of my intellectual development. Moreover, it was not the thought of a cynic, for as soon as it lodged in my consciousness it sent out quick rootlets of despair to all corners of my mind. Indeed, as I vaguely recognized at the time, it was a sign that the mask of my cynicism—I saw then that it was a mask—was wearing thin, and no longer doing its job. If it were, would I even have thought of my heart?

And suddenly my heart filled my entire body. It was not my heart that would burst, but my body, so full was it of my heart, and every beat was sick. Surely it would fail! I clapped my hand quickly to my chest, feeling for the beat; clutched at the window frame to keep from falling; stared at *nothing*, my mouth open, like a fish on the beach. And this not in pain, but in despair!

Here is what I saw: that all my masks were half-conscious attempts to master the fact with which I had to live; that none had made me master of that fact; that where cynicism had failed, no future mask could succeed; that, in short, my heart was the master of all the rest of me, even of my will. It was my heart that had made my masks, not my will. The conclusion that swallowed me was this: *There is no way to master the fact with which I live.* Futility gripped me by the throat; my head was tight. The impulse to raise my arms and eyes to heaven was almost overpowering—but there was no one for me to raise them to. All I could do was clench my jaw, squint my eyes, and shake my head from side to side. But every motion pierced me with its own futility, every new feeling with its private hopelessness, until a battery of little agonies attacked from all sides, each drawing its strength from the great agony within me.

I can't say for how long I sat. What finally happened, when I had become sufficiently demoralized, was that my nerves, fatigued already, succumbed to the unusual strain. My body was suddenly soaked in perspiration; I trembled from head to foot. Indeed, I can't find it in me to deny that, had no other crutch been available, I should very possibly have ended that night on my knees, laying my integrity on the altar of the word *God*. But another crutch was within reach: Jane, now sleeping soundly. And the embarrassment that I feel at telling you how I went shocked and trembling to the bed; how I buried my head blindly in her lap; how I lay there shuddering until sleep found me, my knees clasped to my chest, fighting despair as one fights appendicitis—this embarrassment is not different from that I'd feel at having to confess that I'd buried myself in God. I am in truth embarrassed, reader, but in good faith I recommend this refuge to your attention. There is nothing in it of the ostrich, because the enemy you flee is not exterior to yourself.

I have no idea whether Jane was aware of any of this. At the tick of six I popped awake; my head was on the pillow, Jane's on my right shoulder. In great wisdom I inhaled the smell of her hair: sunshine and salt. There have been no women in my bed since that morning, and yet still at 6:00 A.M. I can summon to my nostrils the smell of Jane Mack. I sat up and looked around me, swelling with incipient wisdom. What had been the problem I'd buried? As was my habit, before I got up I reached to the window sill for my Sherbrook, took a good pull, and shuddered all over, but no answer came. I rose carefully from the bed, so as not to wake Jane, donned my seersucker suit, splashed cold water on my face—and realized that on this day I would destroy myself.

"Of course!"

I grinned at my dripping face in the mirror—dumb, stunned surprise. There was the end of masks!

"Of course!"

There was no mastering the fact with which I lived; but I could master the fact of my living with it by destroying myself, and the result was the same—I was the master. I choked back a snicker.

"For crying out loud!"

III. *There is, therefore, no ultimate "reason" for valuing anything.*

Now I added *including life*, and at once the next proposition was clear:

IV. *Living is action. There's no final reason for action.*
V. *There's no final reason for living.*

This last statement merited some minutes of expressionless contemplation, after which I capped my pen and clipped it in my pocket, put Eustacia's letter where Jimmy would find it, fetched my straw, and left my room without a shred of regret.

The *Inquiry* was closed.

xxvi the first step

Ideally, a new philosophical position, like a new rowboat, should be allowed to sit a day or two at the dock,
to let the seams swell tight, before it's put to any
strenuous application. But no sooner had I taken one
step into the hall than Capt. Osborn called to me from
his room.

"Are ye goin' to the boat show, Toddy?"

"Yes, sir."

Capt. Osborn gave a grunt or two, hocked some
vagrant phlegm into his handkerchief, and hobbled out
of his room.

"I'll jest walk along with ye, if ye don't mind," he
declared. "Ain't seen a boat show for years." He
chuckled. "Young Haecker—I call 'im Young Haecker
now—Young Haecker's been gloomin' around so lately, I figure I better have me some fun while I can. All
set, boy?"

One should not have to make such decisions
quickly; it's like launching a new rowboat into the
teeth of a nor'easter.

"Where is Young Haecker?" I smiled.

"Oh, he ain't goin'," Capt. Osborn sniffed. "He's too
old for such carryin' on! I ain't seen 'im since this
mornin'. Here, I'll jest take yer arm."

Ah. As a boatwright might examine his craft for
leaks, with considerable interest if little real anxiety, so
I examined myself. Can he be called a builder who

shies at launching the finished hull? For what other purpose was it finished?

"Of course," I said, and took my friend with me down the steps.

xxvii   the floating opera

Plain enough by day, the *Original & Unparalleled Floating Opera* was somewhat more ornamented as Capt. Osborn and I approached it across Long Wharf in the hot twilight. Power lines had been run from a utility pole near the dock, and the showboat was outlined in vari-colored electric lights, which, however, needed greater darkness for their best effect. On the roof of the theater Prof. Eisen and the thirteen members of his $7,500 Challenge Atlantic & Chesapeake Maritime Band were installed in their bandstand, rendering, as I recall, "I'm a Yankee Doodle Dandy" to the crowd of several hundred onlookers gathered around—many of whom, particularly among the Negroes, came only to hear the free concert and regard the "Op'ry Barge" with amazement, not having money to spare for admission to the show. The box office was open (it was nearly showtime), and a line was queued up from the ticket window down the gangplank to the bulkheads. Capt. Osborn grew excited and used his cane to nudge small running urchins out of his path, which led unswervingly to the ticket line.

The band wound up George M. Cohan and began a Stephen Foster medley. When we reached the top of the gangplank I looked around at the crowd and saw Harrison, Jane, and Jeannine just taking a place in line. They were occupied with opening Jeannine's popcorn bag, and didn't notice me.

The auditorium was already nearly half filled with the citizens of Cambridge. Capt. Osborn and I took seats about seven rows from the rear, on the extreme starboard side of the theater—he complaining that we hadn't arrived earlier to get really good seats. The hall was illuminated with electric lights, each built into a double fixture along with a gas mantle for use at less progressive landings. Scanning the audience, I saw almost no unfamiliar faces. Col. Morton and his wife sat in the front row on the aisle. Marvin Rose, a showboat *aficionado*, sat a few rows behind. Bill Butler waved cheerily to me from across the theater. My partner Mr. Bishop was there with his wife, whom one seldom saw in public. Harrison, Jane, and Jeannine came in—if they saw me, they made no sign, although I waved to them—and sat on the other side of the theater. Jimmy Andrews, as I'd anticipated, was absent—doubtless out sailing with his fiancée, for a mild but usable breeze had sprung up earlier in the evening.

Above our heads the $7,500 Challenge Band concluded its free concert with "The Star-Spangled Banner." There was some uncertainty in the house as to whether it was necessary to stand, since the band was outside. Some men made a half-hearted motion to rise, hesitated, and sat down embarrassed, laughing explanations at their wives with much pointing of fingers toward the roof. Finally Col. Morton stood unfalteringly, without a backward look, and the rest of us followed suit, relieved to have a ruling on the matter. When the anthem ended there was applause from the freeloaders outside, and much discussion inside about whether it had really been necessary for us to stand. Soon, however, everyone's attention was focused on the small door under the stage, from which the members of the orchestra, resplendent in gold-braided red uniforms, began filing into the pit. When all were in their places, and instruments had been tootled cacophonously, Prof. Eisen himself—lean, hollow-cheeked, Vandyked, intense—stepped to the podium amid generous applause from orchestra and balcony, rapped for attention, and raised his baton, on the tip of which the whole house hung. The lights dimmed slightly, the baton fell, and the band crashed into "The Star-

Spangled Banner." An instant's murmur and then we sprang to our feet again, none more quickly than the Colonel—although Evelyn was a trifle flustered.

No sooner had the final cymbal clashed than the house lights went out completely and the electric footlights rose, playing on the mauve velvet stage curtain. Prof. Eisen's baton fell again, and the sprightly overture was commenced: a potpourri of martial airs, ragtime, a touch of some sentimental love ballad, a flourish of buck-and-wing, and a military finale. We applauded eagerly.

Captain Jacob Adam himself stepped from behind the curtain, bowed to our ovation, and smilingly bade us listen.

"Good evenin', good evenin', friends!" he cried. "I can't say how happy I am to see ye all here tonight. It does my heart good when the *Floatin' Op'ry* comes round Hambrook Light, I'll tell ye, 'cause I know that means it's Cambridge ahead, and I tell John Strudge, my calliope man, I say to him, 'John,' I say, 'get up a good head o' steam, boy, and let's have "Dem Golden Slippers," 'cause that there's Cambridge yonder,' I says, 'and ye'll sail a lot o' water 'fore ye meet finer folks than ye'll see a-plenty in Cambridge!' Now, then!"

We cheered.

"Well, sir, folks, I'm glad so many of ye got out tonight, 'cause we got such a fine new show this year I was anxious for all my friends and even my enemies in Cambridge to see it." He squinted over the footlights. "Guess my friends'll be in later," he mumbled loudly, and grinned at once lest we miss the jest—but we were alert, and laughed especially loud.

"Yes, sir, a brand-new line-up this year, folks, from a crackerjack start to a whiz-bang finish! But before we haul back the curtain and get on with the fun, I'm afraid I'll have to disappoint ye just a wee bit."

We murmured sympathy for ourselves.

"Now I know ye was pinin' to see Miss Clara Mulloy, the Mary Pickford of the Chesapeake, do her stuff in *The Parachute Girl*. So was I, I got to admit, 'cause no matter how many times in a row I watch

Miss Clara jump down in that there par'chute, them legs o' hers is so durn pretty I can't see my fill!"

We laughed more raucously, Capt. Osborn jabbing me in the ribs and exploding with mirthful phlegm.

"But I'm sorry to say Miss Clara Mulloy has caught a germ from someplace—must have been Crisfield, couldn't of been Cambridge—and I swear if she ain't got the laryngitis so bad she can't say a durn word!"

We voiced our disappointment, some of us resentfully.

"I know, I know," Capt. Adam sympathized. "I feel like walkin' out myself. Hey, Miss Clara," he shouted into the wings, "come on out here and show the people yer—ah—yer *laryngitis!*" He winked at us, we roared, and then Miss Clara Mulloy—brown-haired, brown-eyed, trimly corseted—curtsied onto the stage, the sequins flashing on her black gown, a red flannel scarf tied incongruously around her white neck. She curtsied again to our ovation, pointed to her throat, and moved her lips in silent explanation, while Capt. Adam looked on adoringly.

"What do ye say?" he cried to us. "Shall we call the whole thing off? I'm willin'!"

"NO!" we shouted, almost as one man—two or three rowdies cried "*Yes!*" but we glared them down.

"Do I hear *yes?*" the Captain asked.

"NO!" we roared again, our stares defying contradiction from the one or two hoodlums who are forever spoiling honest folks' fun. "No!" we pleaded, hoping Capt. Adam wouldn't judge us citizens of Cambridge by our most unfortunate element.

"*Yes!*" one of the incorrigibles snickered.

"That man should be thrown out!" I heard the Colonel declare in exasperation.

"Well, I say let's be fair and square," Capt. Adam said. "Any man, woman, or child that wants to leave can get up right now and go, and John Strudge'll give ye yer full admission money back at the box office, despite ye already heard the overture!"

We laughed at this last and applauded his generosity. The house lights came up for a moment, but no one dared move.

"All right, then, let's get on with the show!"

The house lights were extinguished, Miss Clara Mulloy rewarded our applause with a blown kiss (her eyes dewy), Prof. Eisen struck up a lively tune, and we relaxed again.

"Now, then," the Captain announced. "Instead o' *The Parachute Girl* I'm proud to present the great T. Wallace Whittaker, one o' the finest singers and actors that ever trod the boards. Ye all know T. Wallace Whittaker as the great Southern tenor—got a voice like a honeycomb in a sweet-gum stump, I swear! But what ye probably don't know is that T. Wallace Whittaker is one o' the best Shakespearian actors in the U.S.A.! Ladies and gentlemen, I have the *great* honor to present T. Wallace Whittaker, the eminent tragedian, in Scenes from the Bard!"

Uncertain applause. The band played heavy chords in a minor key, the curtain opened, and we looked into a Victorian parlor (first set for *The Parachute Girl*), in the center of which bowed T. Wallace Whittaker. He was a broad-beamed, Sunday-schooly young man, and he wore a tight black Hamlet-looking outfit. From the tone of his very first words—a lofty "I shall begin by reciting the famous speech of the duke Jacques, from Act Two of *As You Like It*"—he lost the sympathy of us men, although some wives nodded knowingly.

T. Wallace walked to the footlights, struck a declamatory pose, and closed his eyes for a moment. He did not clear his throat, but some of us cleared ours.

"*All the world's a stage,*" he declared, "*and all the men and women merely players: they have their exits and their entrances; and one man in his time plays many parts....*"

Already Capt. Osborn had the fidgets, and began ticking his cane against his high-top shoe. The rest of us sat uncomfortably as T. Wallace ran through the seven ages of man.

"... *Last scene of all ... mere oblivion, sans teeth, sans eyes, sans taste, sans every thing!*"

Polite applause, especially from the ladies. I thought I heard Jeannine ask shrilly for more popcorn, but it could have been some other child. One of the rowdies made a sneering remark that I couldn't catch, but that set his neighbors chuckling, no longer so hostile to him as before, and rewarded him with a flash of T. Wallace Whittaker's eyes.

"Mark Antony's funeral oration, from Act Three of *Julius Caesar*," he announced. "*Friends, Romans, countrymen, lend me your ears....*"

"Ye can have mine, boy," the hoodlum said loudly. "I've took enough!" He stalked out of the theater, and the rest of us were shamefully amused. Even some wives stifled smiles, but T. Wallace Whittaker went on, blushing, to inflame an imaginary mob against Brutus and company. The oration was long, for T. Wallace went through the whole routine of Caesar's will. By the time he insinuated his desire to move the stones of Rome to rise and mutiny, his audience was on the verge of doing likewise; we were tapping our feet, sneezing, and whispering among ourselves. When he cried at the end, "*Mischief, thou art afoot, take thou what course thou wilt!*" someone whistled and flung a handful of pennies onto the stage.

T. Wallace ignored the insult; rather, he acknowledged it with a defiant glare but refused to be bowed.

"What I shall recite now," he said grimly, "is the most magnificent thing in the whole English language. I shan't expect a noisy rabble to appreciate its beauty, but perhaps a respectful silence will be granted, if not to me, at least to Shakespeare!"

"Where's the minstrels?" someone shouted. "Bring on the minstrels!" More pennies sailed over the footlights.

"The soliloquy from *Hamlet*," T. Wallace Whittaker whispered.

"Go home!"

"Take 'im away!"

"Come on, minstrels!"

"*To be, or not to be: that is the question. . . .*"

"Ya—a—a—ah!"

The audience was out of hand now. Several young men stood on their chairs to take better aim with their pennies, which no longer merely fell at T. Wallace's feet, but struck his face, chest, and gesticulating arms until he was forced to turn half around. But he would not be vanquished.

"*To die, to sleep; to sleep: perchance to dream: ay, there's the rub. . . .*"

One pimply-faced lad, standing in a front-row seat, began aping T. Wallace's gestures, to our delight, until Col. Morton struck at him with his gold-headed cane.

"*For who would bear the whips and scorns of time, the oppressor's wrong . . .*" T. Wallace Whittaker was determined that we should have our culture. I greatly admired him.

"*. . . the proud man's contumely, the pangs of despised love, the law's delay. . . .*"

"Yahoo! Boo! Hsssss!"

It was open warfare now; T. Wallace could no longer be heard, but nevertheless he continued undaunted. Capt. Adam appeared from the wings, disturbed lest we begin taking the vessel apart, but we greeted his conciliatory wavings with more boos. He went to T. Wallace, doubtless to ask him to call it a day, but T. Wallace declaimed in his face. Capt. Adam grew panicky, then angry, and tried to drag him off; T. Wallace shoved him away, still gesticulating with the other hand. Capt. Adam shook his finger at the young man, shouted, "Yer fired!" and signaled to Prof. Eisen to strike up the band. The $7,500 Challenge Maritime Band waltzed into "Over the Waves." T. Wallace Whittaker stepped through the closing curtains, and shaking both fists at us through a copper shower (to which I, too, contributed, standing up and flinging all my change at him), in blind defiance he screamed: "*Thus conscience does make cowards of us all, and thus the native hue of resolution is sicklied o'er with the pale cast of thought!*" Finished at last, he scooped a handful of pennies from the stage, flung them back at us, and disappeared behind the curtain.

A few more late-thrown pennies sailed after him, hit the curtain, and clicked onto the stage. We were all laughing and comparing notes, a little sheepish, but exhilarated for all that—none more so than I, for it is sometimes pleasant to stone a martyr, no matter how much we may admire him. For my part, as I believe I've mentioned elsewhere in this book, I'm seldom reluctant to assist in my small way in the persecution of people who defy the crowd with their principles, especially when I'm in favor of the principles. After all, the test of one's principles is his willingness to suffer for them, and the test of this willingness—the only test—is actual suffering. What was I doing, then, but assisting T. Wallace Whittaker in the realization of his principles? For now, surely, having been hooted from the stage and fired from his job in the cause of Shakespeare, he would either abandon his principles, in which case they weren't integrated very strongly into his personality, or else cling to them more strongly than ever, in which case he had us to thank for giving him the means to strength.

Capt. Adam appeared next from the wings, smiling thinly, and raised his hands. We were willing enough now to be silent, having made our point.

"Oh, well, who likes Shakespeare anyhow?" He shrugged cravenly, kicking a few pennies around the footlights. "If ye think yer gittin' any o' these pennies back, though, yer crazy!"

We laughed, relieved as wayward children who learn that they won't be punished after all.

"Now, then, see if ye can't be a little nicer to the next folks," Capt. Adam grinned. "At least pitch quarters at 'em. Ladies and gents: those knights of the burnt-cork, the U.S.A.'s greatest sable humorists, the chaste and inimitable Ethiopian Tidewater Minstrels!"

We applauded complacently, for this was what we'd come to see. Prof. Eisen ripped into "I'm Alabammy Bound" at express-train tempo, and the curtains parted. The set for *The Parachute Girl* had been replaced by a solid blue backdrop, against which stood out the bright uniforms of a small semicircle of minstrels. There were six in all: three on each side of Capt. Adam, who took his place as interlocutor. All wore fuzzy black wigs, orange clawhammer coats, bright checkered vests and trousers, tall paper collars, and enormous shoes, and sang in raucous unison the words of the song. The two minstrels on either side of the interlocutor assisted with banjos and guitars, while Tambo and Bones, the end men, played the instruments from which their names are derived. With a great rattling and crashing the tune shuddered to its end.

"Gentle-*men-n-n-n* . . . ." cried Capt. Adam, raising his arms to heaven, "BE . . . SEATED!"

Tambo and Bones, to be sure, missed their chairs and fell sprawling on the floor, accompanied by thumps from the bass drum. Knees were slapped, ribs elbowed. Capt. Osborn, beside me, strangled rapturously. Col. Morton's cane banged approval. In his new role as Mr. Interlocutor, Capt. Adam was transformed into an entirely different person—grammatical, florid, effusive—so that one doubted the authenticity of his original character. When the end men, great eyeballs rolling, had regained their seats, the classical repartee ensued, the interlocutor being tripped up in his pomposity again and again—to our delight, for our sympathies were all with impish Tambo, irrepressible Bones.

"*Good evening, Mr. Tambo; you look a little down in the mouth tonight.*"

"*Mist' Interlocutor, ah ain't down in de mouf; ah's down in de pocketbook. New hat fo' de wife, new shoes fo' de baby. Now dat no-good boy ob mine is done pesterin' me to buy him a 'cyclopedia. Say he needs 'em fo' de school.*"

"*An encyclopedia! Ah, there's a wise lad, Tambo! No schoolboy should be without a good encyclopedia. I trust you'll purchase one for the lad?*"

"*No, sah!*"

"*No!*"

"*No, sah! Ah say to dat boy, ah say, ''Cyclopedia nuffin'! Y'all gwine walk like de other chillun!'*"

We were led by the nose through rudimentary jokes, clubbed with long-anticipated punch lines, titillated—despite the minstrels' alleged chastity—by an occasional *double-entendre* as ponderous as it was mild. Negroes were shiftless and ignorant, foreigners suspect; the WPA was a refuge for loafers; mothers-in-law were shrewish; women poor drivers; drunkenness was an amusing but unquestioned vice; churchgoing a soporific but unquestioned virtue. Tambo and Bones deserved their poverty, but their rascality won our hearts, and we nodded to one another as their native wit led the overeducated interlocutor into one trap after another. Tambo and Bones vindicated our ordinariness; made us secure in the face of mere book learning; their every triumph over Mr. Interlocutor was a pat on our backs. Indeed, a double pat: for were not Tambo and Bones but irresponsible Negroes?

We were sung to of heart, hearth, and home by Sweet Sally Starbuck, the singing soubrette, she of the moist eyes, cornsilk hair, and flushed cheeks. What did she sing us? "I Had a Dream, Dear." "After the Ball Is Over." "A Mother's Prayer for Her Son." "Harvest Moon."

"*Y'all so smaht, Mist' Interlocutor, ansah me dis, sah: whut got twenty-nine legs, six arms, twelve ears, three tails, twenty feet, and a passle ob faucets, and say cockadoodledoo?*"

"*Great heavens, Tambo! What does have twenty-nine legs, six arms, twelve ears, three tails, twenty feet, and a passle of faucets, and says cockadoodledoo?*"

"*Three farmers, three milkin' stools, three Jersey cows, and a loudmouf roostah! Ha!*"

We were preached to by J. Strudge, calliopist, ticket collector, and banjo player extraordinary, the Magnificent Ethiopian Delineator, the Black Demosthenes:

"Ladies, gemmen, houn' dawgs, bullfrawgs, an' polecats: de tex' fer today come from de forty-leben chaptah, umpteen verse—borry fo', carry three, give or take a couple, chunk in one fer good measure—ob de

Book ob Zephaniah, whar de two Jedges, name ob First an' Secon' Samuel, done take de Ax ob de Romans an' cut de 'Pistles off de 'Postles fer playin' de Numbahs! Hyar how she go, bredren: *Blessed am dem dat 'specks nuffin', 'caze dey ain't gwine git nuffin'!*"

We were serenaded by banjo and fiddle, bones and tambourine.

"*Mr. Bones, I spoke to your wife today, and she tells me your mammy's been living with you all for three years now.*"

"*Mah mammy! Ah been thinkin' all dis time dat was her mammy!*"

"*No! How can you be so consistently stupid, Mr. Bones?*"

"*Well, Mist' Interlocutor, dat ain't easy fo' a dahkie like me dat's neber been to one ob dem fancy colleges!*"

We were supposed to hear pastoral lays of the corn and cotton fields from the vibrant throat of T. Wallace Whittaker, famous Southern tenor, but we did not, much to the disappointment of the ladies. We heard instead Sweet Sally Starbuck once more, and she sang to us this time "Just a Song at Twilight," "Beautiful Dreamer," "It's a Sin to Tell a Lie."

And Mr. Tambo! And Mr. Bones! Did they pat us the Juba? They did. Did they cut us the Pidgin's Wing? They did. Did they scratch us the Long Dog Scratch? They did.

"*Mistah Tambo, Mistah Tambo! Ah fails to unnerstan'*
How a wuthless, shif'less dahkie such as you, sah,
Kin conglomerate de money fo' a Caddylac sedan,
Jest to keep yo' yaller gal fren' sweet and true,
*   sah. . . .*"

There were banjo exhibitions, comic dances, novelty songs, more jokes.

"And now, ladies and gents," Capt. Adam announced, "for the last feature on our program: the world-renowned imitator Burley Joe Wells, all the way from New Orleans, Louisiana!"

The dead-pan banjoist seated next to Tambo stepped forward, a great black hulk, and held his arms out from his sides. Tambo and Bones stumbled up, and after some pantomimed horseplay, commenced working the arms up and down like pump handles. Burley Joe rolled his eyes and puffed out his cheeks, as though a pressure were building inside him, and when at last he opened his mouth, the blast of a steam calliope rocked the hall with "Oh, Dem Golden Slippers," the *Floating Opera*'s musical signature. A full chorus he tootled, and came whistling to the end accompanied by Prof. Eisen and our applause.

"Looziana sawmill, down in de bayou," Burley Joe grunted next. He took up a stance at one side of the stage, his back against the exit, and after some preliminary coughing, produced a hum like that of an idling buzz saw. Tambo and Bones disappeared into the opposite wing and reappeared a moment later carrying a yellow-pine plank, eight feet long and a foot wide. They tripped, they stumbled, they pulled and tugged, and finally they fed the plank in under Burley Joe's left arm. The saw whined and screamed, and the board disappeared into the wings, followed by the end men. The saw hummed on. Tambo and Bones reappeared ten seconds later with two pine planks, each six inches wide. The process was repeated again and again, the saw chunging against knots and squealing in pine resin, until at last the end men appeared with enormous satisfied smiles on their faces, each holding a single tiny toothpick in his hand; little Bones strode up to big Burley Joe and wrenched his nose as though turning a switch, and the saw's buzz slowly died away.

"Steamboat race," growled Burley Joe, who wasted none of his art on introductions. "De *Natchez* soun' like dis [*A high-pitched chugging, pumping, swishing sound. A shrill whistle*], an' de *Robert E. Lee* soun' like dis [*A low, throaty throb. A resonant bass whistle*]. Hyar dey goes, now."

It was amazing. Ship's bells clanged. Orders were shouted, soundings called. The great pumps thundered. The stern wheel spun. A deep blast of the whistle announced the *Lee*'s departure. Some moments later a deck hand cried "Steamboat 'round de bend!" and a faint shrill whistle identified the *Natchez* ahead. Prof. Eisen insinuated soft, excited music under the throb of the engines. *Toot toot!* The *Lee* flung down the gantlet. *Peep peep!* The *Natchez* accepted the challenge. A race was on! More orders, excited cries, signal bells. The engines accelerated, the music likewise.

I glanced at Capt. Osborn: he was entranced. At the house in general: enthralled. At my wrist watch: ten o'clock. A spotlight directed at Burley Joe was the only illumination in the house at the moment. Quietly, but with no particular attempt at secrecy, I left my seat, slipped down the aisle next to the starboard wall, and stepped out through a side exit, attracting little attention. Inside, the *Lee* gained slowly on the *Natchez*.

It was, of course, entirely dark outside except for the *Opera*'s lights. I found myself, as I'd planned, on the outboard side of the theater. No watchman was in sight. I walked swiftly down the starboard rail to that small companionway in the stern which I'd fixed in my mind during the afternoon's tour, and let myself into the dining room, under the stage, closing the door behind me. Over my head the *Lee* and the *Natchez* were side by side. The music was louder and faster; the minstrels called encouragement to one or the other of the ships; an occasional excited cry broke from the audience. I struck a match and lit three kerosene lanterns mounted along the dining-room walls, then went to the valve labeled DO NOT OPEN UNTIL READY TO LIGHT FOOTLIGHTS and turned it full on, feeling under my hand the rush of acetylene to the stage. Finally I entered the galley, a few feet away, put a match to one burner, and turned the others (and the oven and the broiler) full on, unlighted. A strong odor of bottled illuminating gas filled the little room at once.

Upstairs the *Robert E. Lee* forged slightly ahead of its rival, and the audience cheered. Gas hissed from the burners.

Re-entering the dining room, I glanced around

carefully, checking my work. As a last touch I removed the chimneys from all three lanterns and turned up the wicks. Then I slipped out as I'd entered and took my place again in the audience, now wonderfully agitated as the *Natchez* threatened to overtake the valiant *Lee*. My heart, to be sure, pounded violently, but my mind was calm. Calmly I regarded my companion Capt. Osborn, shouting hoarse encouragement to the *Robert E. Lee*. Calmly I thought of Harrison and Jane: of perfect breasts and thighs scorched and charred; of certain soft, sun-smelling hair crisped to ash. Calmly too I heard somewhere the squeal of an overexcited child, too young to be up so late: not impossibly Jeannine. I considered a small body, formed perhaps from my own and flawless Jane's, black, cracked, smoking. Col. Morton, Bill Butler, old Mr. and Mrs. Bishop—it made no difference, absolutely.

My heart thumped on like the *Robert E. Lee*, and I smiled at the thought that I might expire of natural causes before the great steamboat explosion. The audience was wild.

"*Ladies and gentlemen!*" shouted Capt. Adam, standing in the interlocutor's chair. "*Please make ready for the great explosion of the sidewheeler* James B. Taylor! *Do not leave your seats!*"

Some women cried out, for no transition had been made at all from the one act to the other, nor did the $7,500 Challenge Maritime Band pause for a quaver: indeed, they redoubled their efforts. But the race, apparently, was forgotten. From the pit, under the frenzied music, came a slow rumbling as of tympani, its volume gradually increasing. From Burley Joe—now rising slowly from his knees, arms outstretched, eyeballs bulging—came a hackle-raising hiss like escaping steam. The drums thundered; trumpets whinnied like horses; children grew hysterical; Tambo and Bones hid behind their neighbors. From high on his chair Capt. Adam regarded his brood with an olympian smile—and calmly, more godlike than he, I too smiled.

Like some monstrous black serpent, Burley Joe poised now on tiptoe, arms overhead. The hissing and the music peaked; there was a double flash from the wings, a choked scream, a stunning explosion; the stage filled at once with thick white smoke.

After an instant of complete silence, Evelyn Morton, on the front row, quietly fainted; the Colonel caught her as she keeled. Then Prof. Eisen tore into "Lucy Long," the smoke began drifting away, and the minstrels appeared in a laughing, dancing row on the stage: Tambo, Bones, J. Strudge, Burley Joe Wells (bowing), the two guitarists, Capt. Adam himself (bowing)—and with them Sweet Sally Starbuck and Miss Clara Mulloy, dewy-eyed and blowing kisses. The audience laughed and exclaimed sharply to one another. Husbands looked at wives, wives at children, with an instant's new eyes.

"Lucy Long!" "Lucy Long!" The wonderful pan-ithiopliconica, it turned out, was not more nor less than a grand old-fashioned minstrel walk-around—bones, tambourines, banjos, guitars. The minstrels danced, sang, leaped, cartwheeled. "Lucy Long" became "The Essence of Old Virginny"; faster and faster the minstrels cavorted, to a final, almost savage breakdown. The cymbals crashed, the performers bowed low, Tambo and Bones tumbled into the orchestra pit, and our wild applause saluted the curtains of the Original & Unparalleled Floating Opera.

xxviii   a parenthesis

If you do not understand at once that the end of my
Floating Opera story must be undramatic, then again
I'm cursed with imperfect communication. Say what
you wish about the formal requirements of storytelling;
this is my opera, and I'll lead you out of it as gently as
I led you in. I've little use, as a principle, for slam-bang
finishes like Burley Joe's.

I helped Capt. Osborn to his feet (he was still
shaken with the excitement of the steamboat race) and
ushered him out with the crowd. There was still a
possibility, of course, that the theater might explode—
gas accumulated in the bilges of a vessel is particularly
volatile—but I rather suspected that either some hidden source of ventilation (Capt. Adam had claimed
the *Opera* was safe) or wandering member of the crew
had foiled my plan. Need I tell you that I felt no sense
either of relief or of disappointment? As when the
engine of the law falls sprawling against my obstacles,
I merely took note of the fact that despite my intentions
six hundred ninety-nine of my townspeople and myself
were still alive.

Why did I not, failing my initial attempt, simply
step off the gangplank into the Choptank, where no
fluke could spoil my plan? Because, I began to realize,
a subtle corner had been turned. I asked myself,
knowing there was no ultimate answer, "Why not step
into the river?" as I had asked myself in the afternoon,
"Why not blow up the Floating Opera?" But now, at
once, a new voice replied casually, "On the other hand,

why bother?" There was a corner for you! Negotiated unawares, but like that dark alleyway in Baltimore which once turned me dazzled onto the bright flood of Monument Street, this corner confronted me with a new and unsuspected prospect—at which, for the moment, I could only blink.

We met Harrison, Jane, and Jeannine at the foot of the crowded gangplank.

"How'd you like the show?" Harrison laughed. "The folks really eat that stuff up, don't they?"

"And so do I," I said.

"Oh, well, I enjoy it, too, in a sense," Harrison chuckled briskly. "Hear those horrible old jokes again. Jeannine liked it, anyhow." He indicated his daughter, lying like a sleeping angel in his arms.

"We'd better get her home, I guess," Jane said pleasantly. I believe she and Harrison both were somewhat uncomfortable in Capt. Osborn's presence—though certainly no more so than was that gentleman in hers. "Good night, Toddy," she smiled, still pleasantly, but without warmth. "I guess we'll be seeing you around."

"Of course," Harrison agreed at once, moving off.

"Certainly," I said at the same time, pleasantly but without warmth, and we parted. I've spoken to my friend Harrison on three separate occasions since then; to Jane only once, during a party in 1938 celebrating the final decision of the Maryland Court of Appeals in Harrison's favor (his presence hadn't been necessary when I argued the case, and he sent the firm a $50,000 check via a vice-president of the pickle company); to my beautiful Jeannine, now a twenty-one-year-old debutante of Ruxton and Gibson Island, not at all, though I note her activities occasionally on the society page of the Baltimore *Sun*. Upon their return from eighteen months in Amalfi, Cannes, and Biarritz, the Macks settled just outside Baltimore to live, and so there is nothing remarkable in the fact that I don't see them any more.

Capt. Osborn and I walked back up High Street to

the hotel then, and I bade him good night in the hallway.

"Hold on, Toddy," he grinned. "C'mon in my room here; I got a s'prise for ye."

I followed him in, and smiling broadly he presented me with a pint of Southern Comfort.

"There, now!"

"What's this for?" I broke the seal and sniffed appreciatively.

The old man blushed. "I owed it to ye. That little business we was talkin' about this mornin', for one thing."

"Come on, then, let's drink it up," I said. "You'll need it as badly as I will, because that particular show's all over with."

"Shucks, it would've been all over with anyhow, far's I'm concerned," Capt. Osborn declared.

"How about Young Haecker?" I suggested. "Suppose we cut him in on it, too?"

I went up to the top floor to Mister Haecker's little dormer room and knocked, but though a flickering light shone under the door, he didn't reply.

"Mister Haecker?" I turned the knob, for it was doubtful that a man of his age and circumstances would be either out or asleep at ten-thirty.

The door opened onto a strange scene: a single tall white candle burned in a brass holder on the writing desk beside the bed, and flickered in the small breeze from the window. Also on the writing desk, as I saw on approaching it, were an alarm clock stopped at ten-fifteen; a volume of Shakespeare opened to Act Three, Scene One, of *Hamlet* (with, believe it or not, the words *not all* noted in the margin opposite the line *Thus conscience does make cowards of us all*); a stack of thirteen fat notebooks each labeled *Diary, 19—* (I never had nerve enough to examine those); and a glass bottle with two sleeping pills left in it. On the bed Mister Haecker lay dressed in black pajamas, his eyes closed, his arms crossed in the manner of Miss Holiday Hopkinson, next door, his features calm (*composed* is a more accurate adjective), his pulse and respiration—as

I discovered upon snatching up his wrist and putting my ear to his chest—almost imperceptible.

As far as I could see there was nothing to be done in the way of first aid; I hurried downstairs and notified Hurley Binder, the night clerk, who in turn telephoned the hospital for an ambulance. Then the two of us returned to Mister Haecker's room with Capt. Osborn, who pleaded with us to help him up the stairs so that he wouldn't miss the excitement, and had our drinks there while waiting for the ambulance to arrive. Hurley Binder and Capt. Osborn clucked their tongues and shook their heads and drank their Southern Comfort, mightily impressed by Mister Haecker's elaborate preparations for departure.

"What d'ye think of that?" Capt. Osborn said several times. "And him such a educated feller!"

From time to time I felt Mister Haecker's pulse: he seemed to be losing no ground—but then there was little to lose, for pulses do not beat much more slowly. Presently the ambulance cried up past Spring Valley, and Mister Haecker was carted off to the hospital, black pajamas and all.

"Makes a man stop and think now, don't it?" Capt. Osborn said.

"It does indeed," I agreed mildly, and said good night. What I thought, personally, was that should he live through this foolishness, Mister Haecker might find the remaining years of his life less burdensome than the ones recently past, because both his former enthusiasm for old age and his apparent present despair of it were (judging from appearances) more calculated than felt, more elaborate than sincere. I should enjoy saying that history proved me correct; in fact, however, upon recovering from his generous dose of barbiturates Mister Haecker went from the hospital to a sanitorium in Western Maryland, it having been discovered that he was incipiently tubercular; there, in 1940, he attempted once again to take his life, by the same means and with as much flourish as before, and succeeded.

Alone in my room then, I sat on the window sill

and smoked a cigar for several minutes, regarding the cooling night, the traffic light below, the dark graveyard of Christ Episcopal Church across the corner, and the black expanse of the sky, the blacker as the stars were blotted out by storm clouds. Sheet lightning flickered over the Post Office and behind the church steeple, and an occasional rumbling signaled the approach of the squall out over the Chesapeake. How like ponderous nature, so dramatically to change the weather when I had so delicately changed my mind! I remembered my evening's notes, and going to them presently, added a parenthesis to the fifth proposition:

   V. There's no final reason for living (or for suicide).

xxix *the floating opera*

That's about what it amounted to, this change of mind
in 1937: a simple matter of carrying out my premises
completely to their conclusions. For the sake of convention I'd like to end the show with an emotional
flourish, but though the progress of my reasoning from
1919 to 1937 was in many ways turbulent, it was of the
essence of my conclusion that no emotion was necessarily involved in it. To realize that nothing makes any
final difference is overwhelming; but if one goes no
farther and becomes a saint, a cynic, or a suicide on
principle, one hasn't reasoned completely. The truth is
that nothing makes any difference, including that
truth. Hamlet's question is, absolutely, meaningless.

While finishing my cigar I made a few more idle
notes for my *Inquiry*, which was, you understand, open
again. They are of small interest here—which is to say,
they are of some interest. It occurred to me, for example, that faced with an infinitude of possible directions and having no ultimate reason to choose one over
another, I would *in all probability*, though not at all
necessarily, go on behaving much as I had thitherto, as
a rabbit shot on the run keeps running in the same
direction until death overtakes him. Possibly I would
on some future occasion endeavor once again to blow
up the Floating Opera, my good neighbors and associ-
ates, and/or my mere self; most probably I would not.
I and my townsmen would play that percentage in my
case as, for that matter, we did in each of theirs. I
considered too whether, in the real absence of abso-

lutes, values less than absolute mightn't be regarded as in no way inferior and even be lived by. But that's another inquiry, and another story.

Also reopened were the *Letter to My Father* and that third peach basket, the investigation of myself, for if I was ever to explain to myself why Dad committed suicide, I must explain to him why I did not. The project would take time. I reflected that Marvin Rose's report on my heart would reach me in the next day's mail after all, and smiled: never before had the uncertainty of that organ seemed of less moment. It was beside the point now whether endocarditis was still among my infirmities: the problem was the same either way, the "solution" also. At least for the time being; at least for me.

I would take a good long careful time, then, to tell Dad the story of *The Floating Opera*. Perhaps I would expire before ending it; perhaps the task was endless, like its fellows. No matter. Even if I died before ending my cigar, I had all the time there was.

This clear, I made a note to intercept my note to Jimmy Andrews, stubbed out (after all) my cigar, undressed, went to bed in enormous soothing solitude, and slept fairly well despite the absurd thunderstorm that soon afterwards broke all around.

About the Author

JOHN BARTH was born May 27, 1930 in Dorchester County, Maryland, a region whose memory populates his creative mind. He attended the Juilliard School of Music in New York, played drums with professional jazz bands and returned home to major in journalism at Johns Hopkins University. He began to read the great tale cycles—**The Thousand and One Nights** and the **Decameron**—and started but never finished his own one hundred stories set in the Maryland of his childhood. After receiving his M.A. from Johns Hopkins in 1952, Barth became an instructor in English at Penn State University.

Four years later, **The Floating Opera** (1956), a comic, philosophical novel set in the tidewater areas of Maryland, was published. Greeted by many critics as an oddity, it was nominated for a National Book Award in 1957. Barth wrote **Opera** in the first three months of 1956, and in the last three completed **The End of the Road** (1958), a realistic novel about a teacher at a small community college. His next book, though, abandoned realist conventions: in **The Sot-Weed Factor** (1960), Barth created a seventeenth-century mock epic, the **Marylandiad**, satirizing the style and content of the historical novel. In **Giles Goat-Boy** (1966), Barth returned to the present and the problems encountered by a new messiah at a Maryland university. His experiments with literary forms continue in **Lost in the Funhouse** (1968), a collection of short stories; **Chimera** (1972), three interconnected novellas, which won the National Book Award for fiction; and **Letters** (1979), an epistolary novel.

After teaching at the State University of New York at Buffalo, Barth returned to Johns Hopkins in 1973 where he now teaches English and Creative Writing. He is the father of three children and on occasion can still be found playing drums with a local jazz band.